THE REDEEMED

THE REDEEMED

RV MINKLER

Light Messages
Torchflame Books

Durham, NC

Published 2022, by Torchflame Books
an Imprint of Light Messages Publishing
www.lightmessages.com
Durham, NC 27713 USA
SAN: 920-9298

Paperback ISBN: 978-1-61153-456-6
E-book ISBN: 978-1-61153-457-3
Library of Congress Control Number: 2022901622

In honor to Almighty God, who formed us in His image and loves us; to my patient and supportive wife; to our children and grandchildren, precious gifts from God; to our parents and forebears who did the best they could; and to our family of Christ who nurtured and guided us.

EXORDIUM

At the urging of Abraham Jones, my pastor and teacher, I pen this journal as a faithful retelling of the events that brought us to the new generation. Though not my story, I have firsthand interviews with the principals who experienced the circumstances, and I observed the more recent developments.

In the documentation of our people's saga, I have written primarily about the lives of Nathanael Sinclair, Veena Osborne Sinclair, and Abraham Jones. Most of the eyewitness accounts come from Abraham's lips, as he was before the events that swept in the new era, and he remains our guide, teacher, and spiritual leader.

This testimony records a journey of survival and love while holding fast to the faith. It spans from the last days of the old era, which we now know as "The Thinning," through the desolation and hopelessness of the 'tween years, and culminates in the new era's birth.

The recollections integrated into this chronicle are from those who have been sharpened and strengthened through God's awesome power as He pours out His overflowing grace to secure our future despite our failings.

In the service of Y'shua, may God's mercy restore hope to all readers.

—Ezra Haines,
the sixth child of the blessing
poured upon The Redeemed

THE AWAKENING

CHAPTER 1

Veena rubbed her temples, deep in thought, as Abe and Kath escorted the Lizard King away from the mess kitchen and into the darkness to find him a place to spend the night. The Lizard King was a self-named, scraggly loner who brought startling news to their camp. His appearance was not remarkable as Veena's tribe, The Tierrans, regularly provided him whatever the kitchen had prepared when he showed up, and he would offer information as a token payment. Most of the time, Veena and her team were already aware of the events related by the Lizard King, and frequently they would have to filter his ramblings to mine the nuggets of truth.

Usually, Veena would dismiss the Lizard King's report as part of his predictable, deluded rantings. Soon after sunset, however, drums started pounding from the compound of the nearby ruthless gang known as the Clairens. The savage and mindless Clairens hadn't beaten on their drums in months, and now the timing of the booming seemed to give credence to the Lizard King's sighting.

A boat approaching the shore, I don't think I've heard of anything like that in the last eleven years, she thought. *After years of little change and relative safety from the Clairens, why now?*

The mild and dry Santa Ana winds that swept in from the desert had made this October day warm, and now a shift in the direction brought a cooler, onshore breeze that ruffled a few hairs across her face. She absent-mindedly tucked the stray strands back behind her ears as she said a short prayer. Nearby, Carla put another log in the stove burner, and, in that instant, Veena felt she had an answer to her prayer, and she knew what they had to do.

"Carla," Veena spoke to her sergeant, "tell the squad that we will do a reconnaissance patrol, leaving in the predawn light. Get some rest."

"Yes, Cap," said Carla. Just as Carla Rodriquez held the honorary title *Sergeant*, Veena Osborne, who led their tribe, the Tierrans, was also known as *Captain Veena*, or *Cap*. Carla slipped into the darkness just as Kath returned to the outdoor kitchen.

"Abe's going to make sure the Lizard King is situated," reported Kath, with a slight Southern drawl in her speech. Kathy Haines was Veena's best friend and second in command. Kath was two years older than Veena. She had first met Veena and Abe when she was only thirteen, nearly eleven years ago. Back then, she was Kathy Arlain, a frightened young girl orphaned by the pandemic. Abe and Veena took Kath in, making her part of their extended chosen family, and gave her the training needed to defend and protect herself and the tribe.

Kath came to the mess table and sat down across from Veena. Kath's family had moved to San Diego from Georgia just months before The Fires and pandemic. In contrast to her warrior leadership, she liked to keep a flower inserted in her hair above her ear. Noting the prolonged quietness of her friend, Kath said, "What do you think about the Lizard King's story?"

"If it weren't for the Clairen drums, I'd dismiss it," said Veena. "A small, orange boat appears on the sea and is heading for shore. I'd say that is nonsense, but the Clairen drums disturbing the night suggest that something is unusual. When Rex and the K came south from L.A. and claimed the Clairens, even that event wasn't worthy of drums. You know, I guess we should now call the Clairens the K, but they will always be the Clairens in my mind."

"Well, I'm glad the Clairens haven't become like the K. The stories I've heard of Rex and the K are the beginnings of nightmares. It was pretty unusual that Rex absorbed the Clairens into the K instead of wiping them out."

A grim, weak smile formed on Veena's face as she said, "Well, one of the traders reported it had to do with beer. He said that Rex sparred the Clairens because Dunkin' Donuts could brew beer." She shook her head in disgust as she contemplated the capriciousness of fate.

"Regardless, I'm taking my squad on reconnaissance before dawn, and I want you to strengthen the camp defenses. Ask Roy to assign some of his best men to the outposts." As soon as Veena spoke the last sentence, she regretted it, as she was confident that Roy had taken appropriate defensive measures. Roy Haines was a former military officer, and he remained very competent. Furthermore, Roy was Kath's husband, and Veena realized she may have slighted Kath by implicitly suggesting Kath's husband hadn't done his duty.

Kath knew her friend and overlooked the potential disrespect. "Yes, Veena. Roy already told me his men beefed up the defenses when the Clairen drums started. I'll tell him the Lizard King's story and let him decide if his team needs to do more. You should get some sleep soon, too. In days like this, do you ever wish that Abe was still in charge?"

With a sigh, Veena said, "Every day. I'm sorry for giving you an order for Roy. Your husband has always done more than I've asked; he is a good man."

"Uneasy lies the head that wears the crown," laughed Kath.

"You're lucky that I already set the K.P. roster!" retorted Veena with a smirk. It was just like Kath to lighten the mood.

As Kath disappeared into the night, Veena thought about Abe. Abraham Jones had been a friend of Veena's parents since before The Fires. A young African-American man who had served in the Marines, a knee injury changed his career path at age twenty-three. After being medically discharged, he earned a doctorate in physical therapy. As a physical therapist for the U.S. Olympic camp, Abe met and befriended Veena's parents, African-American decathlete Kyle Osborne and his Caucasian wife, Dawn Johnson, a skilled archer. When Kyle and Dawn learned that Abe was a highly qualified Krav Maga martial arts instructor, they hired him to train their daughter. Veena had trained weekly with Abe for three years before The Fires started. Everything changed during The Fires.

Abe, known by many as 'Old Abe,' became Veena's guardian and mentor upon the deaths of her parents, and he had led the tribe for a few years before he insisted that Veena take the command role so Abe could dedicate himself to spiritual leadership. At first, Veena suspected Abe's knee injury was the reason for the change. Eventually, however, she accepted that he strove to devote himself to holy service, though he still assisted in martial arts training. Begrudgingly, she also realized that her new leadership role forced her to mature. *Still*, she thought, *this is one of those days I wish that Abe made all the decisions.*

―᠁―

The cacophony of Clairen drums booming until the wee hours and the Lizard King –who became more addled and agitated– shouting 'I am the Lizard King' over and over into the blackness of the sky, disturbed the entire camp. Irritated by the fitful sleep, Veena decided to send the Lizard King on his way in the morning. In the predawn light, Veena rose and headed to the assembly point to meet her squad. She noticed a fog had come in, obscuring the visibility across the open and barren camp that had a defensive fence perimeter enclosing the few wooden buildings and lean-tos. She pulled the hood of her loose-fitting camo outfit over her hair to fend off the dampness and hold in her body heat. Veena was almost at the assembly point when she saw Kath appearing out of the vapors.

"The Lizard King has disappeared, and no one saw him leave," said Kath softly.

"What?" Veena exclaimed with a hiss. "Well, I'm glad he's gone, but I'm upset he could clear out without our guards noticing."

"I'll handle it while you're on patrol," Kath responded with an edge in her tone.

Kath split off while Veena continued to meet with her squad. Veena couldn't suppress a grin as she envisioned how Kath would start raising hell because of the guards' negligence. *The sentries are lucky that Carla isn't dealing with the dereliction*, she thought. Veena knew that Kath's anger would pale compared to the discipline that Carla would demand when they returned from the patrol.

Her squad –Carla Rodriquez, Carla's partner MaryAn Hedgemore, and Laoni Wright– were ready when Veena approached. Shrouded by the fog, they departed through the fence and across the open buffer zone before entering the woods and heading to the southwest forward observation post, situated up in the trees. Carla and MaryAn were both about five years older than Veena. Laoni, on the other hand, was the youngest in the tribe at just over fourteen. Still, because Kath and Roy had raised Laoni, her skills were far beyond her years.

As they approached the outpost, Veena was pleased to see the sentries, Chief Virtolli and Vincent Ramon, were alert and ready. After Veena and Carla entered the blind, Chief Virtolli whispered with his Jersey accent: "Except for those infernal Clairen drums, there haven't been any threats. About fifteen minutes ago, we did hear birds rising to flight south of here. So you may want to start there."

Veena nodded, and Carla led the way south along the western ridge as the first rays of dawn crept over the horizon and filled the fog with a diffused glow.

—⁓—

The search that morning was fruitless. The fog not only restricted the squad's vision but also dampened sound. They moved slowly and carefully through the low brush parallel to the beaten paths to avoid stumbling into any Clairen patrols. As the fog dissipated, they did observe several Clairen scouting groups scouring the coastline. It was apparent that the Clairens were looking for something. Veena didn't gain any comfort from the evident failings of the Clairens. Prior to the arrival of the K, the Clairens were not known for their discipline. What she surveyed today regarding the Clairen thoroughness was quite abnormal, and that gave Veena concern. *Perhaps there is a sliver of truth to the Lizard King's report as this Clairen activity indicates they have seen something, too.*

A couple of hours after dawn, Veena's squad ascended Mount Soledad, with its commanding view over the coastline. The early morning fog had burned off completely, but nothing unusual was visible to the team. By mid-morning, Veena decided the scouting was fruitless, and it was time to return home.

"Carla, let's start back along the southern border of the mesas north of Mission Valley. Everyone, keep sharp. There seems to be a lot of Clairen activity. Let's not stumble into an encounter with any of them." Silently, the team descended Mount Soledad, still searching for anything that was out of the ordinary.

CHAPTER 2

The night before, about the same time the Lizard King was loudly reporting his disjointed story to Veena and her leaders, Lieutenant Nathanael Sinclair slogged onward through the unfamiliar landscape that the fog partially obscured. Nate, as he preferred to be called, was exhausted, thirsty, and hungry. *How long ago did I wake up in the lab?* he thought. Everything was fuzzy in his mind, and part of him just wanted to lie down and rest. *I think it was three days ago, but I'm not sure.*

Nate paused and caught his breath. Despite the coolness of the vapor-shrouded night, drops of sweat dripped from his sandy-blond hair. He should be in top physical shape at twenty-three, but his long sleep had atrophied his previously muscled frame.

After his heaving lungs breathed more regularly, he called out, "Hello! Is anyone out there?" Only the muted thumping of drums met his shouts. With this thick fog, he couldn't tell how close the drums were or even precisely the direction of the source of the sounds, but he could feel the concussive pounding nearly as well as he could hear it.

Where am I, and what has happened here?

Three days ago, when he awoke in the lab, everything was all wrong in the facility. The lights were down, and no one else was present. Most of the laboratory's computers' displays were flashing warnings of errors and system failures, yet no one came to fix them. Before abandoning the lab, he had spent nearly a day trying to contact anyone at the central monitoring site. All attempts proved to be futile. Nate decided to return to the base, but the emergency transport pod took twenty-four hours to reach the dock. No one was there either, and, other than the pier itself, which showed considerable wear, nothing looked the same. He would have thought he was dreaming if he hadn't vomited, which thoroughly dispelled that illusion.

When Nate left the lab, it was nighttime. By the time he arrived at the dock, it was dark again. Nate grabbed a flashlight from the escape vessel and started walking, hoping to find someone. He stumbled along without finding any recognizable landmarks or encountering anyone. Somebody had to be pounding those drums, but he couldn't locate them. The fog so obscured the visibility that Nate wasn't even sure which direction he was moving. Several times, he heard scurrying in the nearby shrubs. One time, Nate swept the beam of his flashlight around him and caught the reflected eyes of several large animals, probably coyotes. Fortunately, they didn't threaten him. Still, Nate yelled, "Hey!" to send them scattering.

Having caught his breath, Nate stopped ruminating on the past days and started shuffling along again. The constant use of the flashlight had drained its batteries. In his fatigue, Nate dropped it from his hand and didn't bother to pick it up. He was tired and sore, and everything was so confusing that his head ached. The drums made his headache worse. Nate realized he was becoming dehydrated.

Without the flashlight's beam, the darkness and fog seemed even more oppressive. Nate's anxiousness increased, and any nearby rustling easily spooked him. He kept putting one weary foot in front of another, occasionally having to circumvent marshes and swamps he didn't remember. Then, just as a full moon rose and illuminated the fog's vapors, he smelled smoke. He felt encouraged and started to move with renewed purpose.

As the dawn's rays pierced the night sky, the light within the fog intensified. Nate couldn't see the sun break above the eastern horizon; however, its rising was evident as it filled the vapors with an eerie glow. About mid-morning, he came to the top of a small canyon. The fog that had been all around him now spanned above the canyon to the opposite side. Though a haze obscured the canyon's far side, the air was more luminous in the morning light, and he was able to get his bearings, recognizing that the gully ran north-to-south, and he was on the western wall. He tried to shout, "Hello!" but his parched throat only emitted a raspy croak. Nate started down the steep slope of the cliff and headed toward the canyon floor.

The slope's soil was loose, often cascading when Nate took a step, and he struggled to keep from falling. When a rabbit bolted from a nearby bush, Nate became startled and jumped back. He lost his footing and tumbled down the slope. Bushes and rocks snagged his clothes, tearing them and his exposed skin.

He slammed into a large sage bush, bringing his downward pinwheeling to an abrupt stop. The impact knocked the air from his lungs, and Nate just lay on his side for several minutes before rolling onto his back. His head was spinning, and he felt that, at any moment, he might throw up. Oddly enough, he started giggling and said: "What a silly way to die."

After the hysterics subsided, Nate moved his arms and legs. He determined that he didn't have any broken bones, and none of the cuts were severe. Nate raised himself onto his elbows, and pain shot through his body as he took several deep breaths. After a few minutes, he rolled onto his knees and slowly rose to a stand. Nate looked anew at the canyon and realized he was three-quarters of the way down the canyon wall. The slope broke here and eased into the valley floor fifty yards beyond. From his viewpoint, the canyon was like the inside of a lighted tunnel. The valley floor rose gently to his left, and the corridor appeared to terminate within a mile as the canyon rounded a bend. On his right, he caught the reflective glint of water farther down the canyon. *Probably the ocean or the bay*, he reasoned.

There was firm ground that stretched about three hundred yards to the eastern canyon wall in front of him. Now that he was out of the fog's grasp, a light breeze brushed his face, carrying the scent of cooking food. His stomach grumbled, and Nate felt drawn to continue to the far side.

He carefully tested his footing as he limped down the rest of the slope. The valley floor was uneven and covered with dense, chest-high sagebrush. Picking his way over the canyon floor, Nate kept his head down as he scanned for a path and possibly snakes.

Nate looked up about midway across the canyon and noticed the far side canyon wall ahead of him. He paused and studied the new canyon rim; something was different. It finally clicked in his mind that there were trees on that ridge. He had not seen any trees since reaching the shore. As he studied them further, he got an unsettled feeling regarding the trees' regular spacing atop the ridge. *It looks like somebody planted a fortress wall there.*

Nate yelled out, "Hello, is anyone out here?" No one answered. When a new puff of breeze carried an aroma that reminded him of when his mother baked bread, it encouraged Nate to push forward, and he continued heading toward the ridge. The dense, scraggly chaparral blocked his view of the far side much of the time, and the crossing was fraught with twisty turns and scratching branches.

As he neared the eastern slope, Nate was again panting heavily and dripping with sweat as he struggled up a slight rise. At the top, he was startled to see the remains of a large road. Appearing to be at least four lanes wide, it stretched out on each side as it followed the canyon floor. Nate couldn't tell how far it extended as the dense brush had reclaimed much of the roadway wherever there was a crack in the paving. Crossing the pavement, he recognized it was the remains of southbound lanes of a freeway as he glimpsed the median and northbound lanes. The surface was uneven, but the lane lines were still visible. The road concrete had cracked in many places, and weeds found footing in the fissures. He wondered: *why is this road abandoned?*

Sweating heavily, Nate loosened his shirt in an attempt to let the heat escape from underneath and cool him. Gnats were swarming around his head and buzzing his ears. Mercifully, the breeze gusted and blew them away. Crossing the remaining lanes, Nate started ascending the canyon wall. The steep climb made his heart pound and intensified the aches in his body. Every step hurt as he gasped for air, his head swimming with dizziness.

Halfway up the side, Nate sensed a movement on the slope above him. He paused and struggled to control his wheezing as he listened and looked intently at the bank and shrubs above. There were nearby boulders, and a breeze was rustling the dense foliage, but nothing was suspicious. However, he realized that he could no longer hear or feel the booming of distant drums.

When he had rested enough, Nate restarted up the slope. Just as he was passing beside a large, granite outcropping on the side of the canyon, a man's shout from above shocked him.

"I am the Lizard King. I can do anything. Die, dog!"

From the top of the outcropping, a scraggly, bearded

scarecrow of a man leaped at Nate. Sailing through the air as he plummeted toward Nate, his aim was off. Despite that, his foot struck Nate's head as Nate spun to ward off the attack. Everything went black.

CHAPTER 3

As they returned to camp, Veena and her squad didn't find any evidence of a boat or anyone new. Even though the fog had burned off and the skies were clear, the only human activity they saw were Clairen patrols. Veena felt unsettled that the search had not uncovered anything and sensed her team had similar feelings.

Avoiding the Clairen territory as much as possible, they ascended the western ridge of the Tierran mesa and headed north to the tree line. About one mile south of camp, they entered the grove of trees planted along the crest but stayed close enough to the ridgeline that they could scan the canyon below. Suddenly, Carla dropped into a crouched stance, with her crossbow ready. Veena crept forward to Carla.

"What do you see?" she whispered.

Carla pointed to the sky just ahead and above the canyon. Turkey vultures were circling above that spot. Veena nodded. Carla advanced, and the squad followed. Only fifty yards later, Carla crouched lower and gave the 'hold' signal. Veena looked back to warn Laoni and saw with satisfaction that both Laoni and MaryAn had already taken defensive positions, with their eyes scouring the surroundings. Veena crept closer to Carla at the ridge's edge and followed Carla's stare down the slope to the canyon floor. Carla pointed out a man on the ground, just beyond a giant boulder and about three-quarters of the way down the hill.

"I see him," whispered Veena. "Any others?"

"Not that I can tell, Cap," Carla replied quietly, scanning the area below. "The vultures appear to be circling ever closer to the ground for their meal, so nothing is disturbing their pattern."

Veena used hand signals to direct Laoni to guard the ridge and sent Carla to the north and MaryAn to the south. After Carla and MaryAn moved carefully down the slope into support positions, Veena started a direct route toward the man.

Carla eased into a firing position in a thick bush above the boulder as Veena sidled to the left to establish an effective crossfire defense. When Veena felt that both Carla and she were ready, she signaled MaryAn to proceed. MaryAn slithered within four yards of the man, who hadn't moved, and she stopped to scan the surrounding shrubbery intensely. After confirming no immediate danger of an ambush, MaryAn glanced at Carla and Veena, and both gave her the proceed signal. MaryAn stowed her crossbow, grasped her knife, and crawled up to the man. Holding the blade against his chest above his heart, she felt for a pulse on his throat. Moments later, she slid back and signaled to Veena that he was dead.

Veena relaxed a bit and rose slightly to get a clear view of the body. Even from this distance, she recognized the Lizard King's gaunt body and the ratty clothes he had on when she saw him yesterday. That he was dead so soon after being in their camp was disquieting. Veena moved quickly and quietly towards Carla and the path that wound down left of the boulder. Rounding the rock as she advanced towards MaryAn, Veena stumbled upon the still body of a second man, previously hidden by the granite mass and the overgrown brush. Lying on his back, a trickle of blood seeped from his forehead.

Startled by this man that none of them had previously observed, Veena instantly dropped into a firing position and let out a short, muffled gasp. Carla and MaryAn immediately reacted to Veena's change of posture and increased their state of alertness. Less experienced warriors might have panicked and fired into the next sagebrush branch that moved in the breeze, but harsh lessons had taught the team that even a clear target is not a sure shot.

The air was heavy with uneasiness, and adrenaline pumped into their arteries as they waited for either an attack or Veena's stand-down signal. Veena didn't sense any immediate danger, so she studied the second body a little closer and decided he wasn't a threat. To MaryAn, Veena hand-signaled the command to move into a covering-fire position.

MaryAn moved stealthily up the slope just a few feet and saw the second man's body. Now she understood Veena's stance. With MaryAn in position, Veena edged slowly towards the second man; her crossbow pointed at his heart. *I don't know this guy*, she thought. His apparel and condition were unusual. Though tattered, torn, and dirtied, his clothes were machine-woven and sewn, a rare sight nowadays. As she moved closer, she recognized a NASA logo on his blue jumpsuit. Veena had almost forgotten about that organization, and the reminder was startling.

Veena studied the young man, probably only a couple of years older than she. Though he was rather dirty, his facial hair was minimal, as if he had shaved a few days ago. Here was a man who was unlike any she had seen in the last eleven years, not worn and ragged as all the others.

Veena moved close to touch him, and she could hear his breathing. Assessing him quickly, she noted the shallow slashes on his skin and the large cut and bruise over his left eye. *This guy isn't smart about moving through the brush*, she thought.

Relaxing her touch on the crossbow trigger, Veena shifted and pressed her left knee against the man's right arm and side as she pressed her left fingertips against his right carotid. His pulse was strong but erratic, and his breathing was shallow. She drew back from the man and into the whispering range of MaryAn.

"He is hurt, but not too badly. Do you think these two were attacked?"

MaryAn did a quick scan before she softly said in her sing-song tone, "I don't think so, Cap. It looks like the Lizard King fell and broke his neck. If attackers had ambushed these two, I don't think this guy would have been left alive. Perhaps he and the Lizard King got into a struggle. It seems weird that the Lizard King is dead, and this guy is unconscious."

Not sure how to proceed, but not detecting any threats, Veena signaled 'stand-down' to Carla. Then, without looking up the ridge, she also signaled Laoni and heard the recognition whistle back. Lastly, she motioned for Carla to join them next to the man.

After Carla approached, Veena said in a low voice, "The second man is alive but unconscious. I have never seen him before. He has a large cut and a bruise forming on his forehead but no other apparent injuries. What is exceptional is that he's different in appearance from anyone we've seen since the *Des Moines* crew joined our tribe. He looks relatively well-fed and, though his clothes are torn and dirty, they aren't as threadbare as everyone else's. I wonder if he came from a place that survives and flourishes? Maybe he was on that sea craft that the Lizard King saw. We've got to get him back to camp and ask Abe."

Carla had a deep distrust of unknown men. She said to Veena with a touch of anger in her voice: "Why are we risking ourselves for this man? Let's leave him for the buzzards."

Though she should have known that Carla would respond like that, Veena was irritated with Carla's attitude. "No. This man doesn't appear to be a threat; just look how much he has cut himself up from stumbling through the brush. Look at his clothes: he has a uniform from NASA. I haven't heard of NASA since before The Fires. Where would he get that? Abe will want to question him, and I'd like to know the answers."

"So what, he's stupid, and he steals clothes." Then, Carla noticed the fire in Veena's eyes and backed down. "I'll do whatever you order, Cap."

"All right then, cover the Lizard King's body to keep off the buzzards, and then we'll move this guy."

After Carla put a coarse blanket over the body and secured it with some rocks, the three of them said a quick prayer for the Lizard King while Laoni kept the watch on the ridge above them. Then they lifted the stranger, with Veena and Carla at each arm and MaryAn at his feet and started up the slope. Even though they were sure-footed, the man's body's weight made the ascent a strain. Veena was glad she had such confidence in Laoni's ability to protect them, as they were vulnerable as they struggled up the slope to the ridge. At the top, they set the man's body down for a much-needed rest.

No longer exposed in the canyon, Veena spoke in hushed tones between gasps of air, "Carla, go get Laoni and brief her as you return here. Then I want you and MaryAn to go to the camp for both a burial detail and a medic team while Laoni and I stay here."

Carla acknowledged the commands with a slight shrug and disappeared into the brush. Veena looked to MaryAn, who had started inspecting the man's wounds, and said, "How is he?"

"I'm not sure, Cap. He seems healthy enough. Oddly, he is unexpectedly heavy, as though he's been eating well. His injuries, except for the welt on his head, are minor. His pulse and his respiration are good. That he remains unconscious troubles me, and I hope that he doesn't have a neck injury. He is a strange one."

"Yes, that he is," Veena mumbled as she looked him over again.

MaryAn took out her first aid kit and tended the man's wounds.

Veena looked at the injuries and confirmed that nothing was life-threatening. Remarking out loud to MaryAn, Veena said, "These wounds are consistent with those you get when you're frantically running from something and stumbling. We haven't discovered any pursuers. What is odd is that his clothes are so new." As soon as she said that, Veena wondered if there was something or someone they missed. *If he came from the sea craft, are there others somewhere?*

Just then, MaryAn interrupted Veena's thoughts. "Cap, did you notice how clean-shaven Sinclair is?"

Startled, Veena asked, "What did you say?"

"Did you notice how clean-shaven he is?"

"Yes, I had, but that's not what I meant. Did you just call him by a name?"

"Why, yes, Cap...Sinclair. I mean, I guess that's his name embroidered over his breast pocket."

"Oh, right, good observation," Veena said sheepishly and then blushed. She turned away to scan the terrain around them, angry with herself for missing the obvious. *What is it about this guy that is so distracting to me, and what else am I missing?*

When Laoni returned with Carla, she got her first close look at the stranger and said, "Hey, dude's not bad-lookin'." She quickly shut up when both Carla and Veena threw angry glances at her, but she also kept peeking toward Sinclair.

Carla tapped MaryAn, and they left to retrieve a litter

from camp. Under usual circumstances, Veena would have the team's junior members perform any first aid required to reinforce training. Instead, Veena told Laoni to stand watch while she examined Sinclair's wounds closer.

As she was dabbing antiseptic on his cuts, Sinclair moaned, and his eyes fluttered open. It was clear that his eyes wouldn't focus, and he struggled to talk. For a moment, Veena saw his gaze meet her own. He briefly grinned, and Veena smiled in return. Then, he slipped into unconsciousness again.

CHAPTER 4

Abe watched the western approach as he waited for Veena and her patrol to return. Veena was like his dear daughter, not by blood but by love and joy. Abe had taught Veena well, and he knew she could take care of herself. He was so confident in her abilities that he started delegating command responsibilities to her when she was eighteen. By the time Veena was nineteen, Abe had stepped back to a mentoring role as Veena handled the tribal leadership. Now twenty-two, Veena led the people so well that Abe could dedicate himself to the tribe's spiritual and emotional well-being. Still, even with his faith in Veena, he knew that there are events or dangers for which you cannot prepare, and he was eager for her safe return.

In his late thirties, Abe was one of the oldest in the tribe. As a jest, his congregation affectionately referred to him as "Old Abe," though not usually within his hearing. As he stood waiting and watching for the patrol's return, Abe reflected on just how quiet the forward garrison was. In alignment with the increased defense posture, the camp's defenders reduced the noise within the post, which enhanced their ability to respond to audible commands. The stillness reminded Abe of how much he missed the sound of children playing. *Will we ever be blessed with that joyful clamor again?*

Abe noticed movement at the southwestern corner of the camp. He turned to face Carla and MaryAn as they advanced quickly into the encampment. "Where are Veena and Laoni?" he called out with just a touch of apprehension.

Carla veered off to find Kath while MaryAn continued toward Abe to report.

"They are attending an injured stranger, just over a half-mile beyond the southwestern outpost. Veena sent us to get a stretcher and a burial detail."

Abe's eyes went wide. "A burial detail? I thought you said the person was injured."

"I'm sorry, Pastor Abraham," MaryAn said with embarrassment. "I'm not always good with reporting. Veena and Laoni are fine and caring for an unconscious man we found near the Lizard King's dead body. Pastor Abraham, that man is wearing a NASA uniform."

"What?" Abe spoke with a shocked expression.

"I know, it's puzzling. Anyway, Carla is informing Kath now, and I am selecting a couple of men for burial detail and several others to be litter carriers. I'm headed to the infirmary to get some supplies and the litter."

"I'll accompany you," Abe stated. He was a trained medic when he was younger and a part of a Marine Recon unit.

———

When they arrived back where Veena and Laoni were tending to the injured man, Carla and MaryAn took the two men assigned as the burial detail and started down the canyon slope to the Lizard King's body. Abe looked at the young man that Veena and Laoni guarded. The NASA uniform, and the young man's generally well-kept appearance, struck him immediately.

"Where did he come from?" Abe asked Veena, though he already knew the question was probably silly as the man appeared to be unconscious, and it was unlikely she had an answer.

Veena looked up at Abe, grinned, and said, "Amazing, isn't it? It's like he just arrived, dropped out of thin air. You don't think he came from a spaceship, do you?"

Veena's suggestion about a spaceship made Abe snort with a short laugh. "His uniform doesn't appear to be what you'd wear for space travel. When The Thinning came, as far as I know, the only astronauts who may have remained in space were those in the International Space Station, and he is too young to have come from there. He's a curious one. I'd say that he simply found that uniform in an abandoned storage container and put it on, but he doesn't look like he's been fighting to survive for eleven years as we have. So, what's your assessment, paramedic Veena?"

Veena smirked at Abe's tease of her role. "Nothing appears to be serious. He has a nasty bruise and a large cut over his left eye, which maybe he got from a blow by the Lizard King, who, by the way, appears to have snapped his neck. Otherwise, he has lots of minor cuts and tears, maybe from stumbling through the brush? His breathing and heart rate are robust and regular. I can't quite figure out why he hasn't regained consciousness. I thought he was waking up a moment ago, but then he quickly drifted off again."

Abe bent down and quickly confirmed Veena's appraisal. "OK, let's brace his neck as a precaution and take him back to camp."

Veena gulped when she realized she should have braced his neck before they brought him up the canyon. So, she took extra care as they prepared the man for transport. When the retrieval team lifted the litter and started back to camp, Veena walked on one side of the stretcher with Abe on the opposite side.

—⁓—

During the short trip back to camp, Nate drifted in and out of consciousness. He dreamed he saw a beautiful, light-brown angel on his right and an older, darker, male angel on his left. Nate felt as if he was floating along and felt a peace that he had never known before. Years later, he would remark how exceptional it was that he remembered it all so clearly.

CHAPTER 5

"**D**unkin' Donuts," the latest leader of the Clairens, was seething with anger. One of his miserable thugs had claimed to see a boat on the ocean over a day ago. Since then, none of the Clairen patrols had found anything. *What a bunch of pantywaists*, he thought.

Before The Fires, Walter Duncan was an overweight but meticulously clean night manager of a shoe store. Trying to win favor with his barely sentient staff, he brought a box of doughnuts in the store one evening as a treat. His innocent gift backfired when one of his employees, a pimply, skinny, and ill-dressed teenage boy, guffawed and gave Walter the nickname "Dunkin' Donuts." It was just his curse that the rascal had survived The Fires long enough to pass that horrible brand to the Clairens.

How has life turned out so bad? Before The Fires, he was married, rented a small two-bedroom apartment, and ate to compensate for any slights he endured. After a few years, his wife felt neglected and argumentative. The only thing they shared anymore was a love of toy poodles. They had three of the little dogs, which they pampered and overfed.

The disease that followed The Fires had been the end of his wife. Oddly, he did miss her. Their toy poodles didn't survive beyond the first month; the dogs probably became someone's dinner. He had a couple of new toy poodles, but now there wasn't anyone to clean and groom them. They were dirty, matted, and soiled mops. Regardless, he held an affection for them. Sadly, if his goons didn't find something to eat soon, these two would probably be on the menu.

Walter survived The Fires and disease, and it was an odd twist of fate that allowed him to remain alive with the gangs. Favorably, he knew how to brew beer, and that ability spared his life as the Clairen leader used the libations as a tool to control his punks. So Walter kept his life as long as he continued making more beer.

Moreover, Walter was shrewd. In the early days, he knew his life was at the mercy of the murderous tyrants who led the Clairens. He also recognized that his gang's leader's life was short as challengers, or rival gangs, made the despot a target. Therefore, Walter bided his time while a succession of the brutish bullies died at the hands of others. Finally, these destructive power struggles so effectively eviscerated the more intelligent and stronger leaders' ranks that Walter could assume control of the tribe by poisoning his predecessor and thereby becoming the de facto leader by being smarter than those who remained.

By the time he was able to gain control of the Clairens, they were the dominant gang in the region. At first, they were too far south to be bothered by either Rex and his K or the Riverside Raiders. The mountains and ridges between San Diego and the Los Angeles basin provided natural choke points that were easy to defend against those L.A. gangs' challenges. The pickings in the San Diego area were meager compared to what the L.A. gangs had in their basin. So, the Clairens had little interaction on their northern border.

On the south boundary, The Fires and disease had so savaged the Mexican gangs that those packs were content to defend their territory and not march north. There had been skirmishes in the early years after The Fires, but the Clairens held their own. Regardless, the Clairens no longer ventured south of the Mission Valley swamps. Now, their territory extended from the mesas north of Mission Valley to Camp Pendleton's northern border. Only those damn Tierrans to the east were near their turf and challenging the Tierrans always resulted in a vicious battle NOT in the Clairens' favor.

Walter had thought that things would settle after he had gained control of the Clairens. At first, he didn't have to fear threats to his life every day, and nearby gangs didn't intrude upon their territory. Sadly, that relative tranquility was short-lived. Three months later, Rex led a small band of his K south and demanded three-quarters of their beer and provisions. Additionally, Rex declared that the Clairens would be allowed to exist as a vassal to the K and pay a quarterly tribute of beer and plunder.

Unfortunately, the years of attrition had reduced the Clairens to louts who were barely self-aware, and he had to tell them explicitly what to do. When challenged by the K, Dwayne, the mightiest and fiercest member of the Clairens, rushed Rex. Rex's swift dispatch of Dwayne crushed Walter's rebellious thoughts. Rex smashed Dwayne's throat with such speed and force that Dwayne crumpled to the ground and writhed in pain for several minutes as he asphyxiated from the fatal blow to his windpipe. Walter had never seen such agility and dispatch. Nor had Walter encountered a leader who was so intelligent, lethal, and ruthless. Without hesitation, Walter dropped to his knees in submission, and the rest of the Clairens followed.

Hell, thought Walter, I never suspected that Rex was smart enough to have concepts of vassals, tributes, and fealty. Though he is a hulking brute, he's also more intelligent than I imagined. When I first heard of Rex, I assumed he was just another mindless savage who used his physical superiority to dominate others just like the previous leaders of the Clairens did. No, he appears to be sharp. I've got a bad feeling about my future.

Rex took the beer and provisions and returned to the north with most of the K he had brought. He left behind an evil miscreant, Jamir, and another K member –whom Walter silently branded as "Belligerent Bob"– as enforcers. Jamir was terrifying, savagely beating any Clairen whom he felt didn't defer submission in his presence. Walter realized that Rex must be exceptionally intimidating and cunning to keep Jamir in line. The thought sent a shiver through his body. Fortunately for Walter and the Clairens, Jamir got bored when the Clairens submitted so quickly, and he returned to the K territory in L.A. after three days. The only benefit of the forced inclusion into the K was that now the Riverside Raiders wouldn't even think of striking against the Clairens.

Belligerent Bob, on the other hand, was annoying, and was watching Walter's every move. When the Clairens could not locate the boat or any occupants, Walter felt his days were numbered. *Look what I have to deal with! I'm the figurehead regent in the land of the troglodytes. If these idiots don't find that boat or its occupants, I will soon face a purge myself when Belligerent Bob tells Rex.*

In the first two years after The Fires, stores of quality brew ingredients were exhausted. Since then, Walter directed his crew to pillage fields of grains to make a barely drinkable malt. However, the morons had failed to bring back anything for the last six months. The K had taken nearly all their stores, and soon all the previously brewed beverages would be exhausted. When that happened, Walter realized that things would go badly for him.

He looked down at his miserable body; all the previous fat had wasted away. Only the loose folds of skin draping from his bones divulged how obese he had been. Wistfully, he reminisced of doughnuts. *Those damn Tierrans probably got the boat and its occupants.*

CHAPTER 6

In the Tierran camp, Nate dreamed again of the man angel by his side, with whom Nate now felt complete trust, hope, and peace. The man spoke, and Nate clung to every word as though life depended upon what was said. The man said he was sending angels to watch over him, and Nate felt a calm that washed away any fears or doubts. He rested in sweet peace and assurance.

———

Veena and Abe kept a constant watch over their charge in the infirmary shelter at the forward camp as the morning wore on and the skies cleared. When the sun reached the highest point in the sky, Abe decided that the stranger named Sinclair was not in immediate medical danger, and he rose to step out of the shelter for fresh air. *Now would be a good time for a light lunch*, Abe thought and chuckled, as a light lunch is the only option available anyway. He was stiff and tired as he rose from the vigil, so he stretched before heading for the opening.

"Abe!" exclaimed Veena in a harsh whisper. "Where are you going? You can't leave him."

"Honey, I can't heal what ails him. I've done all that I can for now, and we'll just have to wait and see. You watch him while I get something to eat. When I return, you are going to take a break, too. Staying in here is not doing you, or our people, any good. We'll take turns watching him, and we should probably rotate MaryAn and Laoni into the duty to give us a longer break. For now, we are just waiting for him to heal and awake."

Veena knew Abe was right and that she should be attending to tribe business. Sometimes even her briefest absence would result in whispers and insinuations of new leaders, often initiated by Jody Higgins, a young woman who felt she could do things better. Since they had arrived back at the camp, Laoni had slipped into the shelter several times with dispatches from Kath that the sentries spotted roving bands of Clairens on the far ridge. Clairens coming so close to their camp was atypical. Though Veena had complete faith in Kath as her second-in-command, she wanted to check out the unrest for herself. Increased Clairen activity was disturbing and probably connected to the stranger.

Furthermore, several members of the tribe were idling outside the shelter and not getting their chores done. A couple of times already, Veena had to stand at the shelter entry and motion them away. As the tribe's leader, she knew she should delegate the watch over the stranger while ensuring the camp was secure and confirming everyone was performing their duties. However, she found that she was reluctant to withdraw from the stranger's bedside; she wanted to be there when he awoke.

Abe is right, she reminded herself, and she resolved to take a break when Abe returned. Having decided, Veena felt in control again, though a nagging, uncomfortable doubt tainted her resolution. At the edge of her vision, she detected movement at the stranger's side. After a moment, the stranger's hand twitched, and he sighed. He started to shift his position, moaned from discomfort, and his eyelids began to flutter open.

Veena jumped to the doorway. "Abe! Abe, come quickly!"

Abe rushed through the entry after just a couple of seconds, blinded momentarily by the sudden change from the bright sunlight outside to the dimmed light within the shelter.

"What is it, Veena? What's wrong?" asked Abe.

"I think he is waking up."

Abe had abruptly put down his bowl of soup before he ran to the shelter, slopping some of the broth onto his hands and pants. Keeping an eye on the stranger, he washed his hands at a nearby basin. Then, he bent over the bed and lifted Nate's eyelids so he could examine the pupils. Each iris reacted to the light and each pupil narrowed. He listened to Nate's breathing and heartbeat and then sat in the adjacent chair and relaxed.

"You're right, honey. He's regaining consciousness. Still, he's not awake yet; we should let him gradually come to on his own," whispered Abe. Then with a slightly stern tone, he added: "Now, I'll watch him while you go out and get something to eat. I'll call you as soon as he fully wakes."

"No. I'm gonna remain here."

"Listen, Veena, go," ordered Abe.

Again, Veena knew Abe was right. She rose quickly, left the shelter, and went to the community kitchen for a bowl of chicken broth and vegetable soup and a slice of bread. Each person she encountered asked her about the health of the stranger and what she knew. A stranger in the camp was news, and a stranger in a NASA uniform was big news. To each person, Veena mumbled a reply. Veena quickly excused herself and strode across to the camp center, where the tribe held its community gatherings. As she approached, she saw that Kath was handling the tribe's day-to-day business with the group leaders.

As Veena drew near, Kath dismissed the group leaders so she could talk privately with Veena. Veena sat at one of the rough wood benches around the meeting area, and Kath joined her. As Veena's closest friend, Kath sensed that Veena was troubled.

In some ways, they were so different. Veena was a southern California native, and her vocabulary continued to contain some of the local slang. However, growing through her adolescent years with Abraham Jones as her mentor and guardian, her speech became refined, such as replacing the previously used "yeah" with "yes." In contrast, Kath still had traces of her Georgia roots, even after spending years with Veena and Abe.

"So, how's the stranger?" asked Kath.

"Oh, not you, too. That's all anyone has said to me since I came back into camp."

"I'm sorry, Veena. I perceived you were troubled, and I was just trying to start the conversation."

Veena stared down at her soup, idly stirring the broth with her spoon before she looked up at Kath.

"Kath, tell me how you felt about Roy when you first saw him."

Kath's jaw dropped open in shock before she composed herself, pushing back the flower stuck in the hair above her ear, and answered, "Veena, you're kidding. Do you feel a connection with the stranger?"

"C'mon, give me a break!" Then, Veena relaxed a little. "Look, I'm sorry. It has been a trying and confusing day. He is odd, but there is something more about him than I can identify, and it's bothering me."

Kath lightly rested her hand on Veena's shoulder.

"Well, you'll recall that I first met Roy when the Clairens attacked my patrol. The Clairens had set an ambush, and one of my patrol rookies, who was on point, had blundered into it. They greatly outnumbered us, and, as it was the first patrol for several of the girls, they didn't immediately assemble in a defensive formation. In the first moments of the attack, the Clairens severely wounded half the patrol. I thought we were all lost before Roy and his men burst into the fight at our right flank. At first, I didn't comprehend that they were helping us until I realized they protected our wounded and repulsed the Clairen attack. I'm not even sure if I saw Roy until after we chased the surviving Clairens into the bushes; I was pretty busy fighting for my patrol and life. After it was all over and I gathered the girls and attended to the wounded, I saw a man carrying the youngest girl's lifeless body. Remember her? Her name was Sara." Kath choked with the memory.

Veena nodded somberly, looking down at her soup again. Sara had been a wonderful, bright young girl. *So much death, so much pain.* Her eyes started to water.

"Anyway, Roy was cradling her in his arms as he walked towards me ...and he was crying," Kath continued. "I have seen men cry before, but none have touched me as he did at that terrible moment. Roy set her body down nearby, took off his tattered shirt, and covered her face. At that moment, he was so beautiful, courageous, and like an angel to me that I just broke down and started crying myself. If it hadn't been for Roy and his men, none of us might have returned. Roy stepped close to me and opened his arms. I stepped towards him, a man I had never met before, and we cried together.

"His compassion and tenderness meant incredibly much at that moment. I have loved Roy ever since."

Veena and Kath sat in silence, tears trickling down their cheeks. Then, Veena wiped the tears from her face and spoke softly. "I remember that day. Sara was only three years younger than you. I'll never forget the sight of your patrol returning to camp with those new men helping the wounded and with your Roy walking glumly near you and carrying Sara's body. What I saw filled me with apprehension, concern, and deep aching and sadness."

Kath turned her gaze to Veena. "Yes, that was one of the saddest, most heartbreaking days of my life. It was even worse than The Thinning, as I was so young during that time. Unexpectedly, I found with Roy happiness that I didn't even realize I could have. To answer your question: even with all that was on my mind about the attack, when I first saw Roy, I felt a change in myself, as if I had just found something that was missing."

At that last remark, Veena grimaced briefly. Kath saw it and continued.

"Now, I see that expression on your face. I know we can stand alone without men. Yet, somehow, I grew then, and I felt more whole. Oh, I didn't realize all of these feelings at first, but the transformation was there, and I think I understand it now."

Veena felt a brief embarrassment. "I'm sorry; it's not my place to judge your feelings. I remember how Roy was always near you during those first days after the attack. He even stationed his men outside your shelter until we made him move them away. I know he and his men have been a great addition to the tribe. They all have blended quickly into our people, and it is hard to remember what it was like before they became part of our group. Nearly every man has paired with a woman among our people, and only when they go on patrol will they pull back from their identity within the tribe and reform into the Naval unit they had been when we first met them."

"Yes, it's interesting that we also tend to stick to all-women patrols. I guess using same-sex teams works best for all. Besides, men always think that they have to protect us. Ha!"

With that last snicker, the conversation paused. Veena looked down in contemplation before turning back up to Kath.

"Kath, I am both frightened of, and drawn to, the stranger. I am anxious about his injuries. I have a nagging fear, and I don't understand the reasons I feel this way. Even Abe noticed it and has teased me."

"Don't worry about it, Veena. I hear he is an attractive man. Watch yourself; we don't know anything about him, and he could be dangerous."

"You know, it's funny that you should say that," replied Veena, "because I get the sense that he is dangerous, but not in the way you mean."

"Uh-oh, Veena," teased Kath. Then she added thoughtfully, "Suppress those feelings for now. Abe can take care of him, and you have our people to lead. When the stranger recovers, we will find out more, and I know y'all will make the right decision."

"Yes, that's best," Veena sighed and started to eat her soup.

Kath then brought Veena up to speed on the activities of the camp. The burial party, two men escorted by Carla and MaryAn, had left to take care of the Lizard King's body. Laoni, who was like a daughter to Kath and Roy and lived with them, had insisted on joining Carla and MaryAn on the guard detail. Carla had given her approval to Laoni, and Kath, who didn't want to contradict Carla nor hold back Laoni by being overprotective, had reluctantly consented.

At that, Veena spoke up. "Yes, I wanted to talk with you about Laoni. She did exceptionally well on this morning's patrol. We saw several Clairen groups, and we hunkered down, undetected, to let them pass by us. Laoni performed flawlessly, just like a seasoned pro. When we found the Lizard King's body and Sinclair, she took the high position and guarded us."

Kath, startled by new information about the stranger, teased Veena, "Oh, Sinclair! Is that his name?"

"Oooh," groaned Veena. "Won't you guys ever give me a break? We saw the name on his clothes, and we assumed that's who he was. He may have stolen those clothes for all we know. Now, listen, I'm trying to talk with you about promoting Laoni to unrestricted patrol status."

At that, Kath beamed, "Thank you. Roy and I are proud of Laoni."

"Well, she is ready for advancement. You and Roy should be pleased with her."

No sooner had these words left Veena's lips when one of the sentries came running to the edge of the camp. "One of the men in the burial squad just signaled that they are under attack!"

Veena dropped her bowl as they both jumped to their feet and sprinted toward the southwest edge of the camp.

"Kath, border guard, Blue Team," ordered Veena. Kath, though she wanted to go with Veena to help defeat the attack and protect Laoni, split off to strengthen the camp's defenses, particularly the perimeter fence, against a potential separate attack. She would lead her Blue Team's advance sorties that scour the northern end of the canyon to the west.

With her next breath, Veena yelled out, "Red Team! Red Team, southwest!" Across the camp, Kath was calling out the Blue Team.

As the Red Team members gathered their crossbows and knives and sprinted to the meeting point, Veena met the sentry who called out the alert. "Status," she commanded.

"Unknown, Cap. Joe just appeared below the ridge and gave us the ambush signal," panted the sentry.

Abe came running to Veena, carrying her weapons. "What's going on?"

"Ambush of the burial squad; that's all I know. Watch Sinclair: maybe he's involved in whatever is happening."

"Not likely, but I'll watch him," responded Abe. "He is still unconscious."

Veena turned to face the Red Team and barked, "Ambush of a squad. Weapons on safety. Follow me." With that, Veena and the Red Team ran out of the camp.

CHAPTER 7

Half an hour earlier, Carla had stationed herself on top of the same large boulder that had obstructed their view of Sinclair earlier. She sent her teammate and companion, MaryAn, and Laoni, with the two-person burial detail. The foursome passed the Lizard King's body as they went down the side to the canyon floor and found a level spot where they could easily dig a grave. MaryAn and Laoni moved away from the men and took defensive positions, MaryAn heading toward the opposite canyon side while Laoni maneuvered a short distance up the canyon. The men, Larry and Joe, started digging.

The sun had burned off the fog and heightened the unwashed smell of the Lizard King's body. *Oh, swell, I'm downwind*, Carla thought as the odor reached her position atop the boulder. *I'm sure glad the death stink hasn't started yet.* Fortunately, the canyon floor was deep, coarse sand, and it didn't take the men too long to dig a sufficient grave.

As the men started back up the canyon side toward Carla to retrieve the Lizard King's body, a flurry of arrows and crossbow bolts rained down on them from the ridge behind her. Shocked by the unexpected direction of attack, the team froze in disbelief. Larry yelped as an arrow pierced his left thigh. With that, Carla's reflexes took over, and she whistled to the team as she slid off the boulder where she was so exposed. MaryAn and Joe scooped Larry off the ground and ran to the boulder for protection from the hail of projectiles. Laoni joined them and took a defensive firing position on the boulder's far side as MaryAn did the same on the near side. Carla looked at Larry's wound, decided it was not life-threatening, and that they should wait to take the arrow out later.

"Joe," Carla hissed. "Get to a viewpoint where the sentries can see you and signal for help. Use the boulder for cover as long as you can."

Joe turned and scampered down the slope, keeping the boulder between him and the attackers. An intermittent arrow or bolt flew his way, but he was already out of range when the attackers had a clear view of him.

"How did I let those assholes get behind us," Carla mumbled out loud as she peeked around the edge of the boulder to the ridgeline above them.

"Who would have thought that they would get between us and the camp?" MaryAn whispered to Carla.

"I should have!" Carla took a deep breath and looked again at Larry, MaryAn, and Laoni. She noticed a thin trickle of blood on Laoni's arm. "Laoni. You're bleeding on your right arm. Are you OK?"

"Oh, it's just a grazing cut. It's nothing like Larry's million-dollar wound," snickered Laoni as she grinned at Larry. Larry smiled back, then grimaced in pain.

"All right, then. Keep your eyes open, and don't fire unless you have to." Carla looked back at Joe, who now was partway up the opposite canyon wall, standing in an open area. "It looks like Joe is giving the signal to the sentries. We just have to keep them back until the response team gets here."

Carla cursed under her breath as she realized that she would suffer embarrassment from the tribal leaders in the best scenario. In the worst scenario, the attackers would press the ambush before the response team could get here. *Damn!*

CHAPTER 8

Peering along the edge of the boulder, MaryAn saw movement on the ridge above them. "Carla, two of them just took off along the ridge toward camp. I think they're going after Joe."

"Makes sense. OK, stay steady until our response team arrives. Those bastards have a better position on us."

Laoni spoke up. "Should I go and warn Joe?"

"No," replied Carla, with an air of irritation and resignation. "Joe knows the dangers and how to handle himself. We need you here in case they decide to rush us."

Laoni felt sick to her stomach for Joe; for some reason, she thought he was in more danger than they were, though that probably wasn't true. She concentrated on her view around the boulder, with a periodic glance at the canyon floor below them to make sure the Clairens did not outflank them. After a few minutes, she saw a man run to the canyon floor, about three hundred yards to the south of them.

"Carla, one of the Clairens is trying to circle us," whispered Laoni.

Carla turned and saw the man running across the canyon.

"I see him. I don't think he is trying to circle us, not by himself. I suspect he is going for reinforcements. That, at least, is good news in a sense. They must feel they don't have the numbers to rush us, so we're probably safe for a while. Now, if our help can arrive before the Clairen reinforcements, we'll get out of this fix. So, it's a waiting game. You can relax a little for now; just keep your scans up."

Keeping in the shade of the boulder as the morning sun rose higher, they pulled out camos to protect themselves from heat exhaustion that would weaken them and make them vulnerable. Carla glanced at Larry.

"How are you feeling, Larry?" she whispered.

"I've felt better, Sarge." Like Veena's *Cap* or *Captain Veena*, the Tierrans regularly referred to Carla as *Sarge*, another honorary title. "I don't feel I am bleeding anymore, but I do wish those Clairens would use clean arrows. I'm more worried about infection than any other damage. I would kinda like to get the dirty thing out of my leg; it's starting to hurt a lot."

Yeah, an infection may be the worst problem, thought Carla. Turning to Laoni, she whispered, "Laoni, I'm taking your position. Pull back and check on Larry. See if that arrow can come out so we can treat the wound."

Laoni pulled back as Carla moved to the edge of the boulder. Quickly assessing Larry's wound and the arrow, she whispered back to Carla, "We'd have to cut next to the wound to get the arrow out. The shaft has spurs; it's not gonna come out easily."

"Shit. Well, Larry, you're going to have to tough it out until we get you back to camp. It won't be too long." Carla locked eyes with MaryAn before they both turned back toward the threat.

CHAPTER 9

Nate's head was throbbing. All he could see was a blurry fog. He felt a damp cloth wiping his forehead, cooling it. He blinked a couple of times, moaned, and then narrowed his eyelids to a slit. His vision cleared slightly, and he saw that he was in a dimly lit room.

A voice spoke gently, "Well, young man, it's about time you returned to the land of the living."

Nate turned his aching head slightly to the left and saw a kind, dark face watching him. Hoarsely, he whispered, "Where's Dr. Epstein?"

"Dr. Epstein?" the kind face replied. "I don't think I know him. I haven't heard of another doctor for at least ten years. My name's Abraham Jones. Some call me Old Abe, but I'd prefer it if you would call me Abe. What's your name?"

After a moment, Nate responded, "Lieutenant Nathanael Sinclair, sir, though I prefer 'Nate.'" Oh, his head ached.

"Nathanael. Interesting name. Are you in the Navy, Lieutenant?"

"Yes. Please, where's Dr. Epstein? She should be here. My head is killing me," Nate responded weakly.

"Settle down. You have a nasty bump on your forehead, and you need to rest. Here, take a sip of water."

Cradling Nate's head, Abe lifted the cup of water to Nate's lips. The water was refreshing and soothed his raw throat.

Nate tried to rise to a sitting position, but he got dizzy and fell back on the bed.

"Whoa, young man. You're not in any condition to go anywhere. I told Veena I'd look after you, so you rest."

"Who's Veena?"

Abe smiled. "Veena's the one who brought you here. She found you passed out in the canyon, and she is concerned about you. To be frank, you are a mystery to us. Enough of that for now; rest, and we'll talk later."

Nate felt overwhelmingly weary, and sleep overtook him.

CHAPTER 10

Soon after giving the signal to the sentry post situated on the opposite ridge, Joe saw the unmistakable flash of an arrow zipping past his head. He quickly realized that at least one of the Clairens had come for him and was between him and the camp. A second arrow narrowly missed his chest, and, with that, Joe bolted northward along the canyon floor, hoping to get closer to the sentry post that was just to the northwest and out of the range of the Clairen arrows.

His lungs ached; already hot and weary from digging the grave when the attack came, he had been sprinting ever since. He knew he couldn't keep running at this pace when he spied a sage bush that could conceal him and darted behind it. He crouched low, struggling to quiet his heavy breathing, and waited.

Advantageously for Joe, his pursuers had momentarily lost sight of him. They were puffing heavily, and they couldn't hear him over their gasping. Joe needed any advantage he could get as he had left his crossbow near the burial site. Now, he had to rely on his wits, experience, and the knife he carried on his belt.

Joe watched as the Clairens ran toward where he was hiding. When they reached the large sagebrush, one continued moving in the same direction while the other turned left to ascend to higher ground. Joe kept low, hoping they would both pass. The first was soon out of sight, but the second man slipped as he climbed the steep, loose soil of the canyon wall and tumbled right next to Joe. The Clairen was surprised to see Joe but recovered quickly enough that Joe's first lunge with his knife didn't strike a fatal wound. The man fought like a wounded animal, but Joe's training was better. He finally sank his knife into the man's chest, and the struggling ceased.

Joe heard a noise on the higher ground behind him and turned toward the sound. There, he saw the second Clairen raising his crossbow and moving to a better firing position. As Joe gulped for air, his heart sank as he saw the Clairen carefully aim at him. Trapped, Joe thought it was the end. The Clairen was close enough that Joe could see a smirk spread on the man's face.

Then, before the Clairen fired his crossbow, Joe heard a *thunk* and saw a bolt sticking out of the Clairen's chest. The Clairen was surprised too, and he lowered his crossbow. Joe saw the Clairen looking down at the bolt before the crossbow fell to the ground, quickly followed by his body's collapse as life left him.

Joe couldn't believe he was still alive, and he wondered about the shot that saved him. Then, he saw Kath and another Blue Team member about twenty yards beyond where the Clairen had stood. Kath was reloading her crossbow as her teammate member searched for additional threats. Joe wanted to yell with joy, but his chest heaved in welcome relief as he struggled to catch his breath. Then, he vomited.

CHAPTER 11

W hile Joe fought with the Clairen pursuers, Veena's Red Team was about a mile south of the camp. As they approached the location of the burial team, Veena signaled her team to spread out and advance quietly. They quickly and silently separated from their column and dispersed into a firing line. Continuing south along the ridge, the team stayed within the tree line. They were about one hundred yards from the Clairens when Jody spied the ambushers and alerted Veena with hand signals. Veena motioned to the rest of the team to hold their position while she and Chief Virtolli crept to Jody's location to size up the situation.

They observed the Clairen patrol, five scraggly and filthy men, resting on the ridge and looking at the canyon below. None were over thirty-five, but all looked worn and old from hard living. Veena was relieved to see their technique was sloppy as they hadn't set a rear guard. She could hear them squabbling over the women they had trapped in their attack on the burial squad below them; greed and lust had replaced wisdom.

Leaving Jody to guard their flank, Veena and Chief Virtolli took different approaches to maneuver within forty yards of the Clairens. After surveying the arguing Clairens, Veena signaled Chief Virtolli to withdraw with her about ten yards and then signaled Jody to bring the rest of the team forward.

When they gathered, Veena first whispered to Chief

Virtolli, "Chief, I counted five. What about you?"

"I also saw only five, Cap. That doesn't make sense; don't the Clairens send out patrols of eight? Why isn't there a rearguard?"

"It may be a stroke of luck for us," replied Veena in hushed tones. "I'm guessing that old fart that is leading them is a bit cocky. They are arguing about who gets the women and not acting like a seasoned unit. I'd wager that they sent one man to get reinforcements and at least another to chase whoever sent the signal to our sentry post. Post your defensive guards, Chief, and let's take care of these fools now."

Chief Virtolli turned to his Red Team and whispered, "You three, take defensive positions and guard our flanks and rear. The rest of you, we have seen five Clairens. Close within ten yards of them and wait for Veena's first shot. Keep your eyes open for anything we might have missed. There may be at least one more Clairen nearby."

As silent as shadows, they moved into position.

CHAPTER 12

While Veena's team moved into attack position, Carla's team, unaware that their rescuers had arrived, kept watch from behind the boulder's shielding. Carla pulled her hand away from the crossbow trigger and wiped off the sweat running down her forehead beneath her closely cropped hair. She glanced at her crew and saw how the midday heat and constant tension were wearing all of them down.

For Laoni, MaryAn, and Carla, the day had started just before dawn with Veena's patrol, and they were weary. *Damn, it doesn't feel like it is the same day*, thought Carla. *What strange and awful events.* Carla hoped she could put things right and save her squad.

Abruptly, screams arose from the ridge above them and cut short the waiting. All four of them snapped to full alertness, each one stifling their reflex screams as adrenaline flooded their blood. They squinted, straining to see what was happening above them and whether an onslaught was about to rain down. Laoni briefly glanced away from her scans of the canyon, looking to see if death was coming from the ridge above them.

"Are they attacking? I can't see them, Carla."

Carla scanned the ridge. "No," she breathed with relief. "Something else is going on up there."

A moment later, they heard the all-clear whistle and saw Veena exposed on the ridge. Several of the Red Team members started down the slope toward Carla and her squad. Carla stood up and waved them in.

Veena saw Carla and rushed past her advancing team. When she got within range, she spoke to Carla in hushed words, "We got five; are there any others?"

"One went toward the Clairen camp, and two took off after Joe, who I sent to alert the sentries. Is he all right?"

"I don't know." Veena turned to Chief Virtolli, who had just joined them. "Chief, send a squad to find Joe, and watch out for at least two Clairens who were pursuing him." Chief Virtolli turned and quickly sent off a group led by Jody.

Veena turned back to Carla. "How's the rest of your squad?"

"Larry has a bolt in his thigh. Another arrow grazed Laoni's arm, but she appears to be OK; she's guarding our six. MaryAn is unharmed and guarding the approach on the far side of the boulder."

Veena looked at Chief Virtolli again. "Chief, have your medic do an assessment and evacuation. Leave four of your men with me. We have Clairen bodies to drag to that clearing below and leave them as a warning to any Clairen reinforcements. Then, we're all withdrawing to camp; no more casualties."

Each did as Veena commanded. That is how the first battle ended after the stranger's arrival.

CHAPTER 13

hief Virtolli and several members of the Red Team remained behind to finish burying the Lizard King and watch for a Clairen response. The rest of the team helped Larry back to the infirmary. Veena followed them to relieve Abe so he could treat Larry. There was also her desire to observe the resting stranger that her team had brought in that morning. Constructed with salvaged, manufactured wood and partitioned with reclaimed plastic sheets and bedspreads, the infirmary was the best-built structure in the forward camp. When she entered, Kath was already there with Joe.

Veena stood at the door to the room where the stranger dozed as Kath briefed her, in a low voice, on their rescue of Joe from the two Clairens. Kath had pulled back the Blue Team and beefed up the staffing of the sentry posts. Satisfied that everything was under control, Veena left Kath to monitor the stranger as she went into the room where Abe was treating Larry.

As Abe finished suturing Larry's wound, he saw Veena enter and said, "Larry should be OK in about ten days." As a result of the pain meds, Larry was grinning like a fool. Then, Abe nodded toward the adjacent room. "Oh, his name is Lieutenant Nathanael Sinclair, but he likes to be called Nate. He appears to be OK. He keeps asking for a Dr. Epstein."

With that, Veena returned to Nate's room and sent

Kath to recheck the camp. She sat in the chair by Nate and studied his face. He was young, probably mid-twenties, reasonably tall with blond hair. She recalled that when he opened his eyes earlier, that she had gazed into deep blue eyes. *What a mystery; he has a little stubble of facial growth, but he is considerably more clean-shaven than most outsiders we've encountered. Other than dirt on his jumpsuit and scratches on his face and hands, he is markedly cleaner than anyone nowadays.* Then, she realized that he didn't have the weather-beaten and sun-darkened appearance like everyone else. While she sat there pondering this, she drifted into sleep.

CHAPTER 14

In the late afternoon, Chief Virtolli and the rest of the Red Team returned to camp. Veena awoke as she heard him enter the infirmary to give his report, and she felt stiff and sore from sleeping in the chair. She rose to meet him at the door of the room.

"Your strategy worked regarding leaving the dead Clairen bodies exposed on the canyon floor as a warning," Chief Virtolli spoke in a low voice. "We saw about forty of the Clairens start down from the west ridge of the canyon. They must have spotted the bodies as they stopped in their tracks and then quickly retreated to the top of the ridge. They sent a group of eight to inspect the bodies. After they looked at each one, they stripped the clothing from the dead. We would have let them all go, but one of the eight used his machete to start hacking off the legs of the dead and started shouting how they'd 'eat meat tonight.'"

Chief Virtolli paused. "I can't tolerate cannibalism, so from my concealment, I tried to shoot near that bastard and scare all of them off. Just as I squeezed the trigger, the degenerate stepped forward into my line of fire; the bolt hit him, and he dropped right there. The rest of them took off scrambling like mad up the far slope, and we let them. After an hour, my deep scouts signaled that the Clairens had returned to their camp. We built a fire and burned the dead, then came back."

"OK," said Veena. "Tell Kath to keep the extra sentries through the night, and if nothing more happens, we can stand down to normal alert level at dawn tomorrow."

As Chief Virtolli left, Abe passed into the room to check on Nate. He looked at Veena. "Honey, you look beat. Are you all right?"

"Yes, Abe. I just woke up from a nap. How's Nate? I'm guessing he is the reason for so much of the events of the day, including the Clairen drums last night."

"He is recovering nicely. As you can see, I took out the IV, and his color is much better."

As Abe spoke these words, Nate's eyes fluttered open. He briefly looked at Abe and a slight smile formed on his face. Then, he saw Veena, and his smile widened. "You, ...you are the angel. My god, you are beautiful."

Both Abe and Veena smiled back, though a blush tinged Veena's smile.

Nate raised himself onto his elbows, and Veena saw that he reclosed his eyes and raised his right hand across his face to touch his forehead. It was evident that he had quite a headache.

Abe lightly touched Nate's shoulder. "Easy, Lieutenant. You will be all right, but you have a few nasty bruises that will hurt for a day or two. Here, let me prop you up with some pillows."

Nate relaxed back into them and withdrew his hand from his forehead. He blinked his eyes open again and looked at Abe. "Did I talk to you before?"

"Yes," responded Abe. "How are you feeling?"

"I have a headache, and I feel very sore." Then Nate added, "I thought I was dreaming, but I don't think I'd have a headache in a dream. Where am I, and where is Dr. Epstein?"

Abe hesitated. "You are not dreaming. I do not know Dr.

Epstein, but I'd sure like to meet her. You are in our camp. Tell me your name again."

"Nate. Lieutenant Nathanael Sinclair. I'm in the Navy, and I'm working on a research project for NASA."

"NASA? That is a name I haven't heard in a very long time," remarked Abe. Turning to Veena, he said, "Veena, would you get Nate some soup and fresh water, please? Let's get some food into him before we continue this conversation."

Before Veena turned to leave the room, Nate looked at her. "Veena, what a most unusual name. It reminds me of Venus, and I'd say that is appropriate."

With that, Veena blushed again as she turned to Abe and acidly remarked, "Well, our patient seems to be better. I'll be back in a moment."

Nate watched Veena leave. He took a deep breath and faced Abe. "What do you mean, we're in your camp?"

Abe paused before he spoke. "Let's hold that question until a little later."

CHAPTER 15

Walter Duncan marched in a huff back to their camp. *What a disaster this day had become.* They didn't find the boat nor any of its occupants. A patrol had stumbled upon a Tierran burial squad, but instead of killing the men and capturing the women, the Tierrans dispatched most of his patrol. After the runner from the patrol reached the camp to get reinforcements, Walter personally led all the Clairens to make the battle an overwhelming defeat for the Tierrans. They returned to the site too late, finding only the dead bodies of the patrol.

Leery of an ambush, Walter recalled his bedraggled group; that was enough losses for one day. At that, Loudmouth Larry, a constant thorn in his side and a complete halfwit, argued vehemently to scavenge the clothing. *He's just trying to suck up to Belligerent Bob and the K.* "Well, go ahead," Walter said, and so that nitwit got seven more fools to go down to the bodies with him. It was OK until Larry decided he wanted to harvest his former Clairen buddies for meat. That ended badly for Larry. *At least I won't have to watch out for Loudmouth Larry anymore,* thought Walter. "Damn those Tierrans!" he muttered, and the scraggly shells of men closest to Walter moved away to be out of range of any rage-filled lashings.

CHAPTER 16

After Veena returned with a food tray, Abe instructed Nate to eat. Then, while Nate slowly drank some warm broth, Abe took Veena aside, out of Nate's hearing range, and whispered, "Veena, I recommend you assemble your senior leaders for our discussion with Nate."

Veena gave a slight nod and left the infirmary again.

Abe returned to the chair by Nate's cot. "Lieutenant, we're going to need some answers from you before we continue. Veena is gathering her leaders, and when they have assembled in this room, we will carry on. Until then, finish the soup and water, and rest your voice. We'll need you to speak truthfully and strongly this evening."

Nate nodded slowly back and continued spooning the soup into his mouth. After a few swallows and a gulp of water, he asked, "Are you the leader here?"

Abe smiled. "I no longer lead these people. It was one of many responsibilities that I carried, and I was glad when Veena stepped up to that position. I still have roles as advisor, teacher, spiritual leader, and, oh, camp doctor! Those duties keep me busy enough that my days are full."

Abe could tell that Nate was mulling this over as he finished his soup.

—◦◦◦—

It was late evening before Veena returned with her leaders. The light had faded, and the temperature cooled. Abe lit some oil lamps as the tribe's leadership gathered around Nate's cot. Abe sat on Nate's right, and Veena sat on Nate's left. In an arc around the cot, joining them were Kath and her husband, Royce Haines; Chief Virtolli; and Carla. These people formed Veena's inner circle and were her most trusted leaders.

Abe began, "Let us open in prayer. Almighty God, You are the Way, the Truth, and the Light. Please guide us by Your Holy Spirit, that we may discern the truth and respond according to Your will. In the precious name of our Savior, Your son, Y'shua HaMashiach, amen."

They all said, "Amen," and raised their eyes to look upon Abe and Nate.

Smiling at their guest, Abe said, "Nate, tell us who you are, where you have been, and how you came to be here, please."

Nate again looked at all the faces watching him, lingering a moment on Veena, before turning back to Abe. "I don't understand what is happening or where I am. Everything is so screwed up that I am concerned that I am having delusions. Where am I?"

"Nate," Abe responded, "for us to move forward with you, we have to know about you first. If you can't be honest with us and satisfactorily answer our questions, we will have to send you from camp tomorrow. We are responsible for the safety of our tribe, and we cannot tolerate anyone in camp whom we cannot trust completely."

Nate looked down after Abe spoke before raising his eyes to face Veena this time. He didn't know how to proceed, but he felt that he could trust Abe and Veena. So, he took a deep breath and started: "OK, I am Nathanael Sinclair, a lieutenant in the U.S. Navy. I am part of the Extended Space Missions, Suspended Animation Studies project in the Navy.

We are investigating the possibility of putting astronauts into suspended animation to conserve resources for long-duration interplanetary missions. I have a Bachelor of Science degree in Engineering, specializing in Computer Science and Cognitive Reasoning. As such, I have been a leader in software development and testing within the project.

"I joined the program as a pathway to becoming a mission specialist for NASA. I applied to become one of the suspended-animation test subjects when it became clear that all other paths to enter NASA would not work out. I knew the successes we had in the program, and I was confident of the result.

"Management selected me as a candidate, and I am the last test subject in phase two of the suspended-animation tests. As the final test subject, my suspended animation would last six months.

"However, when I awoke a few nights ago, the test facility was dark and empty. Frankly, I was utterly confused to wake up alone, and I am still a bit unsettled and frightened. I expected to be gently revived by the medical staff but instead was startled awake to a darkened facility with several alarms blaring and red failure lights flashing.

"Before I left the test facility, I tried to contact both the shore and the central labs, but I didn't get any response. I felt disoriented and mildly sick, and I can barely remember getting into the emergency escape pod. I'm even questioning how long it has been since I awoke from the suspended-animation sleep."

Abe looked at those gathered there and saw both the expressions of shock and disbelief. This story was so unusual and detailed that it must have held a seed of truth. He sensed where it was leading. "Nate, when, exactly, did your sleep test start?"

When Nate responded with a date in early October *eleven years ago*, the shocked audience filled the room with a collective gasp. Veena's eyes went wide as she stared back at Nate. Abe motioned with his hands to quiet the leaders. "Nate, where is the test facility, and how did you get here from it?"

"The test facility is isolated underwater just off San Clemente Island. As I said: when I couldn't reach anyone, I used the emergency escape pod to return to the surface. The pod resembles a miniature submersible and has a diesel engine as well as an electric engine. The diesel didn't work very well, and I exhausted the electrical system as it took me back to the Scripps Pier in La Jolla. We use the Scripps Pier as our transit station, and the pod was programmed to arrive after 0400 when it was less likely to be seen by people on the shore. I couldn't raise anyone on the whole trip, which took about twenty hours, and the pier was unoccupied when I got there. I had to tie up the pod as best as possible because the pier appeared to be damaged. Nothing looks like what I remembered, and I've been stumbling through the fog ever since. Where, exactly, am I?"

CHAPTER 17

REVELATION 1

Nate's timeline was so outrageous that Abe and Veena withdrew to confer, taking the rest of the leadership team with them and leaving a stunned Nate alone. Once outside of Nate's hearing, Veena turned to Roy and commanded, "Roy, please have the SEAL team check it out."

Roy understood the implications. "Right. If it's there, I'll make sure we secure it and move it alongside the *Des Moines*." He quickly left the infirmary.

After just a couple of minutes, Abe returned. "Nate, we are going to confirm what you have told us about the pod. Until we do, we won't continue the interrogation. A SEAL team will have more information for us by morning. What you have said is hard to conceive and harder to believe, yet I do believe you. To answer part of your question, you are in the ruins of San Diego. If what you say is true, it has been eleven years since you went into suspended animation. You must be nearly out of your mind with thoughts about what is true and what has happened."

"I am!"

"I need you to be patient, so we can confirm and ensure the tribe is not at risk." Abe extended his hand and revealed a pill on his palm. "Take a sedative. As they are worth more than gold, we rarely use medications whenever we can avoid them. In my experience, you'll need it tonight. Tomorrow, we will need you fully rested and at your best so you can continue your statement."

Nate paused and then took the pill with the glass of water on the small table next to his cot. Abe, pondering the remarkable story revealed so far, remained in the room until Nate drifted off to sleep.

———

There was a commotion outside Nate's room as the early rays of dawn crept past the window's curtain seams. As Nate blinked open his eyes, he saw that Veena had replaced Abe as his monitor. The gentle light magnified her beauty: curly brown hair that was cut above her shoulders and framed by a camouflage scarf, copper-hued skin without blemish, hazel eyes that were wide open in the dim light, and a firm muscle tone that was evident even though she wore loose-fitting, camouflage clothes that nearly covered her completely. As she looked back at him, he sensed a softness that was so different from her commanding presence the previous night.

As he opened his eyes, she grinned and said with a slightly teasing tone, "Well, it appears that at least part of what you have told us is true, so we decided not to kill you... yet."

Nate smiled back. "So, what happens now?"

"Vince," Veena called out. Vincent Ramon, a wiry, clean-shaven young man with buzz-cut hair, stepped into the room. "This is Lieutenant Nate Sinclair. Show him how we clean up around here and escort him to the mess in half an hour."

When Nate had washed up and stepped out of the infirmary hut for the first time, the crisp air and bright sunlight were a welcome change. With Vince at his side as he walked, he felt every cut and bruise. Nate moved awkwardly, working out the kinks in his muscles. After the days and nights of fog and darkness, the camp's openness, with clear skies and fresh air, made him feel like he had just awoken from a bad dream and into an inviting world.

As his eyes adjusted to the daylight, he took in the view of the camp. It appeared to be rather spartan, with few people in the camp's communal area. As they approached the mess shelter, he saw Abe, Veena, and others waiting for him. Abe rose as they entered the covering and pointed to an opening on the bench across from Veena and himself. As Nate sat, he observed an older Latina with closely cropped hair who watched him with an intense stare as she took a spot beside him. On his other side, Nate noticed a burly, muscled African-American man. He felt a bit uneasy as the pair sandwiched him in his seat.

With everyone in place, Abe spoke. "Nate, I'll start with introductions." He reintroduced the people Nate had met before and then added Kathy Haines and First Lieutenant Caleb Gates to the list. "By a series of strange and difficult events, our people have become known as the Tierran tribe, and I'll explain more about that later. By the expression on your face, I can see that you are thoroughly confused and have questions. I ask that you wait a bit before you launch into your questions, as I hope our discussion here will clarify the bulk of them. First, let us give thanks and share a meal."

At that, a man and a woman approached the table with bowls of oatmeal, torn sections of flatbread, and a couple of baskets of small apples. After they served, they withdrew, and the leaders bowed their heads in prayer as Abe led the blessing: "Almighty God, our Sustainer, our Redeemer, our Hope, and the Lover of our souls. We give You thanks for this bounty. May we never take it for granted. Bless the food to our bodies and our bodies to Your service. In the name of our LORD, Y'shua HaMashiach, Amen."

While everyone started to eat their breakfast, Nate, with a mildly confused look on his face, turned to Abe and asked in a low voice, "Abe, may I ask a question about your prayer?"

"Certainly."

"I've heard you pray twice, and both prayers sound like Christian prayers, but end with 'ye-shoo-AH' instead of Jesus. Who is 'ye-shoo-AH?'"

A wide smile formed on Abe's face as he gently said, "You're right, Nate. These are Christian prayers. Y'shua is the Hebrew name for Jesus. You may have heard that Joshua is the Hebrew name for Jesus, and that is nearly correct as Joshua is the Anglicized version of Y'shua. We are Christians, and I just prefer to use Y'shua instead of Jesus. Do you understand?"

Nate nodded. "And what is that word after Y'shua?"

"'Haw-mash-she-ACK.' It is the Hebrew word meaning 'The Anointed One,' commonly translated as 'Messiah,' or for us English speakers, 'Christ,' which is the Anglicized pronunciation of the Greek equivalent. As I said, just my personal preference."

"Ahh," said Nate, with a nod of comprehension.

Caleb finished his food in just a couple of gulps, and Veena asked for his report.

"We found the escape pod at the Scripps Pier. It matches what you told me. My team is towing it to the sub base for further analysis and safekeeping. There isn't any evidence that the Clairens, or anyone else, are aware of it. Before dawn, we moved it beyond the horizon, so it isn't visible from the shore. The team will wait until nightfall to bring it into the sub base."

Veena glanced over at Roy, and he nodded. "Thanks, Caleb, and thank your team. Get some rest." Caleb got up and Vince took his spot.

Veena looked briefly at Abe before returning her gaze to

Nate. Abe wiped his mouth before picking up the conversation again.

"Nate," Abe said, "thank you for holding off on your questions. There is so much to tell you that it is hard to begin. I'll start, and then we'll break for a bit. Until we've confirmed everything that you have told us, you will be assigned an escort wherever you go. I don't think it will take us long to get that confirmation, so we appreciate your cooperation. You will be free to move within the camp, and you can ask questions of your escort, who will answer you as far as she, or he, is comfortable. So, let's begin.

"You said you started your suspended animation in early October, with your revival scheduled after six months. Well, eleven years ago, when your sleep experiment began, it was just before the whole world changed. None of us knows the entire scope of events, but from our own experiences and information that Roy and his surviving crew from the U.S. submarine *Des Moines* brought us, we have pieced together the gist of what has happened.

"After several years of drought, fires erupted worldwide, in mid-October. Probably, a portion of fires started naturally from lightning strikes. A few more were likely ignited accidentally by reckless burning or campfires. But I suspect that arsonists and terrorists lit most of the blazes. In southern California and the northern Baja regions of Mexico, strong Santa Ana winds blossomed. These winds blow westerly from the eastern deserts and accelerate to between sixty and ninety miles an hour as they sweep across the mountain ridges that separate the deserts from the coast.

"The gusts drove long walls of flames that soon overwhelmed the firefighting capabilities of the region. Furthermore, it appears that wind-driven fires were burning all across the country and the world. Consequently, local fire crews were unable to get support from external regions as everyone was fighting fires.

"In San Diego County and Tijuana, brush fires drove a fire line that advanced as fast as thirty miles an hour to the coast. Smoke and flames soon engulfed communities and neighborhoods. The enormous traffic from those fleeing The Fires snarled the roads, and accidents and breakdowns compounded the chokepoints. Thousands died trapped in their cars, including Veena's parents. Flames were everywhere, and almost all the buildings burned to the ground."

Abe could see the shock and incomprehension on Nate's face, and he continued his narrative.

"It was horrifying how fast society collapsed. We witnessed it locally, and later it was confirmed as a worldwide catastrophe. All the television and radio stations were silent within twenty-four hours. Electricity blackouts began about four hours after The Fires started, and all the area was without power before a day had elapsed. Gasoline storage areas exploded in enormous fireballs, and even the Navy couldn't get enough of its fleet out of the harbor before they too were ablaze. The enormity of the death and devastation is hard to comprehend unless you have experienced it.

"Before losing the news feeds entirely, we heard that devastation was happening all around the world. Roy and his crew confirmed our speculation when they joined us about a year later. In the Middle East, the eastern European regions, Africa, and most of Asia, regional war activity exploded during The Fires. Central and South American forests and jungles were ablaze. Overall, only Australia and New Zealand, though they also had enormous fires, escaped armed conflict.

"At first, the governments in the United States, Canada, western and northern Europe, Russia, China, Japan, Australia, and New Zealand continued to function. The infrastructure and supply chains in all countries were severely crippled, and food shortages and riots started within three days. As a result of The Fires, large populations of survivors migrated to metropolitan areas. Sanitation, clean water, and food became immediate problems.

"Then, approximately four days later, the epidemic started. After all this time, we still don't know what the disease was. It was similar to the mumps, but the overcrowding, shortages, and lack of medical staff and supplies probably contributed to a morbidly high mortality rate. There is probably a better scientific name, but we all know it as "Mumps Reaper," or MR for short. From what little we know, everyone who survived The Fires got MR, and about eighty percent succumbed."

Abe took a sip of water and looked at Roy. "Roy, would you recount the experience your crew and you had and your knowledge of the worldwide devastation, please?"

Everyone around the table was grim-faced, and several were weeping. Nate's face showed bewilderment.

—◦◦◦—

Roy drew a deep breath. "The epidemic became a pandemic. International flights and troop movements continued in the first days after The Fires began. The massive relocations probably were the catalysts that enabled the disease to spread so rapidly. When fires exploded everywhere, our nuclear-powered, fast-attack submarine, the *Des Moines,* was on station, submerged in the Indian Ocean. The last contact with the Navy and the U.S. government was on October thirtieth, nearly two weeks after The Fires started. We had reports of what was happening worldwide, but those disclosures became more sporadic after the pandemic spread. That last news was terse. It stated that all governments had collapsed, food was scarce, and riots and anarchy were widespread. Local factions and gangs were taking control of any remaining resources. Fleet Command told us that

Australia and New Zealand were our best refuges, even better than returning to the States. Yet, it also said that those countries were struggling as the pandemic ravaged their populations.

"After two more weeks without any communication from the U.S., we traveled to Perth, Australia. Fires also impacted the city. Drought severely depleted the water reserves, and Perth's rapid population growth overburdened the infrastructure. So, their fire departments were overwhelmed, too. By the time we arrived, the disease was rampant, and soon every member of our boat fell to the sickness. The crew had a higher survival rate than the local population; even so, we lost thirty percent, including our Captain.

"At first, we delayed in Perth as we dealt with the illness, always trying to reestablish communications with Fleet Command, but never succeeding. I was the Executive Officer, and after I recovered from my sickbed, I was the senior officer of the boat. As we could not reestablish comms with the fleet, and since it was evident that Perth's surviving population needed our assistance, we stayed for about six months. It became abundantly clear that the disaster was worldwide and that, indeed, every national government had collapsed. We didn't realize that the local Perth administration's survival was abnormal until we finally returned to the U.S. and couldn't find any authorities. Sadly, when we left, there were widespread food shortages, looting, and anarchy. I suspect that Perth also fell to chaos within the year.

"A handful of our surviving crew decided to remain behind in Perth, mainly the single men who had built relationships with the survivors there. The rest of us gathered what provisions we could and made full speed for the U.S. west coast. When we passed the Hawaiian facilities, we cruised slowly to listen for any activity, friendly or hostile. There was nothing. Though we were anxious to get to San Diego,

I directed the crew to navigate past the entire western coast of the U.S. and search for signs of our nation and civilization. Sadly, we didn't find any electronic signals, electric lights, or any visible activity. Caleb Gates and his SEAL team made several excursions to the major ports and military installations on the West Coast, including Kodiak, Anchorage, and Juneau in Alaska; Whidbey, Kitsap, and Everett in Washington; and California's Concord, Vandenberg, Port Hueneme, Point Mugu, Long Beach, and Camp Pendleton, and finally Point Loma and North Island in San Diego. They were ghost towns, though Gates's team picked up a few survivors who joined our crew. The survivors told us about the collapse in the U.S., and the SEALs confirmed the anarchy that reduced our country to gangs and tribes. Less than a year after The Fires, we knew what to expect when we reached San Diego. Nevertheless, we had hope.

"To keep our boat safe, we kept it over the horizon from the coast. Gates and his SEALs acquired small boats to ferry a landing party into the sub base and secure it. Capturing and defending the facility turned out to be an easy task, though we crushed two skirmishes with roving gangs that appeared after we docked the *Des Moines*.

"With the port secure, we sent expeditions around San Diego County and northern Baja Mexico to look for family and survivors. The searchers didn't find any of their families. We did stumble upon a battle between a gang of men and Kathy and her patrol of women." Kath smiled. "We intervened to aid the women, and that is how we met the Tierran tribe. There is more to the story, especially with regards to our inclusion here, but I'll leave that for another time and speaker."

—∕∿∕—

Abe watched Nate during the entire discourse. He could

see the disbelief and confusion in Nate's eyes and posture. As Nate didn't experience the events, Abe knew it was too much for him to understand. It was time to end the discussion and let it stew in Nate's mind. Abe glanced at Veena and nodded.

"All right," commanded Veena. "That is enough for today. Nate will join those of us who are returning to base camp at dawn tomorrow. Nate, Abe will take you back to the infirmary. Vince, you will post a guard on Nate for tonight and make sure he is ready to travel at first light."

"Wait!" Nate spoke up in an exasperated voice. "I have so many questions. Aren't we already at your camp?"

Veena looked at Nate with a sad but empathetic expression. "I understand, but we have much to do, and we need rest. We will do our best to answer your questions on our journey to high camp, about forty-five miles east and up in the mountains. The surrounding area was originally our base, but now it is just our forward camp and link to the port." Then, turning to her team, she said, "Dismissed."

——

Vince stood and waited for Nate. Abe came to join them and walked with Nate back to the infirmary.

Looking firmly at him, Abe spoke, "Nate, we know it is all too much to comprehend. Even though we have been through all these events, we cannot understand even an inkling of God's plan. I kindly ask you to have patience with us, and we will answer whatever we can. I know you will probably have trouble sleeping tonight, and the best that I can offer you are a couple of old ibuprofen pills. Tomorrow is the start of a two-day journey, and we'll have plenty of time to talk. Until then, Vince will escort you around camp. I suggest you try to rest as soon as it gets dark."

With that, Abe placed two pills in Nate's hand, said, "As for the rest of us, we have preparations to complete for the excursion. Relax for the rest of the day; you'll need your strength if you are to travel with us. Until tomorrow." Abe withdrew and left Nate in Vince's care.

———

Revelation 1: Instead of a six-month suspended animation, Nate awoke eleven years later, and the world as he knew it was "gone."

CHAPTER 18

REVELATION 2

Vince woke Nate before dawn. "Get up and put on your shoes. I'll take you to the latrine, and you'll have to take care of your needs before we start our journey. There's a wash station there. We'll grab a bit of grub, and then we'll be walking for about two miles to meet the rest of our party."

Nate rose slowly, still stiff and sore. After finishing at the wash station, Vince and Chief Virtolli escorted him to the camp kitchen. They briefly described their experiences since The Fires, but both took Abe's caution to limit the information. It was just as well. Nate could barely keep awake and was having difficulty making sense of all he heard. At the mess shelter, they ate a meager portion of eggs and oats. Nate saw that Abe was already there. Veena was there, too, but she rose and left after looking at Nate.

"Did I do something wrong?" Nate inquired of Abe.

"No," replied Abe, assuming Nate's remarks were about Veena's sudden departure. "Veena has to make sure that Kath has everything she needs to secure our forward camp before returning to high camp. Kath is Veena's second, and they rarely spend much time together as they split the camp responsibilities. It was unusual for both of them to be together here at the forward camp, but Veena tries to gather all her leads every three months so they can discuss needs and plans. So, by happy circumstance, all the leads were here when God determined to bring you in."

Before Nate finished his breakfast, Vince got up and entered a nearby hut. He returned with a canteen, a floppy brown hat, and a tall, pointed stick. He gave them to Nate. "Take the water sparingly. The lance doubles as a walking stick."

"Why do I need a spear?" asked Nate.

"In our world since The Fires, we're always on alert," replied Vince. "There is a possibility that outsiders, who want what we have, will launch an attack. Therefore, you may need it to protect yourself and your team. You need to understand that attacks are usually life-and-death situations."

Nate remembered the stories he heard last night about gangs. "I'd probably do better with a gun," he observed.

Vince looked Nate directly in the eye. "We don't have many guns, and firing them tends to bring more unwanted attention. So, another thing: be as quiet as possible as we travel."

Having finished breakfast, Abe excused himself and moved briskly eastward from the mess shelter. Vince directed Nate to follow and then walked right behind him. The first rays of the morning sun were lightening the eastern sky. Nate followed Abe, but the quick pace started burning his lungs with every breath. Soon they crested a ridge and looked down into a small valley. Nate saw several people already there... and horses.

"Have you ever ridden a horse?" Abe asked as they started down the slope.

"Maybe once or twice and only for about an hour each time," Nate said. "Why can't we take a car?"

"Several reasons: roads are impassable in lots of places, and cars create too much noise. Most of all, any gas remaining is so old that it is ineffective. Most people don't realize that gasoline, depending upon its additives, becomes unusable between three months to three years after being produced. We lost most of the stored gas during The Fires and the gang warfare that followed. Since then, we don't know of anyone refining oil, so no new gas supplies.

"On the other hand, diesel fuel is viable for longer if kept in cold, underground storage tanks and with proper additives. Regardless, possessing serviceable diesel is a miracle for every day after five years, and we still have a small quantity. Therefore, since diesel is so precious and limited, when we need a motorized vehicle, we mainly use electric bikes that the SEALs got from their supply depot. We charge those with solar panels that we've scavenged. We also save those for the SEALs and then only for special missions. For the rest of us, horses are quieter and the long-term solution. They also give the rider a height advantage. That said, I hope you are up for a challenge as we'll be riding for two days."

Nate, anxious about his horsemanship, joined the assembly next to the corral. He saw Veena there and temporarily forgot his trepidation.

Veena glanced at Nate and gave him a quick smile. "Gather around, team. Daylight is breaking, the SEALs have already started, and we need to follow quickly. Abe, prayer, please."

The team gathered close as Abe kneeled and prayed. After Abe finished the prayer and rose to his feet, he said to Veena, "We better put Nate on Spackle."

Veena nodded to Nate. "You ride near Abe. He'll get you to a horse." Turning away, she strode into the corral and mounted her horse, a brownish American Quarter stallion, and nudged him out of the corral and along the trail.

Abe guided Nate to a saddled, spotted Appaloosa. He brought Nate near the horse's head and said, "Meet Spackle. She is an exceptionally dependable and gentle horse. Give her neck a soft rub so she can get to know you."

Nate was apprehensive at first but soon became calm as he lightly stroked the horse's neck. Spackle snorted and nudged Nate's shoulder.

"Great," said Abe. "It looks like you two will get along quite well." With that, Abe gave Nate the reins and said, "Wait here." Abe got his horse, a gray Kentucky Mountain Saddle Horse stallion, and led him near Nate and Spackle. Abe showed Nate how to mount his horse and hold the reins. As soon as Nate sat atop Spackle, Abe nudged his mount forward and said, "Follow me." Advantageously for Nate, Spackle knew what to do.

Veena led the twenty-person expedition with Abe and Nate in the middle. Right behind Nate was an older man mounted on a large Quarter Horse and leading two packhorses. Moving stealthily and slowly to keep the dust down, they stayed in the early morning shadows below ridgelines. Abe turned in his seat and spoke softly, "We keep quiet, and below the ridges as much as possible. The SEALs have already scouted our trail, and we like to be as invisible as we can. I'll tell you when we can talk more."

Nate soon found that it was easy to ride Spackle. The saddle kit had attachments to hold his canteen and lance, and he mimicked Abe's technique. Nate needed to adjust the drawstring on his floppy hat, and Spackle stepped along smoothly while Nate fussed with the drawstring clasp. They continued so quietly that they could hear the birds' morning songs over the cavalcade's noise. It gave the impression that everything was peaceful and safe.

Then the trail came to a paved, six-lane, divided road cluttered with the burned-out shells of cars, and Nate looked upon the scene with alarm. One by one, the procession scampered its way across the pavement through a pass made between the rusting wrecks and back into the brush on the far side. As they continued, the trail moved from the west side of the ridges to the east side, and the morning sun began to beat down. The skies became clear with fifty miles of visibility as they could see the distinct ridges of the mountains to the east, a nice change after all the smoke and morning fog Nate had experienced on his trek from the shoreline days prior. Even in the morning coolness, Nate began to glisten with sweat and was grateful for the hat.

CHAPTER 19

After about two hours, they came to a small grove of trees. In the center was a clearing, and the procession stopped. Abe turned in his saddle and said to Nate, "Rest stop. Tie Spackle next to my horse on this tree and follow me."

Nate rode Spackle over to the tree. The packhorses wrangler unloaded some water containers and filled a trough at the base of a tree. Nate rose in the saddle and was shocked that he felt sore. After he swung his right leg over to dismount, his leg buckled under his weight as soon as it touched the ground. Nate was stuck hanging with his left foot caught in the stirrup, and his left hand clenched tightly on the saddle horn.

Abe came over quickly and caught Nate under his right arm.

As Nate disengaged his left foot from the stirrup, Abe chuckled lightly. "Don't worry. You'll get the hang of it. The majority of people fall flat on their asses when they dismount the first time."

Nate grinned sheepishly and hobbled as he tied up Spackle and followed Abe.

—⁘—

They rested about fifteen minutes before Veena rode up. "Abe, would you take the point for the next leg? I'll ride with Nate." Nate couldn't see Abe's gentle smile as Abe turned and mounted Shadow. With considerable soreness, Nate remounted Spackle and followed Veena.

The sun was rising toward mid-morning as they continued from the copse of trees. The trail soon widened enough that Veena could ride next to Nate. "Did you sleep well last night?"

"I guess," said Nate. "The night felt rather short. I remember taking the ibuprofen pills from Abe, putting my head on the pillow, and then the next thing I knew was Vince shaking me awake in the dark."

Veena broke into a broad smile and laughed lightly. "Yes, Vince can be a rude awakening." Nate looked at her and noticed, with that big smile, that her beauty blossomed tenfold. Veena saw Nate's stare, and she quickly turned her face away. "We're in an area where we can carry on a quiet conversation. That must have been a lot to take in yesterday."

Nate suddenly dropped his eyes and became somber. "You're not kidding. I'm having a difficult time coming to grips with everything. If I wasn't so sore from riding on old Spackle" —to which Spackle responded with a slight huff— "I'd think the whole thing was a hallucination."

They rode in silence for a minute or two before Nate said, "Would you mind telling me about whatever happened, as well as you know, please?"

Veena took a deep breath. "For all the years I've had to think about it, it is still a bit fuzzy to me even now. I was almost eleven when The Thinning started."

"The Thinning?" Nate interrupted.

Veena bowed her head briefly. "Well, that's the name we use to describe the whole series of events that started that October. It's just a way for us to simplify and not dwell on it too long. The Thinning sums up the tragedies that killed our families, crushed civilization, and reshaped the world and society. We coined the term 'The Thinning' to cover all the atrocities that have reduced us to such a scrappy, fight-to-survive life."

Nate nodded, and Veena resumed. "Anyway, I guess I was a rather precocious pre-teen. On the day of The Fires, I was at the stadium getting Krav Maga instruction from Abe. My dad, Kyle Osborne, was a former decathlete in training for triathlons and Iron Man competitions. Dad knew Abe early in his Olympian training days as Abe had been one of the team's physical therapists. My mom, Dawn Johnson, competed in marathons and was also at the Olympic training center. So, that's where Dad introduced himself and asked Mom on a date. Eventually, my mom, dad, and Abe became close friends. Abe has been like a close uncle to me since I was born. Mom and Dad wanted me to be courageous, independent, and safe, so they put me into karate lessons with Abe when I was five.

"Abe is the kind of man who surprises everyone. Before completing his doctorate in physical therapy, he was in the Marines and had extensive med training and Recon squad experience. During his time in the Marines, Abe decided to become a physical therapy specialist, so he left the Marines and started college courses. He also worked with the Olympic training center. After Abe met my dad and mom, he invited them to church, where he taught an adult Bible study after the first service. We all went, and loved the people and the worship. Abe became part of our family and was included in our social life. He was like an older brother to my dad. When they found out that he was skilled in Krav Maga, they asked him to give me that instruction, too.

"So, I was training with Abe at the stadium when The Fires broke out. Mom and Dad were at the Olympic training center in Chula Vista at the time, and they never made it back to pick me up." Veena stifled a soft sob.

Taking a short breath, she spoke in a voice that was barely above a whisper, "The Fires made it necessary for us to isolate in the stadium for weeks for safety. Soon after, Abe went scouting the nearby area for supplies and information. It's hard to conceive how quickly everything, including news, broke down. The Fires had started a panic, and all the roads, not just the freeways, were blocked with multiple collisions. Abe told me that it was apparent from the burn patterns that several crashes resulted in leaking gasoline and new fires. People were trapped and killed in those. It must have been horrible. I'm glad now that I was so young and understood so little about what was happening."

Veena paused again. "Abe found my parents' car not far from the stadium. It appears they were in a crash with a fuel tanker. The scene was horrible. The impact had bent their car in half, and they died right there. I made Abe take me to the wreck, as I didn't believe it until I saw it. He resisted my pleas, but he must have realized that I needed to see it with my own eyes to move on finally. What a horrible thing to have to show anyone, especially a child. I continue to have nightmares about it." Veena made a choking sound.

Nate, stunned, decided to change the subject. "So, your mom and dad met in Chula Vista?"

After a moment to compose herself, Veena said with a small smile. "Well, as I said, they met at the Olympic training center. Interestingly, they both attended Arizona State University in Tempe, Arizona, though my dad was a year ahead of my mom. Dad studied as a math major but also had a scholarship with the track team. He did math tutoring to help make extra money. My mom grew up in northern Iowa before she came to Arizona State. I guess she wanted to get out of the snowy winters. Her family roots were from Norway, and she was a tall and athletic blond. She studied engineering, and she joined the archery team for the exercise, though later, she developed a passion for marathons. She also did math tutoring, and that's where Dad first saw her.

However, he was too shy to approach her then. I'm confident that Mom knew Dad was on the track team and was pleasantly surprised to see him tutoring math. She would never make the first move. A couple of years later, they were both at the Olympic center, and my dad finally got the nerve to approach my mom.

"Since my mom already knew who he was, they connected quickly. They both were strong in math and the sciences, and they both loved to be fit. It was an exceptional match." Veena's smile was beaming.

After a moment's reflection, she looked at Nate and saw that he was rather pale, and his expression was downcast. "What's wrong?" she asked.

"My parents live in north Scottsdale, which is north of Tempe," Nate replied quietly. "I hadn't thought of them until you mentioned Tempe. I wonder how they are?" Nate flushed with anxiety and anguish, chiefly as he felt convicted since he had not thought of them till now.

"We don't know much about how the areas outside of San Diego County survived. We've had contact with a few groups from the Los Angeles basin to the north and others coming north from Mexico," she replied softly. "It probably will be challenging to find out any information, even if we mounted an expedition. Let's talk more later."

They rode the rest of the morning in silence.

CHAPTER 20

Stopping for lunch before noon, they rested in the shade of a cluster of eucalyptus trees near a pond on the east side of Poway. Abe told Nate to rest as they would wait until late afternoon to avoid the midday heat before continuing the ascent of the pass near Mount Woodson. Nate, already feeling sore from riding, laid a blanket under one of the trees and stretched out stiffly, nursing his aching backside and legs. Abe did the same nearby and said a short prayer before he crossed his hands on his chest and pulled his hat over his face.

After a short nap, Abe came over to where Nate was reclining. Soon, Veena and others joined them as Abe continued telling the saga spanning the years since The Fires.

"The Fires made it unsafe for us to leave the stadium. Propitiously, the stadium was mainly concrete and surrounded by a large, blacktop parking lot, so the flames didn't reach where we were. We stayed in the underground rooms, which were cooler and the least affected by the smoke. Sadly, all the cars in the parking lot caught fire and became useless. We knew that fires were widespread from earlier news and that the roads were blocked entirely and thus were deathtraps. We lost phone communication, as well as news feeds and the Internet, within a day.

"We kept hoping that Veena's parents, Kyle and Dawn, would show up at any moment. It was unsafe for us to travel away from the stadium, and they knew we were there. Injured and hungry people started showing up at the stadium, but they had to walk there, and nearly all of them died soon after arriving from burns or the effects of smoke inhalation. I did what I could to help them, but I got the feeling that I was mainly there to be with them when they passed on. After a couple of days, I left Veena with the remaining survivors and departed the stadium to get supplies and to search for Veena's parents. Even hiking was challenging because of the smoke and the wreckage on all the roads. I found precious little we could use. I headed back to the stadium, hoping to get there before dark; that is when I discovered the wreckage of Kyle and Dawn's car and their bodies. Telling Veena about that discovery was one of the hardest things I've ever had to do.

"Within a day of my return, the remaining survivors started getting sick, including Veena. Probably eighty percent of the sick died from the disease, mainly from congestion blocking the airways. Blessedly, after three days, Veena started to get better just as I fell victim to illness. I was seldom conscious as my body fought the virus and infection, and as best as we can tell, it was ten days later before I made a significant improvement.

"Veena cared for me during all of that time. It was a tragic way for a child to grow up so fast and take on so much responsibility. When I was well enough to sit up, we left the stadium's lower rooms as waste, smell, disease, and death had claimed all those areas. At that time, Veena encountered and befriended Kathy Haines, though she was Kathy Arlain by name then and only thirteen. We took refuge in one of the stadium's upper rooms as it was the safest place to stay.

"During those first weeks, all of us would go scavenging, and we would meet survivors. Everyone we met was weak from both sickness and starvation. All would beg us for help, and occasionally, we would travel to where they had left those who were too weak to search for food. The smell, sights, and sounds of death were everywhere, and there was not much we could offer. A sampling of the survivors, primarily young girls, returned to the stadium with us. The others stayed with the remnants of their families.

"Then the gangs emerged. The bands formed first based on shared cultural traits: race, ethnicity, religion, or merely a mutual hate of another group. Gang warfare became ever-present. Thousands were killed, including the innocents who were in the wrong place at the wrong time. The fighting reduced the remaining bands to just a handful. We seldom left the stadium anymore, and we sealed up the entrances to defend against the marauders. Veena and I trained the people, primarily children, to protect themselves and each other. That was the beginning of our tribe. After losing several of our members during scavenging forays to ambushes or accidents, we decided to stay within the stadium until spring. That decision unexpectedly saved our lives.

"The seasonal rains started in early December, late for the area, but not that exceptional. What was unexpected was the intensity of the rains as the days progressed. Because of all the burnt landscape, flash flooding and mudslides were commonplace. The San Diego River overflowed its banks near the stadium and covered the parking lot, particularly the south side, with water and mud. The average temperature was much, much colder than any of us had ever remembered, possibly resulting from the heavy smoke layers from the fires that covered the earth. Uncharacteristically, we had snowstorms and blizzards that winter. Snow remained on the ground for as long as a week. We stayed mostly secluded in the upper rooms and rarely sent out patrols to find food and supplies. When the scouting parties did go out, they encountered numerous dead bodies, apparently from exposure or drowning."

Abe sipped a little water.

"When spring came, no one held hope that someone was coming to help us. I knew our scavenged supplies would not continue to sustain us, and we would need to find a place where we could hunt and farm. We also needed to find caches of seed as well as books on how to cultivate. My Marine training had taught me how to hunt, build traps, find drinkable water, and survive. During our winter confinement, I had started teaching that to our people. So, we left the stadium and headed east.

"The entire landscape was unrecognizable, with all the typical landmarks razed by fires and rains. I knew there were large open areas to the northeast of the Tierrasanta neighborhood, and that's where we went. During the next several months, we rarely encountered anyone. Most of those we met stayed with us, though we had to force others away from our tribe because they tried to dominate us to satisfy their selfish desires. Since we stayed in the old Tierrasanta neighborhood's general area, the other local groups called us 'the Tierrans.' It's not a name I would have picked, but we didn't care. By late summer, we started to defend our group from the nearby gang known as the Clairens, as the Clairemont neighborhood was the southernmost extent of their territory.

"By God's grace, soon after we hiked to the Tierrasanta area, we were able to find good game: rabbits, snakes, and a rare deer. One of our early patrols also stumbled upon a sealed trunk that contained farming and survival books and seed—probably assembled by a survivalist who had failed to survive. We recovered farming tools, wagons, and seeds on several extended patrols to the El Cajon area. Then, we found the horses. Looking in hindsight at these blessings, it is one of those times you say, 'God works in mysterious ways.'

"After we planted, gentle rains fell upon the fields, and we reaped meager, though sufficient, crops by mid-June. The lust for that bounty, and our people, prompted the Clairens to attack our community.

"We quickly found out that there wasn't any bartering with the Clairens. We lost all the men and boys in our group in the early skirmishes and probably ninety percent of the older women. Most died in the battles or soon after. A few, particularly the women, were captured, but they died at the hands of the Clairens within days of the assault. We never allowed our people to become prisoners again.

After that, Veena and Kath worked hard to train the girls. They became a disciplined fighting force and soundly defeated the main body of the Clairens in an ambush. God was with us and showed us mercy when, due to that Clairen defeat, the remaining Clairens decided to stay away from us and seek weaker targets. Later, we heard that the Clairens ventured south, where they suffered hefty losses in fighting with a gang from Mexico. Since then, massive hordes haven't challenged us anymore. We have had skirmishes with small raiding parties and those we have always successfully repulsed.

"Also, fortunately for us, ammunition for guns had been exhausted by gang warfare in the early months after The Fires. Our tribe has become skilled in our defenses using bows and arrows, crossbows, spears, and knives. About four months later, when the *Des Moines* crew came upon a clash between one of our patrols and a band of the Clairens, we gained men back into our ranks as well as several guns. Ammo is a rare commodity, and there may come a day when guns are only a visual threat.

"We planted the trees along the western ridge of the Tierrasanta mesa as a defensive position overlooking the canyon that held the roadbed of Interstate 15. It became a natural barrier from the Clairens or any other gang. Nonetheless, we realized that the Tierrasanta mesa was too vulnerable and without a reliable water source to continue our crops. So we moved our main camp to a valley east of Ramona and used the Tierrasanta area as an advance post to secure our link to the Navy base and the *Des Moines*. We are heading to our main camp, and we should reach it by noon tomorrow. Now, it's time to continue as we need to ascend these hills east of us and get to our campsite on the east face of Mount Woodson before nightfall."

With that, everyone quietly got up, and the procession continued their trek.

No one talked during the late afternoon climb. During most of the ascent, the riders were dismounted and leading the horses over the rough terrain. The trek to the Mount Woodson camp was about six miles, but it took them nearly three and a half hours. The SEALs had already ensured the site was safe, set sentries, and started a fire. When the group made the camp, Veena sent pairs out to relieve the sentries and allow the SEALs to eat and rest.

CHAPTER 21

After a light stew of vegetables and a meat Nate couldn't identify (and later learned was rabbit), he heard more stories before they all broke for an early night. MaryAn delivered one of the more horrible ones. She sobbed, describing how she and Carla met when the Clairens captured both of them in late spring and kept them as sex slaves. Though Nate had become acquainted with Carla's watchful, distrusting eyes, it was his first interaction with MaryAn. Carla and MaryAn shared a tight bond, even though their appearance was quite different. Carla had a short haircut and carried herself as though she was ready to spring at any moment. In contrast, MaryAn had longer hair fashioned into a ponytail and moved with the sinuous flow of a dancer.

MaryAn delivered her account haltingly as she described how both Carla and she were in their late teens at the time and were near death when, after just a few days in the Clairen camp, Carla strangled their drunk guard during the early morning hours. Snatching up the guard's machete and grabbing MaryAn by the hand, Carla led them away from the horror. They had heard of a tribe of women, the Tierrans, and raced eastward as fast as they could. They were lucky to be noticed by a Tierran patrol and brought into the camp. They were also astonished at how young the girls were in the patrol, yet so well trained and deadly. Carla, who had developed a hatred of men, was surprised to see Abe in the group and was suspicious of him. She learned to trust him after interacting with him for several months. That trust allowed Carla to begrudgingly accept the *Des Moines* crewmen when they joined the tribe later in the year. While MaryAn told their saga, Carla sulked nearby; the memories and anger were made fresh again after being buried for so long.

The night would have ended on that cruel retelling. Fortuitously, after a moment, Veena told him the history about when the patrol from the *Des Moines'* remaining crew chanced upon the attack of Kath's patrol by the Clairens, how they helped crush the Clairen onslaught, and became a part of the tribe. The encouraging account of rescue and inclusion –which also resulted in Kath's romance and marriage with Roy– smothered the unease Nate felt after hearing MaryAn's horrific tale, and he drifted off to sleep.

CHAPTER 22

Like the previous morn, Vince shook Nate awake in the darkness before dawn. If he hadn't been thoroughly exhausted from the previous day's ride, he probably wouldn't have gotten any rest last night from all his aches. Now, his whole body, particularly his inner thighs, was sore and stiff, and each movement triggered a bolt of pain. He couldn't sit for breakfast. Abe recognized Nate's pained expression in the early light and came over to him.

"Rough night?" Abe queried, barely above a whisper.

"Not really," replied Nate. "I slept like the dead." Then, grinning, he added, "I would have thought certain parts of my body were dead, except the constant pain reminds me that they are not. I'm not sure I have the makings of a horseman."

Abe nodded. "Well, fortuitously, we're in a region where we should be safe to travel at a more leisurely pace. The rest of the trip will be a long, gradual incline, and you can walk Spackle. That should loosen those sore muscles and joints and work out some of the pain."

They finished their breakfast of apples and nuts, saving apple pieces and cores for the horses. As they walked to retrieve their mounts, Abe added, "In the early years, we could only safely make the journey at night, and preferably when the moon wasn't full or was at least hidden by clouds. We have traveled during the daylight for the past seven years, but we never let our guard down, and the SEALs ensure that the path is safe. Now our biggest threat is the snakes warming themselves in the path during the sunny days."

Nate considered the implications as he trudged along, Spackle's reins in his hands. At first, his companions admonished him to pick up his feet and not raise so much dust. After half an hour, his movement became more fluid, and he stepped similar to the rest of the assembly, quietly and carefully. Even the horses embraced the motion, and the procession moved along, raising a dust cloud so small that it didn't rise above the horses' legs.

As the group continued the gradual ascent, Nate intermittently looked up from his thoughts to see those who had shared their stories and marvel at their strength to continue after all the horrors they had seen and experienced. Abe followed just behind him, whereas Veena customarily rode near the front of the procession. A couple of times that morning, she waited on her mount for Nate and Abe to reach her. Then, Veena would engage Abe with inconsequential questions before riding forward again. At first, Nate thought her behavior was typical for the cavalcade, but eventually, he realized she was checking on him. Nate tracked her in the procession, and he glanced at her whenever she dropped behind him to confer with Abe. He soon recognized that while she would speak to Abe, she gazed at him. Several times Nate felt self-conscious, and he made an extra effort to move along stealthily, trying to blend in. Nate had to admit to himself, though, the extra attention from Veena felt pretty pleasant.

They crested a ridge in the late morning and looked down on a wide valley that held the main camp. Planted fields covered most of the hollow, and there was a cluster of shelters on the shores of a large pond. As they descended into the valley, Nate noticed several sentry posts, and he realized that the SEALs were already resting in the camp. Their job was complete.

Nate also observed that the camp's people paused from their chores and gazed at the incoming procession. They waved at the arrivals and, if they were close enough, would say 'hello.' Though they all had sun-darkened skin, Nate saw a kaleidoscope of ethnicities, both adults and teens, most of them women. They all had weapons within reach, and Nate saw a group practicing combat sparring.

"Yeah," he mused under his breath. "Nothing is as it was before I started the suspended animation; everything has changed." Even as he mumbled it, he was troubled that something else was off and different about the scene. He just couldn't identify what was peculiar.

They reached the cluster of shelters, and a small contingent of the tribe retrieved the horses from them. Veena walked over. "You're welcome to explore around the camp; just don't wander too far."

"What are you going to do?" Nate asked as he saw his travel companions head to the largest shelter.

"We give thanks for a safe journey," Veena replied. "You're welcome to join us if you desire."

"Yes, I will." Nate felt grateful for the invitation.

The largest shelter wasn't spacious, and all those who had gathered stood shoulder to shoulder. Abe was at the center, and when he saw that Veena and Nate had joined the assembly, he raised his arms and bowed his head. Those gathered fell silent, and after a moment, Abe spoke.

"Gracious, most Holy God, You alone are God, and You alone can deliver. We thank You for our safe journey. We pray that we will empty ourselves and allow Your Holy Spirit to fill us with Your plans and will. Refresh us, LORD, and help us represent You well in all we think, say, and do. In the majestic name of Your son, Y'shua HaMashiach, we pray. Amen."

All the assembly softly responded, "Amen."

Nate wanted to walk out with Veena, but she moved through the group to talk with several people. Nate felt the presence of someone standing next to him. He turned to see Abe.

"How are you feeling now?" Abe asked as he walked with Nate out of the shelter.

"Well, you were right; walking helped loosen my muscles and reduce the soreness and stiffness. I've had enough horse riding for a while."

"You will need to become a skilled horseman if you intend to stay with us. A horse can be the difference between life and death here. I see them as gifts from God as few tribes have them."

Nate hadn't fully considered whether he would stay with the tribe or not until now. Abe's and Veena's direction had carried him along. He looked down, contemplating the future, and then lifted his head to face Abe. "Am I allowed to stay with the tribe? Will I be welcomed here?"

"Welcomed?" Abe chuckled. "In my observations, Veena, and probably others, would be out of sorts if you were to leave. I'd like to know more about your old life and the events that brought you to us. I sense that God sent you to us.

"I also want to forewarn you. You have not been in this new world enough to fully comprehend that leaving the safety of the tribe can make survival very difficult, perhaps even an implicit death sentence. If you decide to leave, we will help you with supplies and information on areas to avoid. You will need every skill and cunning you have to survive. Still, it is your decision."

Nate was warmed by Abe's introductory words and concerned by the latter warning. His gaze swept over the camp. There was an unnatural quietness for such a large group; something seemed off. He saw Veena approaching them, and a sense of peace replaced that odd feeling.

How young she is to be the leader of the group, Nate thought. An unexpected question arose in his mind and shocked him. Abe is affectionately called 'Old Abe' by the group, though he appears to be in his forties. Nearly all of these warrior women seem to be thirty or less. As Nate thought about the people he had met, he realized that Laoni was the youngest person he'd seen since awakening from the suspended-animation chamber, and she looked to be in her early teens. This size community should have preteens and younger children; perhaps they were in a school he hadn't seen yet.

Nate turned back toward Abe. "Abe, where are the children? Are they in a school somewhere?"

—◦◦◦—

Revelation 2: In the new world, survivors struggle for food and resources and are in constant danger from vicious raiding gangs.

CHAPTER 23

REVELATION 3

Nate noticed a sadness come over Abe, and though it was bright and sunny at midday, he felt a chill. Veena, who had just returned and heard Nate's question, started to tear up; she pivoted and strode purposefully away. Nate felt an emptiness as he watched her depart, and he forced himself to turn back to Abe.

Abe looked down as if he was pondering the dust at his feet. Finally, he raised his eyes to Nate, "What I have to tell you is sorrowful and the biggest challenge to my faith. Let's go sit in the shade, and I'll describe what I know."

Nate followed Abe as he moved to a freestanding veranda and took a seat at the picnic-style table in the shade. Abe took a moment to compose his thoughts before starting, with a slight tremor in his voice.

"As far as we know, no child under two survived the first year of The Thinning. Laoni, at fourteen, is the youngest person in our camp, and we haven't heard of anyone younger anywhere else. No couple has conceived a child since that first year. We have had countless heartbroken discussions about it, and it appears that we are all sterile. Perhaps the infertility is related to diet or environmental poison, but we don't know."

Nate was stunned.

"You said this is the biggest challenge to your faith. What do you mean by that?"

Looking intently at Nate, Abe responded, "I continually study Holy Scripture, as published in the Protestant Christian Bible. I suspect that a sampling of people might feel the events are the final days of the end times before the Rapture, but scripture does not prophesy the morbid trials we've witnessed over the past eleven years. Therefore, I don't think we are in the days immediately preceding the Rapture. It is beyond my comprehension the reasons why God has closed human wombs. Let me expand on that. Only people appear to be sterile; all other animals are breeding and producing offspring. So, I wonder about God's plans for our future. I know God's ways are not our ways. I guess you could say that I am struggling with patience or, more precisely, my lack of patience.

"I reflect on and consider all that we have endured and the daily grimness of our existence. We have strived through devastation by fires, disease, storms, and starvation. Gangs, such as the Clairens, challenge our survival with attacks. The last six or so years have been better as the outsiders became so weakened that they rarely bothered us, and God has provided us with our needs as He blessed our hunting and farming. Without children, gangs will probably disappear within twenty years. Neither will we last for much more than that. In a sense, I identify with my namesake, Abraham, when he trusted God to provide the appropriate sacrifice in place of his son, Isaac. Even though scripture records his unwavering faith in God, I have wondered if Abraham felt sick in his heart that God told him to sacrifice Isaac. Thus, the childless curse weighs enormously heavy on me, and I know it is a great heartache for our people. I pray unceasingly about it, and I hope to live to see how our LORD will show His grace. I hold onto what the Apostle Paul wrote in Romans 5, 'Suffering produces perseverance; perseverance, proven character; and proven character produces hope.'"

Nate's mind raced. None of these trials made sense. Nate believed in God, though now was the first time he clearly understood God was confronting him.

"No children anywhere?"

"None that we are aware of," Abe repeated softly. "We have infrequent contacts with travelers and traders. Almost all are seeking a safe and thriving community. 'Thriving' has come to mean children and a future. None of these pilgrims has found one. There may be children somewhere. However, radio communication with the outside world no longer exists, so our interactions beyond our territory are limited to the information we get from the wanderers. As I mentioned before, fires burned up nearly all gasoline supplies, and any remaining gasoline became unusable after two years. Diesel fuel is the only fuel still usable, and whatever we have is getting so old, soon it won't be viable anymore. Even on horseback, the range of our exploration is limited. Arizona, southern Nevada, Utah, and areas just north of Los Angeles, are about the extent of our source of interaction and knowledge. No group from outside that region has come to our area for the past ten years. So, maybe there are children somewhere, but there hasn't been even a rumor of a child for at least ten years."

How can it be? thought Nate. He asked, "How can God allow it? Why doesn't God hear the prayers and grant children to people?"

With tenderness, Abe offered, "There are people who like to think that God will grant every wish and prayer, and then chose not to believe in God when He doesn't. Granting wishes is the mythology of a genie. God is not a genie. He is God, and we are His creation. He made us in His image, so our desire to know His plan and be like Him is part of our being and His creative touch. We are not God; we exist to worship Him. Still, He loves us so much that He has accepted us into His family when we believe in His Son, Y'shua HaMashiach. As such, we are His adopted children, and we are more than just His creation. He always does what is best for us, even if it is unpleasant for us in our time. His timing is not our timing. God exists outside of time; thus, He is the first and the last, and ever-present. As hard as it is for us mortals bound by time, we must wait patiently for His plan to unfold. It is a difficult path for us, self-important people, to follow."

Nate sat in silence with Abe for a couple of minutes. "What do we do?"

"As I said, the only thing we can do," Abe sighed heavily, "is to wait, patiently, on the LORD, and lean not on our understanding. We're human, mortal on this earth, and waiting is a challenge for most of us. We do the best we can and pray for strength. Someday, God will reveal His plan for our future."

Nate tried to comprehend Abe's disclosure. Finally, Abe got up. "If you want to talk more, I will make time. Be gentle in broaching the topic to those you meet as it raises deep and troubling feelings. When you're ready to get settled, see Vince, and he will set you up. It's a lot to absorb, so take your time." With that, Abe strode quietly away.

—⁓—

Revelation 3: No surviving children have been born since the disease, humanity is sterile, and it appears that people will eventually all die off.

CHAPTER 24

INTERLUDE: EZRA'S COMPILATION OF
NATE'S AND REX'S BACKSTORIES

My apologies, dear reader, as I interrupt this storyline to include information regarding Father Sinclair's and Rex's background information. We who have come after The Thinning have an incomplete understanding of the old world. The material in this Chapter is necessary to comprehend the contextual experiences that shaped Father Sinclair and Rex. As children, starting with our third-grade social study and science classes, we gained a deeper understanding of daily life in the old world and Nate's life events that brought him to our new world. In completing this frame of reference, Rex and others have supplied the details recorded in this Chapter.

–Ezra

Four years before The Fires

The program wasn't the astronaut training Nate had desired since adolescence, but NASA had stopped actively recruiting. The opening in the U.S. Navy project for Extended Space Missions, Suspended Animation Studies (ESM-SAS) at least offered the possibility of advancement into the astronaut program. Nate had just graduated with his B.S. Engineering degree, specializing in Computer Science and Cognitive Reasoning. The university previously named that specialty 'Artificial Intelligence.' However, the general populace considered that label had negative connotations, so Cognitive Reasoning became the new term.

Nate completed his Navy-sponsored Reserve Officer Training Corps (ROTC) program. The ROTC supplement had helped pay for his degree, and now he was obligated to serve in the Navy. His Engineering degree expanded his service options to several elite disciplines, and the ESM-SAS project appeared to be his best shot to qualify for a future astronaut selection.

To the uninformed observer, the Navy's participation in the ESM-SAS project may have seemed inconsistent with the Navy's mission. Nevertheless, naval aviation had delivered copious, well-qualified Navy and Marine aviators to NASA, and the Navy wanted to continue and expand its role in space operations. Nate considered a naval aviation career but felt that path would not give him a competitive edge if NASA opened additional astronaut training in the future. It was likely that the criteria for astronaut openings would be intensely selective, and Nate thought his engineering and computer experience might give him a boost in priority over competing astronaut candidates. He also knew he would have to work hard and put in long days to stay at the top of the candidates' list.

Concerning his entry into the ESM-SAS program, his personal life made the timing right. Six months before graduation, Laura, Nate's girlfriend for several years, broke off their relationship. If Nate was honest with himself, their relationship was always strained and challenging. The prospects for a successful marriage required that he suppress his desires and support only Laura's. The most significant obstacles were their different views on religion and children. Nate believed in God and wanted children; Laura didn't. He knew all these issues, but, in the end, it was Laura who initiated the breakup.

Since then, with the final push to graduation, Nate had completed his degree and obtained his Navy commission. Social life, even electronic social life, was pushed aside as he strove toward the goal. He had graduated and needed to consider his commitment to the Navy. So, the ESM-SAS program was the right fit at the right time.

The ESM-SAS project had already been underway for four years when Nate joined. Construction of the suspended animation facility started near San Clemente Island and finished two years after Nate joined the team. It rested about ninety feet deep on the seafloor on the continental shelf of the island's leeward side. As the Navy controlled and protected the island, it was far enough away from the California coast to be out of sight of curious eyes, yet close enough to be readily serviced by the Navy installations in San Diego. Its isolation from civilian areas allowed the Navy to power the facility with a dedicated nuclear reactor.

Within three months of the facility completion, the first volunteer entered the chamber for a four-hour, suspended-animation sleep. Though management promoted the test as a complete success since the volunteer showed undiminished abilities within a week after being fully revived, she was disoriented and confused for the first seven days after the test.

The team refined reanimation and revival procedures, and in each subsequent test, the volunteers completed the ever-longer suspended animation periods of sleep. The second volunteer, also a woman, awoke to bright lights, soft background music, and rapid, increased body temperature for the final five degrees Celsius. Her disorientation and confusion were reduced to just hours, though she was exceedingly weary for the first three days. The reanimation and revival processes changed to introduce a mild sleep narcotic to the volunteer's IV line. This drug triggered a short period of "standard" sleep to complete the restoration process. The last three short-test volunteers awoke from their suspended animation as though they had just taken a short nap.

No volunteer was allowed to repeat the experiment. Follow-up monitoring confirmed that the volunteers came through the suspended animation procedure without any apparent harm. Although all the team members had conviction in their work, several harbored concerns about the long-term effects on the volunteers. Among those researchers who held a firm belief in God, His divine plan, and the human soul, doubts arose regarding what happens to the soul during the suspended-animation process. For those staff members who denied God and the soul, there were questions about what it means to alter a person's life process by suspended animation and how that affects their Id. Whatever their beliefs and inner struggles, the team members were elated at the volunteers' successful revivals and restoration. The weak attempt at humor was the common jest of "no soulless zombies."

The Phase One experiment plan had only three more studies, lasting two weeks, one month, and six months, respectively. The project leadership selected Nate as one of the candidates for the six-month suspended-animation sleep experiment.

—◦◦◦—

Around the same time in South Los Angeles, fourteen-year-old Rex was forming his gang. Rex wasn't his real name; his parents saddled him with Linus —which in South Los Angeles was a name that made him a frequent target of beatings by the neighborhood ruffians. If they had been smart and known Linus's dad, Lawrence Johnson, the bullies wouldn't have picked on Linus.

Lawrence was a mountain of a man with a quick temper. Lawrence, or Larry (as his fellow truckers knew him), was a long-distance truck driver and wasn't home much. Linus's mother, Shanice, was a nurse who always worked the night shift for better pay. Linus and his younger brother, Tyler, grew up fast and took care of themselves. Shanice tried her best for her boys, but working all night and raising the boys left her continually exhausted. During the brief periods between trucking jobs when Lawrence was home, his "hands-on" parenting style was habitually more severe than the bullies' beatings. When their father was home, Linus and Tyler made themselves scarce.

When Linus was eight and walking home from school with Tyler, the neighborhood tormentors jumped them to take their pocket money. Linus fought bravely and tried to protect his brother, but he was smashed to the ground and pummeled mercilessly. He was barely aware of the older boys smacking Tyler around. When Tyler could, he broke free and ran into the street. Tragically, Tyler ran in front of a car. Linus heard the screech of brakes and the horrific sound of the impact. The ruffians dispersed as Tyler's life ebbed away, and Linus couldn't even drag himself over to his brother's body before he lost consciousness.

When he awoke in the hospital, the first thing he heard was the uncontrollable sobs of his mother from the hallway as she wailed with grief. Linus felt so alone and guilty. The following two days at home, Linus stayed in his room with his door shut to muffle his mother's continuous weeping. Lawrence returned home from his cross-country trucking job and poured his rage upon both his wife and Linus. Lawrence blamed both Shanice and Linus for failing to protect Tyler. As soon as the funeral was over, Lawrence left, never returning. Later, when he overheard some neighbors, Linus found out that his father had another family in northern Texas. After that, Shanice turned into a shell of her former self and ignored Linus.

Linus started bodybuilding. By the time he was fourteen, he was big enough that nobody laughed when he called himself Rex. Two years later, he was over six feet tall and two hundred sixty pounds, and his gang, which he called the "Killers," controlled the neighborhood. His former tormentors either were vanquished by his wrath or had fled the district. Rex deserted his mother.

※

Two months before The Fires

The two-week and one-month suspended-animation sleep experiments were successful. Those volunteers awoke as though they had just taken a long nap, and their physical, mental, and psychological characteristics were undiminished. During that same time, the candidates for the six-month test underwent four weeks of intensive training. After the training, leadership approved proceeding with the six-month final experiment.

Nate and the three remaining candidates assembled with the scientists, medical staff, testing staff, and Naval officers into the conference room. Initially, each finalist had started the program with the rank of Lieutenant Junior Grade, and now the superior officers promoted each to Lieutenant. Nate was called up last to receive his promotion. The program managers, with a flourish, brought out a NASA jumpsuit with Nate's name on the breast patch; Nate was the selected volunteer. The other three finalists would remain assigned to the program, assist in monitoring the six-month sleep, and be ready to replace Nate if he could not begin the experiment.

Bursting with joy, Nate wished to share the news with more than the people gathered in the room, but the program's secrecy prohibited that. He called his parents and informed them of his promotion, but he also had to tell them that he was on a classified assignment and would not contact them for nine months. To Nate, the secrecy wasn't a burden as there wasn't anyone else whom he would have told.

———

Three weeks before The Fires

In preparation for the commencement of the six-month study, the medical staff quarantined Nate to a "clean" room on San Clemente Island. All his interactions with the staff became limited to either computer-linked communications or team members in isolation suits. During those last days, he endured considerable jesting from the other three finalists who, though envious, had bonded as a unit. Finally, the medical staff confirmed Nate was fit and ready for the experiment, and they gave him preparatory medications the day before the test began. The last thing that Nate remembered was a euphoric yet drowsy sensation.

———

The Fires

The drought had been ongoing for at least five years before The Fires. Whatever had caused the strange weather pattern, the impact of the devastating effects was worldwide. Though scattered regions had above average snowfall in the winter, even those areas were without additional precipitation until the following winter. Crops failed, forests were dying, and near-starvation was widespread. Whole regions were so dry that fires were already an explosive threat.

Just one week into the six-month suspended-animation test, the world caught on fire.

Extreme heat and dryness left the land vulnerable to lightning strikes, as well as uncontrolled blazes started by careless individuals and pyromaniacs. Whatever fires Mother Nature didn't spawn, human fools stepped in to ignite. Infernos quickly engulfed the northern hemisphere from coast to coast, and the southern hemisphere did not fare much better. Firefighting capabilities were overwhelmed rapidly, and efforts to stop the conflagrations failed. In populated areas, traffic entangled all movement on the roads, crushing any escape. Thousands died stuck in their cars, and millions perished from smoke and flame. It was as if the infernos of Hell were let loose on the Earth.

Amid all the chaos, some nations used the catastrophes as a tactical advantage over their neighbors. Skirmishes broke out on every continent, and even Antarctica was affected by fighting among the "scientific expeditions." The fighting just added to the chaos, and, as a result, nations and governments collapsed within days. All human efforts were ineffective in stopping the raging infernos.

During the ensuing catastrophe of societal collapse, Abraham Jones was too busy ensuring that he and Veena survived to consider the enormous oddity of fires erupting everywhere. From his knowledge of the Bible, he realized that these events were not part of the Rapture. Abraham couldn't determine whether God was directing these flames or simply allowing the conflagrations to consume everything in their paths. Nevertheless, Abraham trusted in God and that He would bring good from this sorrow and evil.

Meanwhile, at the ESM-SAS facility on San Clemente Island, Command gave the test staff emergency leave to return to the mainland to safeguard their families. The facility was automated and only needed monitoring, which could be done remotely from the larger facility at San Diego's Point Loma. Whatever aircraft was available had been diverted to fight fires, deliver supplies, or evacuate people fleeing the flames. However, the smoke effectively grounded all the flights except those that originated from the desert areas. The San Clemente Island-based staff boarded a shuttle boat to transport them to the mainland. A replacement crew was waiting in San Diego to return to San Clemente Island on the shuttle boat and continue the test. The shuttle boat never returned.

Meanwhile, Nate slept.

———

After The Fires

No one was there to monitor Nate nor revive him at the end of his six-month sleep. Without human intervention or system fault, the computers and hardware automatically kept Nate in suspended animation.

The ESM-SAS researchers would have been fascinated to know that the suspended animation volunteers did dream; at least Nate dreamt. After The Fires started, which marked The Thinning's initiation, none of the researchers survived.

In a typical six to eight hours of sleep, a person's brain

activity "moves" through stages of a cycle, and a person's mind may experience four or five cycles during that time. During the Rapid Eye Movement stage, consciousness rises, and dreams occur. Commonly, a person only remembers a dream if they awaken or become nearly conscious during the dream. The researchers wondered if any of these stages applied to someone in suspended animation.

Months later, Nate would vaguely recall visions of conversations with a man in whom Nate felt complete trust. Those dreams were odd to Nate because he couldn't identify him though he suspected he knew the man. In these visions, he remembered the man telling Nate he had a purpose for him.

Meanwhile, in L.A., Rex and the Killers, now better known as the K, used the chaos spawned by The Fires to dominate all of central and south L.A. Within a year, they controlled most of the L.A. basin. Everyone hid or fled when the K approached. Rex was indeed the king.

—*⁓*—

The Awakening

The contractor who built the facility did a good job, using quality parts and experienced subcontractors and people. The facility was watertight and well-constructed, and it stayed in excellent condition even though it was unattended. Time and heat weaken even the highest-caliber parts. The redundancy built into the systems to monitor and handle critical subsystems eventually became insufficient as there wasn't anyone repairing the initial failure.

Over the years, as the components heated and cooled, a microscopic crack formed and grew in one of the electronic components' ceramics. Two weeks before The Awakening, the part failed. Prompted by a hardware indicator, the software logic raised an alarm that should have started a maintenance action to replace the faulty part, but there wasn't anyone to notice the breakdown and start the repair.

By design, redundant subsystems kept the facility in a fully operational state. In the Phase One experiment plan, the medical staff would initiate the test subject's reanimation. However, the system was over-stressed by the first part malfunction, and when a second component failed thirteen days later, the computer system automatically started the revival process. After eleven years, Nate would wake from his long sleep.

CHAPTER 25

ACCEPTANCE

A refreshing, cool breeze swept across Nate as he rested atop a boulder on a slope overlooking the valley and settlement, and the occasional cloud gave a brief respite from the intensity of the sunlight. Nate drank water from his bota and wiped the sweat from his forehead and face. He gazed at the encampment and all the people working there.

It had been six months since they arrived at the high camp. Toil, training, and a couple of painful sunburn episodes banished any thought he had previously held that his experience was an illusion. He was assigned to duties only around the camp for the first four months as he developed his skills to survive in the new world. Every day, after he awoke and washed the sleep from his face, there was an optional prayer and Bible-study time, followed by a light breakfast, farming, and combat training, all before lunch. Lunch was the main meal of the day. Following the lunch clean-up, the daily schedule allowed an hour of quiet time. At first, Nate slept heavily during quiet time. However, within several weeks, he grew hardened to the daily rigor and altered his routine to take a short nap and read whatever he could find. Books were precious resources and guarded as well as their food stocks and weapons.

During the mid-to-late afternoon, camp chores regularly involved Nate's horsemanship and horse care training. Nate and Spackle had finally grown into a skillful team. Later in the day, if he didn't have kitchen duties, Nate had one-on-one training with either Carla or Veena. With a quick wash-up before dinner, he sat at a table with other tribe members to share the meal and a bit of stimulating conversation. At first, people gathered around Nate to hear about his experience with NASA, the Navy, and the suspended animation experiment. About half of the camp members were adolescents when The Fires started, and they longed to know about the life that existed before. Now, more often than not, Nate was the one who asked questions of the tribe members. He especially enjoyed listening to the SEALs, the remaining members of the *Des Moines*, Abe, and Veena. Yes, he savored anything Veena had to share.

Soon after he arrived, Jody and Laoni gave Nate additional attention. Nate was naïve, and at first, he thought they were just trying to help him adjust and fit in. Jody would sit by him whenever they gathered for a meal or a discussion. Vince had to tell Nate that Jody was flirting with him and trying to nurture a relationship. Though Nate had a suspicion and was flattered, he didn't feel a spark with Jody. Rather than address the unwanted attention directly, Nate distanced himself from Jody. She took the hints and no longer came around.

Laoni, on the other hand, was so much younger than Nate that he missed her signals completely. Nate was Laoni's first crush, and she volunteered to teach Nate combat skills. She would sit at his feet during the evening campfire discussions. Unlike Nate, Carla recognized Laoni's fawning after Nate and sent the girl to the forward camp for a month. When Laoni returned, her crush on Nate was over, and Nate was clueless that it had ever happened.

There were breaks in the routine. Sometimes, storms swept in and interrupted the prevailing schedule, followed by several days of hard labor to complete the chores preempted by the weather. In the fall, there were several three-day trips to the Julian area and the surviving orchards, primarily for apples. These excursions broke up the drudgery of camp chores, though Nate missed the participation in the training sessions, which he found invigorating even though they were exhausting and bruising. *The Julian trips are a refreshing change of pace, but I miss the time with Veena*, thought Nate.

After four months, Carla had begrudgingly decided that Nate could now participate in the patrols, though she assigned him to her squads to keep an eye on him. When he performed satisfactorily for a month of short patrols and sentry duty close to the settlement, Carla let him join her expedition to the Tierrasanta forward camp. In truth, Carla would have preferred to keep Nate on sentry duty, but the mission was Veena's patrol, and Veena had directed Carla to bring Nate. Nate was glad that he and Spackle had bonded so well before that month-long expedition, and he rode with ease wherever they went.

Now, they were back at the high camp, and Nate settled into the camp schedule. He looked forward to another quest in four weeks; camp duties were essential to survival, but patrols were more exciting. He looked across the valley from his perch on the boulder and saw Veena walking near the slope base.

CHAPTER 26

Veena finished the morning inspections and strode across the camp towards the training area to lead the morning's combat exercises. As she walked, she thought of how well Nate had acquitted himself on his first long patrol. *I really should congratulate him. He's taken the training to heart and then demonstrated it*, she mused. Then Veena felt a flush on her face, realizing she was focusing on Nate. She looked up the nearby slope and noticed that Nate was resting on the boulder there.

She waved him down, and he came quickly to walk by her side.

"You did well on your first long patrol," was her greeting as Nate approached. "Are you headed to training?"

"Yes, may I walk with you?"

Veena nodded, and they strolled in silence to the training arena.

Unhappily for Nate, Veena challenged him much more severely than she had previously, and the morning's session resulted in a collection of bruises and sores.

All afternoon, Veena felt guilty about how harshly she had attacked Nate during their one-on-one sparring session. He had improved considerably over the last six months, but her internal embarrassment about her feelings for him, which she didn't understand fully, had loosened her restraint. She had charged him aggressively, and —though he had become more of a match for her—she had effortlessly slammed him to the ground. She resolved to make amends over the evening meal.

"Nate," Veena greeted him as she approached where he was sitting with his plate. Then, in a softer voice, she asked, "May I join you?"

"Please," Nate responded with unguarded enthusiasm.

"Are you feeling sore?"

"Only when I breathe." The chuckle made him groan.

After a moment's silence, Nate said with a jesting tone, "So, do you initiate all novices this way?"

Veena let out a hearty laugh and teasingly shoved Nate's shoulder, to which he immediately let out an overstated groan, and they both broke into a howl.

Nearby, Abe noted the closeness of Veena and Nate.

CHAPTER 27

As each day passed, Veena and Nate spent more time together, sitting side by side in Bible study, sparring with each other during training, sharing mealtimes, and walking together after the evening meal. They'd talk about the times before The Fires, and when Veena felt strong enough to discuss it, she would recall more of the events of the last eleven years. Veena was envious that Nate had the experiences of high school, college, and the old-world career, whereas the ruination of The Thinning stole her adolescence and young adulthood. Conversely, Nate, overwhelmed by the devastation and the atrocities that followed, was fascinated by the tales of survival and the formation of the tribes.

"How did you have the courage and strength to endure all those horrors?" Nate asked in a soft tone as they strolled in the chilly night air one evening just an hour after sunset.

The question, more than the briskness of the evening, sent a cold shudder through Veena. She stopped, looked directly into Nate's eyes, and whispered, "Only by God's grace was I blessed to be with Abe when The Fires erupted. Abe trusts in God and has taught me to trust Him, too. Now, eleven-plus years later, I can see how God has cared for us in each challenge and tragedy, how He kept us safe from the worst of the terrors and evils. Innumerable people suffered horribly. God gifted Abe with knowledge and skills, which Abe has taught to me and our tribe. When God sent additional victims to us, we grew stronger, and God's hand protected us, even in the worst battles with the ruthless, hateful gangs that tried to overcome us. Looking back, we should have all perished, but He has kept us. He even sent you to us, and, though I don't understand His reasons, I am happy He did." Tears watered Veena's eyes, and she looked away.

"I can't comprehend what you have endured, but I'm thankful that you are here, and you have accepted me into your group," Nate whispered gratefully. He moved closer to her, took her hand, and squeezed it.

Though momentarily stunned by his boldness, Veena did not snatch her hand away. Instead, she shifted closer to Nate, and they stood together in the quiet of the night. Then, she gave his hand a little squeeze back, said, "Good night," and pulled away to walk to her hut.

Nate watched her leave, a thrill pulsing through him at both his nerve to hold Veena's hand and at her affectionate squeeze back. He let out a silent sigh as he watched her walk away, illuminated only by the camp torches and kitchen fires. *Wow* was all that he could think.

CHAPTER 28

Over the next two weeks, Veena and Nate continued to walk together in the evenings. Though they enjoyed each other's company, there was a tension present now, and both felt a bit awkward.

It was a welcome change in the daily grind when Veena included Nate in the northern patrol scheduled for the next day to check their traps, the presence of game, and any signs of intruders. Habitually, Veena would take her squad known as the Archangels, with Laoni as her teammate and Carla and MaryAn as the rest. This time, though, Veena suggested to Nate that he join the mission in place of Laoni. Nate jumped at the opportunity and fidgeted like an overexcited child. Laoni didn't mind being left behind, as there wasn't much excitement in the routine patrols around the settlement, and they customarily didn't take the horses for those local patrols. So she was just as happy to stay and train with Abe to improve her Krav Maga techniques.

Following standard procedure, the squad arose before dawn, had an early breakfast, and headed out of camp at first light. Veena took the point, followed by Nate and Carla, and MaryAn guarded the rear. They moved stealthily through the tall sagebrush dripping with the morning dew as they ascended the hills around the valley. They slipped out the north side of the camp just as the morning's rays kissed the tops of the western ridges.

Nate drew in the crisp, clean air, and he felt a renewed vigor as he practically skipped along the trail, trying to keep Veena within sight. His enthusiasm overtook his discipline, and he scuffed up a small puff of dust.

"Knock it off, Sinclair," snarled Carla in a hushed tone. "It may be a routine patrol, but you're making enough noise to scare away the game as well as let any enemies plan an ambush in leisure."

Taken back a bit, Nate sheepishly focused his awareness on the surroundings and stepped cautiously. He slowed down so that Carla closed the distance between them. He matched her pace and looked at her over his shoulder. "Why are you on my case, Carla? I've never done anything to hurt you or anyone else."

Carla glared at him briefly before sneering, "That's Rodriquez to you, Sinclair." A moment later, she added, "No, you haven't done anything against me. You're a man, and that's reason enough. You're a leech, a worthless curiosity that eats our food and distracts our leader. You are putting us all in danger with your sloppiness."

Nate knew of Carla's justifiable hostility toward nearly all men. After hearing her account of how the Clairens had appallingly abused her and MaryAn, he even understood it. Until now, Nate hadn't associated himself with that animosity. Part of him boiled at the unjust, sweeping categorization that grouped him with the loathsome monsters that had preyed upon Carla and MaryAn, and, instead of letting that anger slide, he bit back with a touch of sarcasm. "Look, Rodriquez, I may indeed be a man, but I had nothing to do with the events of the past. As for being a leech, I didn't expect to wake up in a world gone mad." Then, a little ashamed of his outburst, he added, "I try to pull my weight, and I hope to make you see that I'm here to serve and contribute. Lastly, I'm sorry you feel that I distract Veena, but I happen to care deeply for her."

Surprising himself at his impromptu declaration of affection for Veena, Nate's anger faded.

Not pacified, Carla's rage was only fueled by Nate's response. "Those events of the past," she intoned with scorn, "killed most and forever scarred the survivors. We continue to struggle with that terror, as our skirmishes with the Clairens demonstrate. As for you, I haven't seen anything to suggest that you are any different or better than that scum. Now, get back in formation." She gave Nate a shove, and she dropped back until she could barely see him anymore.

They continued in silence for another half hour, with Veena at least one hundred yards in the lead, and Nate intermittently lost sight of her. Nate let his attention drift as he fumed at Carla's accusations. Carla remained far back from Nate, suppressing her rage while maintaining her vigilance. MaryAn was so far behind the squad that Nate hadn't seen her since they left camp.

———

MaryAn, though, could tell there had been bad words between Carla and Nate. She was upset by that friction; Carla was her partner, but MaryAn liked Nate and thought Veena benefitted from his company. She understood Carla's hatred of men better than anyone else, and she knew that Nate wouldn't escape that rage just because he wasn't there during the last eleven years. MaryAn prayed, inwardly, that Carla would grow to tolerate Nate, just as she had the other men in the Tierran tribe.

CHAPTER 29

They covered a lot of ground and were now about three miles from the settlement. They were near the outermost border, in a region still considered safe due to its proximity to the nearest sentries. Veena decided to signal a rest, and she paused to let her squad approach. From here, they would move into the outlands. She was just about to tell Nate to keep silent and careful as they moved from the rest when a commotion broke loose back down the trail near MaryAn.

Nate was looking at Veena when he heard a startled cry from behind him, and he spun to see four men rush toward MaryAn, far back on the trail. Stunned, he saw one of the attackers collapsing, clutching at a bolt in his chest that MaryAn had released from her crossbow. Before MaryAn could reload her crossbow or draw her knife, the remaining three men tackled her.

Nate froze. It was the first time he had been in a combat situation. Carla immediately charged down the trail, screaming so shrilly that the attackers looked up. Nate bolted after her, pulling out his knife and letting out a war howl.

Carla's fear for MaryAn's safety overrode her discipline as she charged blindly down the trail. Then two new attackers broke out of the brush on the right side of Carla. The first attacker leaped through the air at Carla, and she ducked and spun, grabbing his arm and flinging him to a backbreaking crunch on a nearby rock. During her maneuver, she lost her grip on her crossbow, and it arced away from her, dislodging the arrow bolt and releasing the readied drawstring as the crossbow bounced on the ground. She had just flung the first attacker as the second thug slammed into her with a tackle that would make a linebacker proud. Locked together, they smashed to the ground.

Nate broke stride to help Carla. However, Carla was back in full command of her combat skills and had already gained an advantage on her attacker. She noticed Nate's slowing and screamed out, "Go!" as she drove her stiffened hand into her assailant's solar plexus.

Nate noticed Carla's crossbow and bolt on the trail ahead of him, but he ignored them as he returned to a breakneck speed down the path toward MaryAn and her attackers.

MaryAn's attackers were overconfident, thinking that the rest of their gang would subdue the two people running down the trail. They beat MaryAn savagely, already savoring their prize. Nate sailed through the air, catching them unaware and smashing into all three as they clustered over MaryAn.

Nate rolled to his feet and charged the nearest assailant. He caught the thug by the head and snapped his neck with a quick twist and a forward thrust of his arms. The other two jackals shook off the initial stunning blow and turned toward Nate just as the sickening snap of their comrade's neck pierced the air. One rushed Nate, while the other, frightened by the quick death of his buddy, held back.

Nate dropped the limp body of his first victim and moved just in time to deflect the lunge of the second assailant. They fell to the ground, spun around, and crouched into a defensive posture as they faced off. Nate kept glancing at the third attacker as he maneuvered to counter the second thug's movements. Abruptly the second assailant jumped forward and swung a roundhouse thrust at Nate's head. Now, the months of training of Krav Maga with Veena and Carla paid off as Nate swiftly dodged the blow. Catching his attacker's arm with both hands, he twisted the limb and snapped it at the elbow with a vicious, upward thrust of his knee. The creep howled in pain as Nate now pivoted, dropping the attacker to the ground and smashing his ribcage with a driving heel stomp. Fueled by rage, he killed his assailant by driving his clenched knuckles into the thug's larynx, crushing the windpipe.

Quickly, Nate turned to face the third ruffian, who had moved into a position with a knife held over the limp body of MaryAn. "Back off, man!" he shouted at Nate. Rage coursing over him, Nate ignored the challenge and charged his foe while filling the air with a bloodcurdling cry. Frightened by the killing demon, the thug forgot his threat and raised his arms in defense as Nate hurled toward him. Instinctively, Nate twisted in midair and brought his feet into a slamming impact on the bushwhacker's chest. With the air forced from his lungs by the tremendous blow, the thug flew backward and collapsed. Nate was on him in an instant, grabbing the goon's hand that still clutched the knife and driving the blade into his belly and up into the chest cavity.

Panting, Nate rose from the third kill, with blood splattered on his hands and clothes. Gasping for breath as he realized he had killed all three attackers, he stumbled over to MaryAn and knelt beside her. Her face was puffy, her body covered with welts, but she didn't appear to be bleeding. The sounds of a nearby scuffle made Nate snap his attention behind him on the trail. *Carla, Veena*, he thought as he realized the fight wasn't over, and he sprinted up the path.

CHAPTER 30

Carla was still wrestling with her second assailant, a man much bulkier than she. He threw her to the ground, straddled her to hold her down, and started pounding his fists into her face. As Nate came running up, the gorilla looked toward him. Carla quickly kneed her assailant in the groin, causing him to fall off her as he writhed in pain. She snatched her knife free and drove it home through the base of her attacker's skull.

Before Carla could ask Nate about MaryAn, they heard a piercing cry of pain from further up the trail. Nate looked, nearly panicking, as he saw Veena struggling with a man armed with a large knife. The man had managed to wound Veena on the thigh with a swipe of the blade. He lunged at her, driving the weapon toward her chest while she braced with her hands locked onto his arms to force the edge back.

Concerned he probably couldn't cover the sixty yards in time to break the attack, Nate noticed that Carla's crossbow and bolt were there in front of him. Scooping them up, he quickly drew back the drawstring and locked it into the trigger mechanism. As he raised the bow, he slapped the bolt into the barrel slot and swiftly aimed. When Nate squeezed the trigger on the crossbow, the bolt sprung toward the target and whistled through the air. It felt like it took forever to cross the distance, but the path was true, and the bolt embedded deeply above the attacker's jaw. With the attacker momentarily stunned, Veena got control of the knife and drove it deep into his chest. Veena pushed him back as he collapsed to the ground, blood streaming from his ear, nose, and mouth.

Veena then dropped to the ground as exhaustion and blood loss overtook her. Nate swept down beside her and cradled her head in his hands as he gasped in panic, "Veena, are you all right? Veena, answer me." He noticed the blood oozing from her leg wound.

Veena embraced him and began to weep, softly at first, then building to sobbing. "I'm all right, Nate," she choked out between sobs. "What about Carla and MaryAn?"

"Carla appears to be all right. MaryAn is alive but savagely beaten. I didn't see any bleeding wounds or broken bones. We need to assess her condition more closely. Do you know if you have other cuts?"

Veena clutched Nate closer and sobbed. Nate was weeping now himself, and he wanted to just hold onto Veena. He carefully checked for other wounds, finding none, and then inspected the gash on her leg. "It's deep," he said, "but I don't think any arteries are damaged. Let me clean and bandage it, and we need to get everyone back to camp." Veena nodded as Nate retrieved his first-aid kit and gently cleansed the cut before applying antiseptic and a tight bandage. "If you keep off the leg, you should be OK till we get back to camp and treat it properly."

He looked around and saw that Veena had been in quite a fight by herself. There were three bodies in addition to the one that Nate had shot. For the first time, he noticed that they had Asian ancestry.

Veena wiped her eyes and face and looked again at their assailants. "They must be an Asian gang that we haven't encountered before, possibly from the Los Angeles area." She looked at Nate with admiration and affection. "Next time," she tried to say with levity, "don't aim for the head; the shot is too risky."

"Oh, Veena," he stammered. "I was so frightened for you. I just pointed and shot. I don't know what made me think I could hit anything from that distance. I could have just as easily hit you." He shuddered.

Veena looked intently at Nate. "You didn't hit me, and I'm grateful that you are here. We have much to be thankful for." She reached for Nate, and they held close.

Gathering up their weapons, Nate kept an arm around Verna's shoulders to help her hobble along. They started back down the path toward camp and where Carla was with MaryAn.

Carla looked up as Veena and Nate approached. MaryAn's head rested in Carla's lap, but her eyes fluttered open, and she weakly smiled as she saw Veena and Nate.

"She's battered and bruised, but she's not cut, and there aren't any obvious severe injuries. We need to get her back to camp for a thorough examination." Then Carla looked directly at Nate and softly said, "Thanks."

Nate nodded. "If you can help Veena keep off her leg as we go back to camp, I can carry MaryAn."

Carla studied Nate, assessing this unanticipated behavior, and eased MaryAn's head back to the ground. She rose and took Nate's place in supporting Veena. Nate knelt, tenderly lifted MaryAn over his shoulder, and rose to his feet. Together, they all started the trail back to camp.

CHAPTER 31

MaryAn, with no cuts, broken bones, or internal injuries, recovered faster than Veena. Within a week, she could resume her complete set of duties, whereas Veena's gash required sutures and four weeks to heal to the point that it wasn't likely to tear open if she stressed it. As a precaution, Abe restricted her duties for an additional two weeks so that her muscles would fully heal.

The six weeks of limited duty gave Veena and Nate more time to spend together. Since the attack, they had grown incredibly close.

One evening, during the sixth week of Veena's recovery, as they sat side by side in the night and gazed at the stars, Nate embraced Veena and declared, "I love you. I want to spend my life with you."

Veena needed a moment to reply, "I love you, too, Nate. You need to know that I believe in commitment and marriage, and I will be uncomfortable sharing my life with you in just a casual relationship."

With only a moment's reflection, Nate dropped to his knees. "Veena, I am in love with you, and I want to grow old with you. Will you bless me by becoming my wife?"

"Yes," Veena gushed, and she embraced Nate tightly.

"When shall we get married?"

"Every day is a blessing," Veena said tenderly. "We don't know the length of our days on the Earth. I say we should marry within the week."

"Yes!" exclaimed Nate, squeezing Veena tighter. "Let's do that."

CHAPTER 32

The next day, Nate sought Abe to talk with him, get his blessing of marriage with Veena, and request that he perform the ceremony. He made his approach after the morning Bible study.

They sat at the table in the veranda's shade, and Nate spoke of his desire to marry Veena.

"Well, actually, I'm not surprised," said Abe with a broad smile. "It's mature of you to ask for my blessing, even though I have no claim to give it. Joyfully, I do give my blessing and offer both of you hearty congratulations. What a wonderful celebration it will be."

"Thank you, Abe. I know you aren't Veena's father, but you are the closest she has to family, and I hope it's obvious that your blessing means so much to Veena and me. I have great respect for you, and I marvel at your steadfast walk in faith."

"That is dearly kind of you to say, and it warms my heart that both of you care for me so. As for my faith walk, my journey is not without trials. May I tell you a little about it?"

"Yes, I'd genuinely like to hear that," said Nate.

"OK, from the beginning, then. I've always had a belief in God, and my family made sure I went to church as a child. Despite that, I never really developed a close, personal relationship with Y'shua, Jesus, until after the Marines. You see, when I left home and joined the Marines, I was pretty full of myself, and it was easy to put God in a dusty corner. Then, during one mission, I injured my left knee. It wasn't too bad until a week later when I overstressed it while training. As a result, I needed surgery and physical therapy, and my suitability to go on missions was eliminated.

"As part of the post-surgery recovery regiment, I was given prescription pain medication. The loss of being able to go on missions meant my reassignment to desk duty. It became clear that even with the successful surgery, I would never really be effective in the field again. I became despondent, and during that time, I also developed a dependency on pain meds. Miserable and repeatedly depressed, I didn't reenlist, and I pretty much just holed up in my apartment. Can you understand how I let my life spiral out of control?"

"Yes," Nate said softly. "Though I've never experienced the depth of despair you are describing, I have had bouts of sadness, especially after a breakup with my old girlfriend. I also knew a buddy who had an alcohol dependency, and it was tough to watch his life collapse."

"Well, yes, that would be similar," replied Abe. "So, one day, I ran out of all my pain medication, and my outlook hit a low spot. The depth of that despair is challenging to describe. I finally surrendered to God. I lay prone on the floor and prayed that He would enter my life and rescue me. An odd thing happened, or so I thought then; my tears of sadness and pain changed into tears of relief, love, and joy. Until you've experienced that, it probably sounds incredulous. Yet, I tell you, it was a landmark turning point in my life.

"The withdrawal from the pain meds was awful, and I regularly felt sick. Yet, I had a renewed strength and purpose. I started going to church again, and I felt that each week's message personally targeted me and my journey. I enrolled at the University of California San Diego in their physical therapy program, and I found considerable enjoyment and affirmation in education. What I still savor the most, though, is my relationship with God—Father, Son, and Holy Spirit—and the examination and contemplation of His Word."

In the silence, the sounds of the camp and nearby birds filtered in. Finally, Nate said, "Wow, I had no idea. I'd like that type of personal relationship with God, too."

"You can have it, Nate. All that you need to do is to ask Y'shua to reveal His truths to you, accept His love, and let the Holy Spirit work in your life."

"I will, Abe," said Nate. "Will you pray with me?"

"It will be an honor," Abe said with a smile and a glad heart.

After they prayed, Abe asked, "Nate, I have two questions. First, have you been baptized, and second, when would you and Veena like to get married?"

"No, I haven't been baptized. Do I need to be?" Nate replied.

"When we just prayed, you received the baptism of the Holy Spirit," said Abe. "Water baptism is simply a declaration of your commitment to Y'shua and a symbolic cleansing by God of your sins. It is an outward sign of a personal pledge. In a way, both baptism and the marriage ceremony are demonstrations to the community of your dedication and love."

"Then, I'd like to be baptized."

"Good. About the second question, when would you like to be married?"

"Veena and I would like the marriage ceremony to happen as soon as possible."

"That is also good. We could hold the baptism and marriage ceremony on the same day here in the high camp. May I suggest that we plan it for a week from now as that will give those who want to come, and are currently at the forward camp or the sub base, time to travel here?"

"For me, the answer is yes," said Nate with a grin that went from ear to ear. "I need to check with Veena, but I suspect she will be pleased with that date, too."

CHAPTER 33

Seven days later, under sunny skies, pleasant temperatures, and a refreshing breeze, Nate's baptism and the later wedding were a grand celebration in the camp. Abe presided, Nate chose Vince to be his best man, and Veena chose Kath to be her matron of honor, with MaryAn, Laoni, and even Carla, standing with her. All exclaimed with a joyful gasp as Veena strode into the communal hut wearing a dress and with her hair laced with flowers. Nate realized he had never seen Veena in a dress. Nate was nearly overcome by her beauty and by his joy that she would consider him worthy.

Abe quieted the assembly, called them to stand, and opened with prayer. "Almighty, most Holy God, Your mercies and grace are without end, and new every morning. We bless Your holy name that You have brought this dear woman and dear man, precious children of Your creation, together to be wed in holy matrimony. We rejoice that You have allowed us to be witnesses of their blessed joining, a bright hope in these times of shared despair. You remind us that You are our hope and that You have not forgotten us.

"LORD Y'shua, one of the first miracles You performed is recorded in John 2 at a wedding. You bless weddings, and they are part of Your loving plan. We humbly ask that You send Your Holy Spirit to bless this wedding and all who are here celebrating. In the blessed name of Your son, Y'shua HaMashiach, we pray. Amen."

All the assembly echoed, "Amen."

Abe came close to weeping as he beheld Veena and Nate standing before him. "Veena and Nathanael, marriage is a lifelong partnership and bonding. It is the foundation on which we build communities. Do not take the ceremony nor this commitment lightly. Embrace it fully, giving your partner your total pledge and duty every day of your life that your marriage may be a shining beacon of God's love to us and His faithfulness. May your love for each other be an effective witness, and may you have a bounty of reasons to acknowledge that you are blessed."

Then, turning to Nate, Abe smiled widely and asked, "Nathanael, who could have foreseen your entry into our lives? You truly have been sent by God, and we are all enriched because He did. Will you take Veena as your wife, a gift from God, to love, honor, and obey? Will you be her companion, partner, and helpmate? Will you faithfully serve God by listening to her counsel, and will you cherish her as long as you both shall live?"

"I shall," Nate declared heartily.

As Abe faced Veena, tears formed in his eyes, yet a loving smile shone upon his face. "Veena, how could I have even imagined how our lives would be linked when your mother and father introduced me to their young child? We have struggled and survived so much. Still, here we are, gathered with dear friends at a truly wonderful miracle in our lives. Without any reservation, I know that your parents and the whole host of heaven are rejoicing right now.

"Will you, Veena, take Nathanael as your husband, a gift from God, to love, honor, and obey? Will you be his companion, partner, and helpmate? Will you faithfully serve God by respecting him, and will you cherish him as long as you both shall live?"

With tears streaming down her face, Veena took a breath

to compose herself and confirmed in a resolute voice, "I shall."

"Then, by the grace of God—Father, Son, and Holy Spirit—I confirm you as husband and wife, blessed children of His family. May He grant you reasons to celebrate beyond measure. Amen."

All the tribespeople heartily responded, "Amen," and a great cheer shook the gathering.

CHAPTER 34

GRACE

Life in the new era didn't favor perks such as honeymoons. Every day, the camp duties and chores continued as demanded by life. Nonetheless, Veena and Nate enjoyed their dedicated time together, the closeness that marriage stimulates and nurtures, and the security of shared struggles, dreams, and intimacy.

What Nate had not anticipated was that he was no longer allowed to go on patrols with Veena. Except for Carla and MaryAn, who had a legacy exemption, Tierran policy separated couples into different squads. The protocol was Abe's wisdom and one that Veena had fully embraced, though now it pained her.

One morning, six weeks after their wedding, Veena awoke later than she ever had before. She could hear the morning sounds of the camp and realized that breakfast was already over. Feeling tired, though exceedingly good, she stretched in bed and loosened her muscles. The morning air's fragrance was refreshing, and she couldn't remember ever feeling so joyful. She turned her head to study Nate, who continued to doze, and a smile formed on her lips as she remembered last night. Rolling over on her side to face him, she reached to stroke his cheek.

"Ewww, whiskers cover your face," she teasingly whispered as the bristles of his beard scratched her fingertips.

Nate's mouth fashioned a mischievous grin that steadily grew wider. His eyelids fluttered apart, and his eyes focused on hers. "Well, good morning to you, too," he bantered back as his grin now seemed to reach ear to ear. "Most men's faces have beard growth overnight."

"I know that," she stated with amusement. "It's just that you have more beard growth than any day I've seen since we first found you. Now that I think about it, your scarcity of facial hair that first day made you look remarkably different than other men. Maybe that cooling for your suspended animation sleep temporarily changed your biology. Perhaps our intimacy is re-stimulating that growth."

"Ha! I'm sure that's the reason," he laughingly rejoined. "Seriously, what time is it? Aren't we usually up and out by now?"

"Oh, are you complaining?" she teased. Then she felt sick to her stomach, jumped out of bed, and raced for a bucket. Nate was startled by her movements and frightened as Veena vomited the contents of her stomach.

"Veena, are you all right? Shall I get Abe?" Nate rushed over and knelt beside her.

"No, don't get Abe," Veena said in a coarse whisper. "I'm feeling better now. Let me lie down; I'm just a little tired."

Nate gently grasped her arm and helped her over to the bed. Grabbing a cloth, he wet it with clean water and dabbed her face and forehead. Only as the color started to return to her face did he realize how pasty her skin had become.

Seeing his concern, Veena smiled faintly. "Thanks, Nate. I'm feeling better now. You go ahead and get cleaned up. I'll be up shortly."

Nate begrudgingly left. Veena did feel better soon, and after a brief rest, she also got up to face the day.

CHAPTER 35

The following day, Veena roused closer to her customary time, and then, nausea returned. Again, Nate helped her back to bed and cleaned her up. Nate was anxious, as he knew how vulnerable they all were to any illness. Medications were limited, and the tribe didn't have a medical doctor. Abe's medic training and Hospital Corpsman Douglas Ames, a member of the *Des Moines* crew, were the best they had. 'Doc' Ames was currently in the forward camp. Nate stayed with Veena while she briefly dozed. When she awoke for the second time that morning, she pronounced herself "fine" and left to face the day. Nate, however, resolved to consult Abe.

Nate forced himself to complete his chores before he set out to find Abe. By then, it was late morning. Abe had just finished leading about a dozen tribe members in a reading of a scene from Shakespeare's *Julius Caesar*, a technique he employed to entertain his charges while also teaching them.

As soon as Abe finished the session, Nate approached him and, in a whisper, said, "Abe, I've got to talk with you."

"Sure, Nate, what's on your mind?"

"Privately, if you don't mind, Abe."

Abe looked seriously at Nate and nodded. "Let's inspect the cornfields."

As Abe turned and walked toward the farmland, Nate

quickly jumped into step by Abe's side. They walked in silence until Nate felt they were out of earshot. Gossip was a big entertainment commodity, even for a disciplined camp.

"Abe, Veena has been sick to her stomach, though it appears to pass quickly."

Abe looked again at Nate. "You said 'appears.' Has the sickness happened more than once?"

"Just twice, yesterday and today. After she vomits and rests a bit, she says she is OK, and then she goes out for the day's activities."

"Do you know if she has a fever?"

"No, 1 haven't felt a fever, though her complexion paled briefly."

"If there isn't a fever, then she might just have an allergy, though 1 don't ever recall her having any allergy troubles. In all probability, she is just overtired and needs additional rest. If it happens again, come get me as soon as you can."

"Thanks, Abe," Nate said with minor relief, and as they walked back to the shelters, they made the small talk that one makes when you don't want to discuss the graver concerns.

———⁓⁓⁓———

That evening in their shelter, Veena jestingly reproached Nate. "1 heard about you wanting a private conversation with Abe. What's that about?"

"Sheesh, is there anything in the camp that you don't know about?"

"No, dear," Veena teased. "Especially if it concerns my main man."

"Ha! 'Main man,'" Nate teased back. "There better not be any others."

"You know that there aren't," Veena spoke, feigning hurt. "Now, quit stalling. What did you and Abe talk about?"

Nate looked down. "I'm concerned about your health. 1 told him..."

"What?" Veena cut him off. "I told you I'm OK."

"Veena," Nate said with a worried tone. "I care deeply about you, and our new world, with its lack of medicines and doctors, makes me apprehensive. I don't want anything to happen to you."

Veena's anger subsided. "I understand, Nate. I guess I'd do the same thing. Listen, I'm OK, and we're OK. I love you, too. Let's forget about that now and rest."

Their hug was long and tender. They slept that night locked in an embrace.

CHAPTER 36

Abe was just getting out of his bedroll when Nate burst into his hut. Abe had always been a morning person, but such an awakening was startling, and Abe was so shocked, he yelled, "Nate!"

Nate didn't notice as he yelled back, with a touch of fear in his voice, "Abe, Abe! Veena's sick again."

"Go, lead on," Abe exclaimed as he cinched up his pants, grabbed his medical kit, and followed Nate out the door. As he trotted behind Nate, he said a silent prayer: *God, please hear my prayer and keep my little girl safe.*

When Nate and Abe arrived, Veena remained sitting on the ground next to the bucket holding the watery remains of her stomach's contents. She looked up, saw Abe, and protested, "Abe, I'm OK. Nate's worrying about nothing."

Abe lightly pressed his fingertips against her forehead. "Listen, dear sweet Veena, in case you forgot, while you lead the tribe, I handle the doctoring. So, let me judge your health. Hmm, you don't have a fever, but you do look faint. Tell me what is going on."

"It's nothing really. I have felt tired and sick to my stomach a few mornings. I just need fresh air, and I will feel better."

"Well, the blood's returned to your complexion, and you're pretty feisty. I don't think there is anything seriously wrong, but I want you to rest in bed for a little longer this morning. Let me check your vitals."

Veena nodded, and Abe did a quick examination. Satisfied with his initial readings, he said to Veena and Nate, reassuringly, "Everything checks out as OK. Please take it easy. There is something I need to investigate, but it's not serious." Then, in an attempt to inject a bit of levity and allay any concerns, Abe added, "You two might need to take it easy for a while, or I'm going to have to separate you into different huts."

"C'mon, lover," Veena retorted as she reached for Nate to help her get up. "Let's take a walk together to breakfast and give these idle people something to talk about."

While Nate and Veena walked to breakfast, Abe headed to the greenhouse in search of Miriam Cohen. Miriam was the chief botanist of the tribe and, at forty-six, was the oldest woman in the camp. He found Miriam humming tunes while working with her soybean seedlings. Apprising her of his observations of Veena's illness, Abe postulated what the cause might be. Miriam looked at Abe with a shocked expression and agreed that she should also interview Veena. Together they walked down to the kitchen shelter where Veena and Nate were sitting.

Veena saw Abe walk into the shelter with Miriam in tow, and she didn't like it one bit. She was also a little frightened, and when Abe suggested that Miriam also evaluate Veena's symptoms, she agreed. Back at Veena and Nate's hut, Miriam sent the men outside and then examined Veena. After about ten minutes, she came outside and sent Nate in. When Nate was out of hearing range, Miriam whispered to Abe with excitement in her voice, "You may be right."

Together they reentered the hut and faced Veena and Nate.

"Well, doctor," Veena challenged, though a ghost of fear crept within her. "Am I going to live?"

"Veena and Nate," Abe spoke in a soothing tone. "First off, we don't think that you are ill." Then, struggling to hide his fears, Abe smiled broadly as he softly said, "We think you are pregnant."

CHAPTER 37

Veena's eyelids opened so wide it appeared that her eyes would pop from their sockets. Her head swam, knees buckled, and nausea started to knot her stomach again. She would have collapsed to the ground if Abe had not anticipated the reaction and prepared. He grasped her arms as she started to sink, guided her to her bed, and helped her down.

"Oh Jesus, Abe!" exclaimed Veena. Nate just stood there, immobilized.

"Yes, dear Veena," Abe said gently. "Though I don't think you meant to say our LORD's name in that way, I am sure He is guiding this miracle. God has answered our prayers and granted us hope amid our sorrow on the earth."

Staring transfixed at the ground in front of her, Veena muttered, "Abe, are you sure? We've only been married for two months."

"As sure as we can be. We don't have the equipment to run positive tests, but your recent symptoms match what we call morning sickness. Miriam has experience with pregnant women, and she confirms my suspicions."

Miriam nodded.

"I've heard of morning sickness. Abe, if it is true, what are we to do?"

"Well, first, we need to keep the suspicion to ourselves until we have confirmation. We do need to wait a while to ensure you are pregnant." He didn't verbalize the concern that he and Miriam shared about whether the baby would survive. "I don't want you to worry. Furthermore, on the chance that Miriam and I are wrong, we must restrict the news before we have solid facts; otherwise, we could raise false hopes, crushing people's already fragile and tested faith. Miriam will also meet with you daily to see how you are doing and help you understand what is happening."

Abe paused. "Before Nate told me of your sickness, I already felt that God had touched my mind and soul and blessed me with the knowledge of this miracle. I don't have the words to explain it more than that, and I feel assured."

Veena drew a long breath and looked up at Nate and then Abe and Miriam. "I implicitly understand. I missed my period, but I discarded the possibility of pregnancy because, well, because no one has become pregnant for years. As soon as you told me the news, I believed it. I'm shocked, terrified, but I also have peace and confidence." Then, with a teasing grin, she added, "I guess we may have to change your nickname from Old Abe to Grandpa."

When Veena finished speaking, Nate sank to the bed next to Veena as the shock of her words made it all real to him. He felt he should say something, but he couldn't form the words.

Abe looked intently at both Veena and Nate. "Do you want a baby?"

Nate and Veena exchanged looks, searching for a sign in each other's eyes. Then, Veena nodded slowly and giggled. Nate relaxed and looked back at Abe. "I never thought of it before, but hell yeah, I want this baby." Veena and Nate embraced in a tight and gleeful hug.

"Good," Abe acknowledged with conviction. "Remember, please keep the news to yourself until we can confirm that you are pregnant." Turning to Miriam, Abe said, "Let's go out and let these two have time alone."

CHAPTER 38

Miriam followed Abe out of the hut, and they walked to an isolated spot before Abe spoke to Miriam in low tones. "Now, there is another reason why I don't want anyone else to know that Veena may be pregnant." He paused. "If Veena is pregnant, then it's possible that not everyone is sterile as we previously thought."

With a thoughtful expression on her face, Miriam mulled over Abe's last statement. What Abe had said and its implication disturbed her peace of mind. Finally, a revelation came to her, and it frightened her. "Abe, what exactly are you inferring?"

Abe took a deep breath and collected his thoughts. "Remember the illness that swept through everyone who survived The Fires?"

Miriam nodded, concern growing on her face.

"Do you remember that it was similar to the mumps but much more virulent?"

After nodding again, Miriam's face became distorted with a pained expression.

"Well, since Nate was in that suspended animation, he did not suffer that illness. Therefore, perhaps only the men who recovered from the disease are sterile, similar to how the mumps make a small percentage of males infertile. That may also mean that all females are potentially fertile." Abe let that thought sink in.

Miriam suddenly caught her breath. "Merciful God!" she gasped. "What about the baby?"

"I don't know," Abe said with caution. After a moment's reflection, he continued, "If Veena is pregnant, then I must trust that God, in His infinite wisdom, will pass on Veena's acquired antibodies of the disease to their baby. As regards Nate, he might still be susceptible."

Miriam stood next to Abe and thought about it for several minutes. "You're right; we need to keep it quiet for now. Still, I tell you, I have hope now greater than any I have experienced in the past eleven-plus years."

Abe smiled. "'Proven character produces hope.' Amen."

CHAPTER 39

Four weeks later, and ten weeks after the marriage of Veena and Nate, Abe, Miriam, and Veena were confident that Veena was indeed pregnant. Nate could hardly grasp the enormity of the blessing. In the camp, rumors circulated as people noticed the additional attention that Abe and Miriam were giving to Veena. At Miriam's urging and with Veena's and Nate's permission, Abe held a camp meeting after the evening meal. When all who were not required on guard duty or essential tasks had gathered in the community shelter, Abe stood and quieted the crowd by raising his hands and signaling silence.

"Let us open in prayer," Abe invited, and all the assembly bowed their heads. "Almighty God, our true Deliverer, and our ever-present Help, we thank You for Your sustaining love poured out in great compassion upon us. We pray for Your wisdom, Your guidance, and Your patience to help us comprehend Your latest blessing upon us. May we be led by You and protected by Your mighty hand. LORD, in Your perfect timing, You have revealed a new blessing to us. Fill us with Your Holy Spirit, that we might be ever faithful, and act according to Your Will. In the matchless, blessed name of our Savior, Y'shua HaMashiach, we pray."

In unison, they all said, "Amen."

Abe then said, "Please sit. I am about to tell you something overwhelming, and I humbly ask that all of you hold your questions until later. Indeed, we will not take questions tonight. We will meet tomorrow evening, and as many evenings as we need after that, to discuss any questions or concerns you have. Tonight, as I just prayed, we are revealing a new blessing, and we ask that each of you spend the next day in prayer, and listening to God's wisdom, before we meet again."

Abe looked over the people. He saw the concern, and maybe even fear, on their faces. He motioned for Miriam to stand beside him before he continued, now with a smile on his lips. "Veena and Nate, would you sit before Miriam and me, please?" After they sat, Abe, with eyes shining bright and wet, clearly spoke, "Veena is pregnant, and we estimate that Nate and Veena's baby will be born in approximately seven months."

Gasps, along with scattered shrieks and "Hallelujahs!" erupted in the assembly. Abe had to raise his hands again to get the people to quiet down.

"Dear saints," Abe said in a softer tone. "How long have we prayed for such a miracle. My faith, and my hope, have soared enormously, and I feel so blessed to witness God's kindness."

Again, "Amen!" resounded in the room.

"Nevertheless, we face a potentially perilous road ahead," Abe continued, and the assembly quieted down again. "When news of the blessing spreads, I expect that we will face numerous trials and be tested severely, possibly harder than we have before." The room got noticeably somber now, and people could hear everyone's breathing.

"We must pray for safe and successful delivery. We desire that mother and child are healthy, and we all need to assist in nurturing that result."

Abe looked at the compassionate, hopeful expressions of those looking at Veena. "None of us have heard of a pregnancy in the last twelve years. More than a few have given up hope; I know I was deeply troubled by the absence of children. However, the news may not be met with joy by all, particularly those outside our tribe. When they hear the rumors, some will travel here to be a part of the outpouring of grace. We will need divine wisdom regarding interacting with them, especially those who wish to join our body.

"Hate and envy will fill others. Just as we have had to defend our tribe, camps, supplies, farms, and faith, we must expect that there will be those who would come against us to destroy what God has done. We must commit to a renewed vigilance. We shall protect Veena, Nate, and their child."

Murmurs of agreement flowed through the crowd. Veena and Nate fidgeted at the pronouncement, grasping hands and looking at one another with concern. They had been consumed with shared joy and excitement about their baby and hadn't fully considered the risk they would face from outsiders. Both knew that Abe was right, and each must always be on guard and alert.

"Now," Abe commanded. "We will send out messengers to the rest of the tribe, those on duty here at high camp, those in the forward camp, and those at the naval base. Additionally, if any of you have pregnancy-related knowledge or experience, and I mean real knowledge, please contact Miriam as she will assist Veena and Nate. A strong word of caution: if anyone interferes with or troubles Veena, Nate, or Miriam, there will be immediate consequences. If we consider the interference minor, we will give you just one warning. If we consider the interference to be more than minor, or if we warned you already, we will banish you from the tribe." Abe looked across the people and let that sink in.

"As I said at our opening, we will not address any questions tonight. After we close in prayer, open your heart and soul to God, and pray for wisdom. Listen patiently tomorrow and bring any non-malicious questions to tomorrow night's gathering."

Abe led them in prayer, rejoicing in the miracle of this baby and asking God for wisdom in how to proceed with this blessing. After the prayer, the people were contemplative, and they drifted into the night.

Soon, everyone had left the shelter except for Veena, Nate, Abe, and Miriam. Abe took a seat near Veena and Nate and motioned Miriam to sit near him. Looking briefly at Miriam before he started, Abe gazed contently at Veena and Nate and spoke softly. "Veena and Nate, Miriam and I must discuss something with you before tomorrow evening's gathering. This child is a miracle, yet the pregnancy will also cause considerable turmoil within the camp."

Veena, already suspecting where the conversation was leading, looked down, and her eyes became copiously wet. Nate was puzzled, and he looked from Abe to Miriam and back to Abe. Finally, he asked, "Why will our child cause turmoil within the camp?"

Abe looked at Miriam, and she picked the response. "Nate, think about it for a moment. Of all the couples in the tribe, you and Veena are the first to conceive a child. I can assure you; couples have earnestly sought a pregnancy and have been heartbroken by the lack of conception time and time again."

Veena continued to look down as Nate tried to piece together what Miriam and Abe were suggesting. Finally, with anguish, Nate asked softly, "Are you telling me that Veena is the only woman who can have a child?"

"Well, that is a possibility, but we don't think that is what is happening here. Nate, we suspect you are the only non-sterile man we've encountered since the disease afflicted all of us just a week after The Fires."

Nate's face drained of color, and Veena started to weep openly.

Abe continued, "If that is true, first there will be jealousy and anger that Veena has you and a child, and the other women don't. Then, there will be demands that you father children for them." Abe stopped to let Nate fully understand that prospect.

"Abe...Miriam...there must be a different way," protested Nate.

"When we had access to great medical equipment, there was," replied Miriam. "Now, however, we only have the way that God provided between woman and man."

Nate blushed. "It isn't right; I'm dedicated to Veena. I won't lie with anyone but Veena."

"Nate," Abe said soothingly, "it is a miracle from God. We don't have the answers or understand His plan now, but I don't believe God would have you test, or defile, your marriage. I believe that God is 'Yahweh Yireh,' the One and only God who foresees and provides. Remember the testing of Abraham in Genesis 22, where God told Abraham to sacrifice his only son, Isaac. When Isaac asked his father, 'Where is the lamb for the sacrifice,' Abraham replied, 'God Himself will provide the lamb.' I have faith that God will provide us with a solution, and we need to wait patiently. It will be unexpectedly tough for those who now see God's blessing upon both of you. In the days to come, we will face unforeseen challenges. Regardless, I have faith, and I am asking both of you to pray for a strengthening of your faith, too. Now, go and rest. I have asked Kath and Royce to ensure that you are not disturbed."

CHAPTER 40

There was little sleep that night for anyone in the tribe. Questions, renewed sorrow, and, despite all that, a glimmer of new hope consumed everyone's thoughts. The tribe respected Abe's admonishment not to disturb Veena and Nate; nonetheless, the following morning, the constant stares eventually drove Veena and Nate to isolate themselves at one of the sentry posts. Several women approached Miriam to volunteer to assist. After interviewing the candidates, Miriam found that only two had any experience with pregnancy or birthing. Even so, Miriam noted the women as potential trainees. Auspiciously, Doc Ames had training in women's health issues, including pregnancy. Still, to say that his experience with women's health and childbearing was a bit stale was an understatement.

The meeting that evening started boisterously. Abe and Miriam convinced Veena and Nate to stay away, and they did. They hiked to the safe blind on the trail to Julian, accompanied by Carla and Doc Ames. MaryAn, who usually was always by Carla's side, wanted to attend the meeting, and she sat with Laoni.

Abe finally got the attendees to settle down. After the initial prayer, which helped get the people focused on a constructive gathering, Abe asked Miriam to describe how pregnancy alters a woman's body, psychology, and emotion. Except for the *Des Moines* crew and maybe half-a-dozen others, most of the tribe was under thirty. Hardly anyone in the tribe had experienced or witnessed a pregnancy. Though informative and fascinating, Miriam's tutorial shocked half of the people. Chief Virtolli relayed the information via their encrypted radios to both the forward camp and the *Des Moines*. As he heard the details of childbirth, he occasionally looked squeamish or embarrassed, which was pretty unusual for the Chief.

Then Abe reclaimed the floor. Knowing the main question that was on everybody's mind, for it was undoubtedly on his, Abe preemptively stated, "I'm sure that most of you are wondering the reason that Veena was able to become pregnant when previously no woman has become pregnant for the last twelve years. The truth is, we don't know. Regardless, Miriam, Doc Ames, and I suspect the reason is Nate. Nate was never ill with the disease that swept through the population after The Fires, and, therefore, he might be fertile when all the rest of us men are sterile." Though several suspected it, too, there was a collective gasp in the room.

Abe raised his hands again to restore order. "Again, I want to emphasize that WE DON'T KNOW! We do not have the resources and tests to confirm the conjecture, but implicitly it is the logical conclusion. Even if this is the reason, we, as a people adopted and loved by God, must wait on Him for direction on how we proceed. I believe that God will provide us answers, just as He has blessed us with the miracle after twelve long, arduous, and overwhelmingly perilous years. Remember that and acknowledge that He has always provided in His good time. Now, we are the safest that we have ever been since The Fires. We have a secure camp, a good source of water, plentiful fields and livestock, the most negligible threat from outsiders that we have ever known, and an intimate relationship with God: Father, Son, and Holy Spirit. So, I call on you to persevere, and I believe that God will grace us with knowledge on how to proceed.

"Finally, Miriam and I have discussed our situation with the leadership team. In their new role of caring for their child, Nate, and especially Veena, will not be as available in the leadership and protective duties. Under Veena's supervision, Kath and Caleb will split Veena's defense oversight. Veena has agreed to stop participating in patrols, and we will restrict Nate's defense duties to high camp. It is time to consider an elected administrative leadership. We propose we have a ballot to elect a president in one year. We have asked Royce, with Veena's guidance, to act as administrator until that election.

"Now, please respectfully raise your questions, and we will try to answer as best we can."

There were only a few questions as Abe had preempted the expected, unspoken questions: when the women who desired a child could become impregnated, and what would be the mechanism to achieve that. Abe, Miriam, and the leaders all knew the yearning undercurrent was there, but they had nothing to offer except prayer.

CHAPTER 41

For nearly a week after the announcement of Veena's pregnancy, MaryAn was morose and depressed. Carla suspected the reason for her partner's attitude; even hardened Carla felt a twinge of the empty-womb syndrome. That feeling angered Carla; she didn't desire to have such a response to Veena's pregnancy news. Nevertheless, she was unprepared for MaryAn's request one evening as they lay in their shelter before going to sleep.

MaryAn was oddly reserved that day, and her demeanor already put Carla on edge. In the evening, as they lay there, letting the duties and burdens of the day drift away as they eased toward sleep, MaryAn gently stroked Carla's arm and whispered, "Carla, I want to be a mother."

"Honey, you're talking to the wrong person."

"Carla, please be nice to me. You know I care for you. It isn't easy for me to say."

Carla received MaryAn's words, accepted them, and they warmed her heart. She turned towards MaryAn, brushed back the bangs that hid her eyes, and smiled. "I'm sorry. Go ahead."

After a moment's silence, MaryAn meekly whispered, "Carla, would you ask Nate to father a child for us?"

"What!" shouted Carla, and she sat up in bed.

"Carla, please don't be angry," MaryAn pleaded, tears

forming in her eyes. "I want a child for us. Only Nate can give us a child."

Carla's rage burned. "So, what is it you want? I suppose you want me to move out so Nate the Stud can service you. Then, after the baby is born, I can visit every weekend as the queer auntie." Venom was coating every word.

Tears now streaming down her face, MaryAn sobbed, "Please stop it. I don't want you to leave. I need you, and the baby will need you. Please, Carla, I want us to have a baby."

Carla bit back her bile and tempered her words, which was a considerable strain for her. "But MaryAn, he's a man. I may respect him now, especially after he proved himself during the ambush. I probably regard him as well as I do Old Abe. But he's still a man."

"I know, but what else can we do?" MaryAn sobbed in shaking breaths.

Carla jumped out of bed, dressed quickly, and raced out of their hut as MaryAn started to cry loudly. She fought against her hatred of men, recognizing that there were men such as Abe, Nate, and Vince, who had shown they were not monsters like the Clairens. Fighting her anger, she forced herself to admit that all the men in the Tierran tribe were decent persons. She reluctantly acknowledged that it was easier to fuel the rage than deal with the difference between these men and those in the hideous gangs.

Over and over, she mulled MaryAn's humiliating, yet honest and necessary, request. While she started with agitation, as she sat in the dark under the starlight, shivering a bit as cold air helped drain her bitterness, Carla begrudgingly accepted MaryAn's desire and that Nate was essential to granting that longing. As the first streaks of dawn licked across the dew-wet grasses and warmed Carla's huddled body, she knew she had no recourse. Carla loved

MaryAn too deeply to keep her discouraged and realized that the request was probably exceedingly painful for MaryAn. If she failed to follow through now, Carla ruefully foresaw that she might drive MaryAn away and lose her forever. Then, a surprising insight, a deeply buried yearning for a child, rose within Carla, and she understood MaryAn's desire.

When Veena and Nate left their hut later that morning and arrived at the mess for breakfast, Carla was waiting for them.

CHAPTER 42

YAHWEH YIREH:

GOD FORESEES AND WILL PROVIDE

"**A**be." Veena's voice disturbed the early morning solitude that Abe enjoyed as he read, spending those precious moments in one-on-one communion with God. Abe was always an early riser; he savored the peace and tranquility of the dawn as the sun gently awoke all living things from their appointed slumber and rest. Now, the disturbance Abe had expected all week burst upon his morning, and he sighed, knowing he would have to face the people and be firm. He looked up from his Bible as Veena pushed aside the entry covering and entered his hut without being invited.

"Abe, it's starting already. Carla just asked me to allow Nate to impregnate MaryAn."

Rising from his crude desk, Abe motioned Veena to sit on his cot while pulling the desk chair close. "Did you say that Carla...Carla, of all people, asked you to let Nate know MaryAn?"

"Yes, she was waiting for Nate and me when we left our hut just a little while ago to get breakfast. Abe, I'm so mad and upset. I didn't expect such a request from Carla and MaryAn."

"No, though I expected someone would bring such a

request, I also didn't think that it would come from MaryAn and Carla first. How is Nate handling it?"

"He is unmistakably embarrassed and, oddly, ashamed. I asked him to join the men in the morning sweep outside the camp."

"Understandable," Abe said thoughtfully. "Well, it is not surprising that we would have a disturbance; please consider that and try to calm yourself." Abe looked down but rested his hand on Veena's shoulder, seeking to console her. After more reflection, he continued, "I am just so shocked it is Carla that would first bring the appeal. It appears that Almighty God has shown us mercy in dealing with the issue. I struggled with a foreboding that one of our women would try to seduce Nate."

Veena gasped and started to rise, but Abe tenderly guided her back to a sitting position. Veena looked sharply at Abe and said, "Abe, I don't think Nate would ever be untrue to me."

"I'm sorry, Veena, I did not mean to imply that. I see Nate's strong character, and I believe he will always hold to you, and you only. I am thinking more about how weakness and overwhelming desire for a child would tempt some women to seduce Nate. Although Miriam and I hinted a forewarning to Nate and you, I realize that all recent events are beyond what we could have prepared.

"In Holy Scripture, in the first Chapters of Genesis, it records God saying, 'Let us make mankind in our image, in our likeness.' We, woman and man, are made in the image of God, but we are not God. Our desire to create, including the passion for cocreating children, is part of that image of God. Yet, we are fallen people, forgiven, but less than God. I believe that God will provide a solution that allows us to have more children, but it will be in His time, not ours. That is where the difficulty for us arises. We are not all-seeing, all-understanding, and beyond the scope of time. I'm not sure if any of what I'm telling you is a help or comfort for you. Perhaps I'm just trying to get a better grasp on what we, as a people of God, are facing."

Veena was visibly calmer. She thoughtfully looked at Abe. "It helps a little bit."

"Veena, have you and Nate talked about how childless couples might react?"

Veena glanced nervously at the floor and then around the room. She had difficulty looking directly at Abe while she talked about the subject. Suspecting Abe's question might be related to the desire of other women to mate with Nate, Veena felt a knot in her stomach, and the tightening of her throat choked her words as she replied, "Sort of, it's been a difficult topic for both of us. We were both truly hoping that you and Miriam were wrong and that we wouldn't have to face this dilemma. Neither of us anticipated a situation where Carla and MaryAn would want a child. That request certainly caught us unprepared."

"Yes, as I said, me also," Abe said softly. "In a way I did not foresee, Carla and MaryAn's appeal may help us prevent similar demands within the tribe. Carla and MaryAn are highly respected and seen as members of our close personal circle of friends and confidants. A publicly-delivered caution to them will resonate throughout the tribe."

Veena now stared directly at Abe as he took a breath and continued, "God has provided us with an opportunity to handle the challenge until He graces us with a solution. I need to talk with Miriam. Would you please call for an assembly of the leaders at the mess shelter at noon today? Also, have Kath insist that Carla and MaryAn attend."

Veena nodded and left. Abe prayed for wisdom before he got dressed. Abe knew how Veena treasured Carla and MaryAn's friendship and patrol skills. Abe tried to model a loving servant posture as he interacted with Carla and MaryAn, and he waited on the Holy Spirit in their relationship. Expelling Carla and MaryAn would effectively be their death sentence and would alienate Veena. Such an expulsion could also fracture the tribe. He thought about all of this as he went to find Miriam.

CHAPTER 43

At noon, in front of the Tierran leaders, with Miriam, Veena, and Nate sitting behind him, Abe called Carla and MaryAn forward. "Carla and MaryAn, you have been stalwarts in our people, and you are senior members. Notwithstanding, you have allowed your desire for a child to supplant God's timing and gift, and your request would disgrace Veena and Nate's marriage. You disturb our walk and faith in God by this intrusion, and you have violated my request. Therefore, we caution both of you. If either of you trespasses again, then the consequence shall be banishment from the people. Is that clear?"

Carla and MaryAn nodded.

"I want you to acknowledge that you understand publicly," commanded Abe.

"Yes, I understand," Carla and MaryAn both stated, though sniffling tinged MaryAn's response.

Abe looked at them and then looked across the leaders to ensure that all understood the consequences. Then he softened. "Please take a seat."

After they sat, Abe motioned for Miriam to stand next to him. Addressing all the leaders, he spoke. "Tell our people what happened here and our expectations of behavior. None of us are insensitive to our shared, deep-seated desire for children. We must wait upon Almighty God, the Creator of all things, to reveal His plan and solution to us. Pending His revelations, I have asked Miriam to list those couples who desire a child. We will then prove ourselves faithful as we have invested in acting upon His plan when He divulges it. Is that clear to everyone?"

A chorus of "Amen" answered Abe.

"There is another directive that I ask you, as the leaders, to consider and approve." Abe looked at Miriam before continuing. "When our LORD provides us with wisdom on how to move forward with additional pregnancies, we will need discernment, cooperation, and support to ensure that we are sensitive to the needs of our people and the safety of the camp. When the Holy Spirit moves, and we gain additional pregnancies, we will become extraordinarily wealthy in the eyes of the world. Make no mistake about how Satan will use this gift of God to incite hatred toward us. We must pray for wisdom and courage. Before we do, are there any questions that cannot wait until a later time?"

A woman in her late twenties and recently elected to leadership stepped forward. "Abe, Miriam, you talk with confidence that God will bless us with children. After all that we have been through, my faith is shaky, and I don't want to be crushed by false hope. How are you so sure?"

Abe bowed for a moment before he tenderly spoke. "The Holy Spirit has brought peace and joy to my soul. He has given me confidence that the Father's gift is not just for Veena and Nate alone but is a plentiful blessing to flow across our people. Additionally, I feel assured that God will bless groups outside our people with children, ensuring our children will have future mates. Lastly, I believe that if the Holy Spirit is truly bringing me to such knowledge and assurance, then the Holy Spirit will make it known to more than just me. Is anyone else here acknowledging such a blessing of the Holy Spirit?"

One by one, several of the leaders stood and declared, "I also have sensed this confirmation, assurance, and blessing." With at least ten standing, and after a pause when no one else stood, Miriam turned toward Abe and stated with tears in her eyes. "I, too, have felt the presence and blessing of the Holy Spirit, and my soul sings with joy."

The crowd shouted with glee as wonder embraced them.

Knowing now was the right time to close, Abe raised his hands and prayed, "Almighty God, Holy God, You are the Alpha and Omega, God outside of time, God Eternal, Creator and lover of our souls. LORD, we humbly give You our lives and our plans. Lead us, dear LORD, and protect us from evil. First, we pray for wisdom. We rejoice in the miracle You have graced upon us, and we desire Your wisdom to live according to Your will and plan. Help us to choose wisely, and may our service be pleasing in Your sight. In the blessed name of Your son, Y'shua HaMashiach, we pray. Amen."

All the leaders heartily responded, "Amen."

—⁓—

Stung and unnerved by the reprimand, Carla and MaryAn respected Veena's and Nate's privacy from then on, though MaryAn did approach Miriam early the next day to add her name to the list. For the rest of the people, the public rebuke of Carla and MaryAn was a sufficient deterrent to preclude anyone else from surrendering to the temptation to approach Veena or Nate. Veena and Nate appreciated the consideration of their privacy that the rest of the tribe gave them, though they were acutely aware of how everyone in the area now watched their every move. Having more experience in a leadership role and how closely the tribe looked to her for guidance, Veena adjusted to the scrutiny more easily than Nate. Eventually, Nate was able to take it in stride, too.

CHAPTER 44

One month later, as the Tierrans were still reeling from the news of Veena's pregnancy and the possibility of more pregnancies, hostilities with the Clairens took a very sudden change when their ragtag army advanced toward the high camp. The Clairen mob took the easiest and most direct route and scrambled up the pass at Mount Woodson as they marched east. Caleb Gates, his SEAL team, and other highly trained Tierrans hid in an ambush in the brush on the sides of the pass as the Clairens blundered forward. The Clairen advance was so sloppy and slow that Veena, Nate, Carla, MaryAn, and Laoni could observe it from a concealed position higher on Mount Woodson.

The Clairens, in a disorderly fashion, picked their way up the narrows of the pass. Walking in the middle of the pack, Walter Duncan thought, *if you want anything done right, you have to do it yourself.* Though he had long passed caring about the Tierrans, it was a practical method to coalesce his motley mob. Walter would have preferred to stay at their encampment rather than lead these fools against the disciplined Tierrans. However, Belligerent Bob had replaced Loudmouth Larry as an agitator against Walter's leadership, and he spoke loudly to the multitude.

"Dunkin' Donuts isn't a leader; he's a tool," Bob would tell anyone who got within ear-range of his booming mouth.

It's bad enough that I have to tolerate Belligerent Bob and be wary of what he tattles back to Rex, thought Walter, *but the fool also thinks he has authority from Rex by proxy. Well, I'll lead the attack and make sure that Belligerent Bob isn't around anymore to call me Dunkin' Donuts.* So, here they were, three days later, weak from hunger and thirst and huffing and puffing up the broken road.

Walter was near the front of the pack, and just as he wondered, *where is that idiot Bob, anyway?* he felt a sharp pain as a *thunk* shook his body. He looked down at his chest and saw that an arrow had pierced his right chest. As he collapsed to the ground, he recognized the missile had Bob's distinctive marking on it and that the arrowhead protruded out the front of his chest. *Bob shot me in the back.* Just before his sight went gray and his eyes glazed over, he saw Bob's face inches from his own as Bob hissed, "I'm the top dog now. Speaking of dogs, I'm going to have yours as appetizers tonight."

Bob's claim was premature. After Walter dropped, the Clairens thought they were under attack and let their arrows fly haphazardly. The Tierrans, rising from their concealed positions, fired back with deadly accuracy. Bob dropped, clutching at one of the three bolts that penetrated his body.

When the Clairens realized they were under fire, they broke formation and ran back down the road. Per Kath's standing order, the Tierrans allowed those fleeing to leave unhindered. The Clairens were never a threat again, and word of the overwhelming defense had the effect of inhibiting any other outsiders from an assault. Since that battle, the only nuisances were meddlesome traders who used any excuse to visit the camp. Those annoyances were easy to handle.

CHAPTER 45

Less than two weeks after the Clairen assault, Abe's hope that the reprimand of Carla and MaryAn would be sufficient for the whole tribe proved to be fleeting. Jody Higgins, who had earlier sought to win Nate's attention, was now partnered with one of the single crewmen of the *Des Moines*, Johnny Gerkin. Jody had previously grumbled about the leadership of Abe and, particularly, Veena. Ever since Veena had won Nate and become pregnant, those developments inflamed Jody's jealousy and ambition.

Her earlier rants about the Tierran leadership fell overwhelmingly on deaf ears. Despite that, using the shared envy of Veena's pregnancy as an underpinning, Jody would murmur discontent to anyone who would listen, but always away from the main body of the camp and those tribal members who trusted Abe and Veena.

"Why should the privileged leadership be able to tell us who can be impregnated by Nate? Is it right that Veena gets to have a child while we are denied? It should be a gift to all of us, and we demand immediate access to Nate. It is our right, and it's time for a change in leadership. We've defeated the Clairens and listened to God. We don't need Abe or Veena to guide us."

Jody easily swayed Johnny, and soon he was just as indignant and driven as she. Jody would ply Johnny with dreams of camp command but intentionally led him with counterfeit suggestions as the authority dreams were for her alone. She just needed Johnny as a male figurehead and an agent to bring more brawn into their ranks.

CHAPTER 46

Abe, Veena, and the rest of the Tierran leadership knew of Jody's previous history and ambitions to sow discontent. So they were saddened but not surprised when Hasan Malik approached their table with unpleasant news one evening.

Hasan was one of the senior members of the people in the Tierran tribe who were not Christians. Though the group was a minority portion of the tribe, they lived and contributed fully with the rest and accepted Abe and Veena's leadership. The believers and non-believers had coexisted in harmony for years, mutually supporting the defense and enrichment of the tribe. Hasan, and the people he represented, were always welcomed at the leadership meetings. Jody and Johnny, seditiously, had sought to build support for their schemes in these people, saying, "You are disenfranchised people, and you deserve a leader who understands and appreciates your needs and contributions."

As supper was finishing, Hasan approached the supper table occupied by Abe, Miriam, Veena, Nate, Kath, and Roy and said softly, "May I join you for a moment?"

Abe smiled and said, "Please, Hasan, sit with us. We have already eaten. We will wait if you want to get something to eat."

"No, I have also already eaten. I would like to offer you counsel."

Abe recognized the seriousness of Hasan's tone and

exchanged looks with Veena. "Perhaps we should take an evening stroll."

"That would be wise. You all should hear it."

After they were out of earshot from the dining area, Hasan spoke. "Let's continue walking to make the conversation less obvious. Jody Higgins and Johnny Gerkin are gathering people later tonight near the northern outpost. They've asked people to gather in the upper field when the moon rises. Perhaps you should be there."

Though Abe already had a suspicion of Jody's intent, he asked, "What is the purpose?"

"Jody is trying to collect support for a change in leadership, using the guise of demanding Nate's seed as a widespread motivation."

Nate's face went pale, and Veena nearly shouted "What!" before Abe could guide the group along and calm the emotions.

"Thank you, Hasan. Your integrity and foresight are appreciated. We shall pray on how to receive this unfortunate news. May God bless you and all those you hold dear."

As Hasan walked away, Abe could see the rage building in both Veena and Nate. He led the remaining five in prayer, requesting wisdom, clarity, and peace. That brought down the emotions in the group. Then he looked at their faces as he said, "Veena and Nate, please stay in the high blind until we come to get you. Kath and Roy, please assign guards for Veena and Nate, and return to me with trusted sisters and brothers in faith. We should present ourselves at the meeting and see if we can defuse the dissent and restore harmony."

As Veena and Nate left, Abe was saddened to acknowledge that the unity the tribe had enjoyed might be beginning to fray.

CHAPTER 47

The high blind overlooked the road to Julian that rose eastward from Ramona and was staffed continuously by sentries. The sentries moved out of the blind when Veena, Nate, and their escorts of MaryAn, Laoni, and a couple of the SEALs appeared just after sunset. The SEALs also disappeared into the night before the moon rose, but just far enough away to not be obvious. Though the upper field near the north outpost wasn't visible from their location, Veena and Nate sat quietly, looking in that direction and listening.

Soon after the moon rose over the eastern ridge, they could hear a commotion coming from that direction. It lasted only about a minute before the silence returned. Nate could see Veena straining forward, and he knew that she was agitated that she wasn't there with Abe, Kath, Roy, and Carla. Nate also wanted to meet the challenge directly, but he knew that Abe was right and that they should stay away. Not only would they both be vulnerable at that gathering, but their presence might additionally provoke simmering tensions. Suppressing a sigh, Nate massaged Veena's head to help them both cope with the stress.

—⁓—

About an hour later, the SEALs escorted Abe and Miriam into the high blind.

Veena immediately stood, and Nate followed.

"Well?"

"The crisis has passed, for now. Let's all sit and let me catch my breath; then, I'll tell you how it resolved." The SEALs went out of the blind as Abe and Miriam sat, and Veena and Nate quickly gathered near them.

"We stayed in the shadows to observe at first. There were about thirty people there, though I suppose most of them had come just for entertainment. As the moon rose, Jody started into a rant, claiming injustice and the need for new leadership, which meant her. Johnny was next to her and would sporadically shout, 'Yeah!' Despite that, no one joined in their message.

"I stepped in from the outer edge of the crowd, and Jody became incensed that I was there. Johnny came running to face me, though I don't think he had any idea how he had placed himself in danger. Before I could say a word, Carla, Chief Virtolli, and Vince came out of the crowd and stood shoulder-to-shoulder with me. Johnny backed up so fast that he crossed his feet and fell on his backside. Jody accused me of shoving Johnny, but it was clear that no one was buying that.

"I tried reasoning with both of them, but Jody had worked herself into such a frenzy that she wasn't listening. Finally, I had to tell them that they either live with the current leadership or leave the tribe. I told them that if they came to us directly, we would listen and consider their proposals. I also told them they had no right to make any demands upon Nate."

Abe paused for a moment, and it was evident a sadness was upon him.

"Jody looked around and saw that nearly all of the crowd had drifted away. It was clear she couldn't let go of her pride, so she announced she was leaving instead. Though it appeared that Johnny didn't want to go, he followed Jody's lead. Their departure was not how I wanted to resolve the crisis, and I hoped they'd reconsider if they spent the night thinking about it. Therefore, I tried to get them to wait until dawn, but Jody left in a huff, and Johnny followed her.

"We followed them at a distance and watched as they gathered provisions, clothing, and weapons from their shelter. Chief Virtolli tried again to get them to think overnight about their decision, but Jody just stomped off with Johnny trailing her. The whole situation saddens my heart."

"Abe, we always knew that Jody was ambitious. I don't think any of us expected these events. Do you think we are safe?"

"We are safe. Chief Virtolli and Vince followed them discreetly and will make sure that, if they return, they do so peacefully. Sadly, I don't think Jody and Johnny will be safe, not outside the tribe on their own. Their departure is harder to accept than those we previously experienced."

"Well, Jody did serve well and was a valued member of our tribe. She has been with us for the past eleven years, and she is part of our family. As for Johnny, I wonder if Chief Virtolli and Vince are surprised. The crew of the *Des Moines* went through a lot together. Do you think I should try to reason with them?"

Abe looked at Veena, taking joy in her compassionate heart. "No. Certainly not tonight. Perhaps if they cool off and return, we could talk with them. Now, let's get you and Nate back to the safety of your shelter and secure the camp."

As they left the high blind, Kath and Roy were waiting and joined them on the trail back to camp. That night was the last that anyone ever saw Jody and Johnny.

CHAPTER 48

When Veena's pregnancy was six and a half months, Caleb Gates brought news of a well-organized caravan of about forty people headed toward the high camp from the north. One of Caleb's roving patrols observed the procession as they traveled at night along the San Gabriel Mountains' southern slopes, north of the Los Angeles basin. Caleb reported that the expedition continued along the base of the south slopes of the San Bernardino Mountains before turning south and moving along the foothills at the San Jacinto Mountains' western slopes.

"They are now crossing along the north slopes of Palomar Mountain, and they should reach Lake Henshaw in about a week."

"Do they look like a military troop?" asked Veena.

"Not really," replied Caleb. "They are moving with a defensive posture and taking care not to draw attention to themselves. They have discipline and have avoided both the K and the Riverside Raiders. Only the outer circle is armed with more than defensive weapons. If I had to guess, they are coming here as representatives of a larger group."

"That's quite a stretch, Caleb," remarked Veena. Then, looking at Kath, Veena inquired, "What do you think?"

After a moment's reflection, Kath stated, "We should meet them on the harvested fields east of Lake Henshaw. We can observe them from the nearby hills and mountain slopes with hidden squads in case they aren't friendly."

Veena now looked to Abe. "Your thoughts?"

"I agree with Kath, and I should go along. You and Nate, however, should observe from the southern hills."

Veena wasn't pleased with that suggestion, but now advanced in her pregnancy, she knew she would be a greater liability than an asset. So she just nodded and said to both Caleb and Kath, "Make it so."

CHAPTER 49

Caleb kept the leaders apprised of the progress of the caravan. Five days later, the team assigned to make the first contact left to position themselves on the southern hills overlooking Lake Henshaw. Caleb and his SEAL teams were already in place to secure the site and observe the outsiders' movements. Kath and her squad assembled a tent awning near the southern hills in the pasture and placed a pole with a small, white flag. Then, she joined Roy, Abe, and Miriam in the shade to wait for the new arrivals while her squad sat behind them and out of sight when viewed from the north. Veena, Nate, Carla, MaryAn, and Laoni observed these preparations from their camouflaged shelter on the hillside.

By mid-afternoon, the outsiders had reached the top of the climb, traveling on the remains of Highway 79. They paused there and looked over the harvested fields and pastures east of Lake Henshaw, where the tent shelter and flag stood out like a facial mole with an errant white hair. When all of their group reached the summit, they formed into a defensive posture. Veena felt a tremor of concern wash over her until she saw three persons separate from the group and proceed, also bearing a white flag, down the gentle slope toward the awning. Caleb and two of his SEALs seemingly appeared out of nowhere when the three outsiders were halfway to the shaded canopy.

"Please, we come peacefully, and we are not armed. We

would like to talk with the leaders of your group," said a middle-aged Asian man from the newcomers' assembly.

Caleb looked over the three: the speaker, a middle-aged Asian woman, and a younger Caucasian man, probably a teenager. Not seeing any weapons, Caleb nodded. "Follow me, please."

Kath, Roy, Miriam, and Abe rose and stepped forward to greet them as they approached the tent. Caleb signaled the newcomers to halt when the two groups were about twenty feet apart. The Asian man raised both hands and spoke.

"Grace and peace to you from God our Father, and the LORD Jesus Christ."

The tension level dropped immediately as smiles spread across all the faces. Abe stepped up to the Asian man and said, "I greet you with a holy kiss." Then Abe hugged the man and put a light kiss on his cheek. He released the man and smiled broadly at all three emissaries.

The Asian woman whispered to the Asian man, "These are part of the Body, and they are the people we seek."

The Asian man rejoiced and said, "Hallelujah! Let me introduce ourselves. I am Eric Zhang, my wife, Hope, and our adopted son, Thomas McCoy."

"Welcome, dear sister and brothers in Christ Jesus," said Abe warmly. Then, turning so he could introduce the leaders, he said, "Kath Haines, her husband Roy Haines, and Miriam Cohen, all part of our leadership team. You have already met Caleb Gates and two of his SEALs. I am Abraham Jones. Where are you traveling?"

"We have heard stories that there are people who have a pregnancy in their group. We have heard that they are Christian sisters and brothers. Hope and several members of our group confirmed the news by the Holy Spirit, and, just now, Hope has determined that you are among the people we seek. Is that so?"

"Yes," said Abe. "Though not all our people are believers, we are the recipients of that blessing."

Just then, Kath spoke, "What is your intention?"

Hope looked afresh at Kath. "We humbly seek to join our people with your people, and we, submissively, appeal to share in that blessing."

Kath was not quite prepared for that response. After a moment, she said, "Is that group all of your people?"

"No," Eric said. "We are just the envoys and our traveling defensive troop. We could not bring all of our people as we needed to care for and protect our crops. There are about one hundred sixty people at our home near Camarillo. We beseech you to let us share the blessing. As a token of our good and sincere intentions, we have brought gifts, including a pediatrician doctor."

Kath looked at Roy, Abe, and Miriam. Finally, Abe said, "I believe you are sincere. I also believe that we need to pray and seek guidance from our LORD. We will withdraw to do just that. You may stay in the shade of our awning until we return."

"Peace and blessings be upon you," said Eric. "If you'll permit us, we would like to return to our companions and also join in prayer."

"Go, and may Almighty God grant us all wisdom. Caleb, would you go with them so we can call you back when we have God's direction?"

As Caleb escorted Eric, Hope, and Thomas back to their group, Kath, Roy, Abe, Miriam, and their guards withdrew to a Live Oak tree behind the southern hills. Veena, Nate, Carla, MaryAn, and Laoni joined them there.

"Did you hear all that?" asked Kath as Veena and Nate approached.

"Yes, the radios carried the conversation clearly," said Veena. "Abe, shall we pray?"

They gathered together under the shade of the tree and joined in prayer. After praying for about fifteen minutes, they sat in silence for another fifteen minutes until Veena said, "I have a peace that I had not expected. What guidance have the rest of you received?"

"I also feel serene with the prospect of this group joining," said Nate. "I may be the newest member, but I acknowledge that much is now expected of me, and that has disturbed my rest. I'm excited that there is a pediatrician in their group; it is a great blessing for our child. Perhaps there is also an answer to our prayers for a means of more pregnancies."

Nods of assent and amens came from the leaders. Abe looked at his friends, his charges, and his people. "I am led to receive these sisters and brothers in Y'shua. Nevertheless, our current camp is already insufficient, and especially for so large a group. We need better water sources, more farmland, and defensible space. I know that what I'm saying seems off-topic; even so, I feel God is calling us to relocate. The local area has been our home for over twelve years, but I sense God is calling us to a new land. Furthermore, a vision keeps coming to me of a new home near the mountain slopes of the eastern Sierra, near a small community called Bridgeport. Will anyone else confirm that?"

Miriam spoke first, "Yes," and Veena, Nate, Roy, and Laoni soon echoed Miriam's confirmation. Abe looked at each of their faces; even Carla nodded. Abe felt a wonderful glow in recognizing that God had provided a miracle with a shared vision.

Veena spoke. "We should get an agreement with all of the leaders. I don't think I could travel that far before our baby is born."

Miriam quickly agreed, and then Abe said, "Yes, it will probably be about five hundred miles of travel, and there are several passes we'll need to negotiate. We'll have to wait until late April to give us the best travel weather."

"Veena, you and I should contact the leaders," said Kath.

Just then, Laoni spoke up. "We should first verify that they have a doctor."

Everyone looked at Laoni. Abe chuckled and said, "Don't take it wrong, Laoni, but 'out of the mouth of babes.' That is an extraordinarily wise insight. Yes, we must do that."

Since Kath had previously decided to keep the radio channel active during all the discussions, including the prayer time, all leaders quickly gave unanimous approval of the plan. Kath called Caleb and told him that they wanted to interview the doctor and meet Eric, Hope, their doctor, and whomever else they needed to bring back to the canopy in half an hour.

CHAPTER 50

Caleb and his two SEALs returned with Eric, Hope, Thomas, and another Asian woman, pretty and young, probably in her mid-thirties. Thomas pulled a garden wagon, on large wheels, that carried medical supplies. When they got near the tent, Eric said, "We have prayed, and a strong movement of the Spirit met our prayers, and our confidence is high. May I introduce Dr. Joy Shimizu, our pediatrician."

"Welcome," said Kath. "We were also blessed with a clear leading of the Spirit. It is our duty, additionally, to interview your doctor. Dr. Shimizu, would you like to sit here?"

"No, I would prefer to stand. It's been my experience that I think better when I'm standing. May I ask, where are the pregnant women? I could examine them if you will let me."

Miriam spoke first. "You seem rather young to be a pediatrician."

"I am thirty-eight. I had just finished my residency when The Fires started. I have experience with the children who survived The Fires, such as Thomas here." Thomas blushed. "That said, my medical experience has been primarily with adults. My last interactions with pregnancies were during my residency."

"I understand," said Miriam. "I don't know why I would have expected anything else. My apologies. I did not mean to offend."

"No offense is taken. Who could have predicted the

calamities of the last twelve years? I have brought with us a portion of our medical supplies, which Thomas has in the wagon. Now, again, may I examine the pregnant women?"

Miriam looked at Abe and Kath before she said, "We have only one pregnancy. Regarding how we received the blessing, we suspect that a newcomer to our people, a man who missed The Fires and disease and is the child's father, is also the only fertile man. We have waited for the LORD's guidance on how to proceed."

Dr. Shimizu thought about Miriam's disclosure, and she began to understand. Finally, she said, "That is a sound decision. I have equipment that will help us ascertain if, indeed, the man is virile. I can tell you that I surmise he is because all the men I've examined before are sterile, and they were all afflicted by the mumps-like disease. I'm curious; you said he missed The Fires and disease. What do you mean?"

Abe joined in the discussion then. "It's a long and fascinating tale and one we shall share in conversations after dinner. The short version is that he was in suspended animation for eleven years."

Dr. Shimizu's eyes widened fully. "Wow. I don't even know how to respond to that."

Abe smiled. "We had a similar reaction, and we can only acknowledge that it is by God's grace and mercy."

"Amen," said Dr. Shimizu. "If it is acceptable, I would like to examine both the mother and the father."

Abe looked at everyone assembled there and got nods of confirmation from the leaders. He pulled up his radio. "Veena, Nate, are you agreeable?"

The radio crackled with the sound of Veena and Nate answering in unison, "Yes."

Abe turned to Eric, Hope, Thomas, and Dr. Shimizu. "We do feel led by the Spirit to join our peoples. However, our current camp does not have adequate water or farmable land to support all of us. I feel sure that God will bless us with additional children. Furthermore, the Spirit is guiding us to relocate to a more secure site. If you agree, we suggest that your group's representative stay with us while the rest return to your camp with a squad of our SEALs. Then, in late April, both groups will leave our current camps to meet in the high desert, between Lancaster and Victorville, to travel as one people to a better site in the eastern Sierra near Bridgeport. Do you want to ask your group?"

Eric smiled and opened his arms. "Praise God. Dozens of our people have had a similar vision. In answer to you, my group empowers me to say, 'Where you go, I will go, and where you stay, I will stay. Your people will be my people, and your God my God.'"

Abe's heart leaped with exhilaration. "'Where you die, I will die, and there I will be buried. May the LORD deal with me, be it ever so severely, if even death separates you and me.' I do so cherish that statement of love, loyalty, faith, and service in the book of Ruth. Please tell your group to follow us to our camp. Caleb, would your men guide them, please?"

The two people were now one, and they hugged members of this new family as if they were greeting long-lost relatives. Seeing the agreement from their hillside vantage point, Veena, Nate, Carla, MaryAn, and Laoni started back to the camp.

CHAPTER 51

In the afternoon, Dr. Shimizu examined Veena and Nate. She pronounced that Veena and the baby were in great shape and did not foresee any pregnancy complications.

Abe assembled the leaders and asked for Dr. Shimizu's assessment. After she confirmed the great news of the pregnancy, she spoke, "If you are willing to consider artificial insemination, I believe we have the necessary equipment and washing chemicals back home in storage. In the early days after The Fires, we tried to collect as much medical equipment and supplies as possible. I would like our team to collect those instruments and supplies so we can explore if such a procedure is an option."

Veena and Nate looked at each other, and both nodded.

Abe considered the plan and said, "May I suggest your team go with Caleb and his SEALs. They have boats that depart from San Diego and arrive in Ventura, bypassing L.A. It should also reduce the transit time to less than a week."

Everyone agreed, and Caleb left to make the preparations for the journey.

Looking at Miriam and Doc Ames, Dr. Shimizu said, "You have told me about your plan to wait until a successful birth, and I agree. I have every confidence that the baby will be healthy and robust. I would appreciate your support in all that we will be facing. If God continues to bless us, we will all be wonderfully busy."

"Of course, Dr. Shimizu," said both Miriam and Doc Ames.

"Please, call me Joy. We will be working closely together, and I will depend upon each of you, too."

Miriam and Doc Ames smiled at the warm invitation. Nonetheless, despite her protestations, from that time on, Dr. Shimizu was called Doctor Joy.

Later, after the evening meal, and as everyone gathered in the assembly shelter, Abe told them about Nate's arrival. "Amen!" and "Hallelujah!" were shouted numerous times during the narration, both from the emissary team and from the fellow Tierrans who had heard the saga countless times before.

CHAPTER 52

Discussions and plans for the future merging of the groups filled the following day. Every time Veena and Nate passed within sight, people from both groups would strain their necks to get a better view of the pair. Veena and Nate joined Eric, Hope, Kath, Roy, Doctor Joy, Doc Ames, Miriam, and Abe, who had gathered in the common room for a meeting.

"I feel like I'm on display," lamented Veena, gently massaging her bulging midsection.

"Yes, I completely understand that, too," griped Nate, and a mild chuckle flowed around the group.

"Eric, how did your people come together?" asked Abe.

Eric looked around at those gathered. "I believe you'll understand and be empathetic," he said, "that we came together because the majority of us share an Asian heritage. Even though almost all of us are at least third-or-fourth-generation Americans and Christians, it seems that the overwhelming majority of non-Asians only see us as Asians. So, we gathered for our mutual protection. We have descendants of Chinese, Japanese, Koreans, Filipinos, Vietnamese, and other Southeast Asians in our group. Also, in our assembly are non-Asians who don't hold a bias but share our love of Jesus. Even among ourselves, previous cultural norms where one group wouldn't typically associate with another—Chinese and Japanese, for example—were put aside by our need for protection as well as our united belief.

Several in our group were originally at Point Mugu Naval Air Station and joined us after The Fires and disease collapsed society."

"That makes sense," said Abe. "Veena and I originally gathered young women and girls together to form a protective unit for survival. Decent men have joined us, and together we've fought off attacks from gangs. We became known as Tierrans because of the region we occupied. I've always hated that nickname. Is there a name for your group?"

"Well, as you can imagine, we've been called pretty awful names," said Eric. "We, humbly, call ourselves The Redeemed."

"The Redeemed," said Abe. "I truly like that; we should keep that name."

With smiles and nods all around, the people unanimously adopted the designation.

The following morning, nearly all of the emissary group, Caleb Gates and three SEAL team members, resupplied and started the journey to the San Diego base. From there, they would cross the ocean to The Redeemed camp north of Camarillo.

THE REDEEMED

THE JOURNEY TO RESTORE CIVILIZATION

CHAPTER 53

Soon after Caleb arrived at the Camarillo camp, he and his fellow SEALs offered advanced military training sessions for anyone who desired it. The response was overwhelmingly positive, and they had to offer multiple sessions to limit how many attended and still ensure the camp's responsibilities received attention. Four weeks later, Caleb and one of his SEALs led the six best trainees to scout out the route to Bridgeport as well as the suitability of the Bridgeport area itself. They took two diesel vehicles and traveled at speeds no more than thirty miles per hour to safely navigate the roads while keeping as quiet as possible.

They had barely completed the survey when the first snows of winter started falling heavily around Bridgeport. Unexpectedly, the scouting patrol got winter survival skill training as they navigated across the passes and headed south down the Owens Valley to return to the Camarillo camp. Caleb was exceptionally pleased with how the squad performed, and, more importantly, the Bridgeport site was a perfect candidate for their future relocation.

Over the next two and a half months at the high camp, Veena grew increasingly uncomfortable while her ability to contribute to the camp defense dropped to nil. She became restless, grumpy, and frustrated. Doctor Joy periodically examined her, using those checkups to train Doc Ames, Miriam Cohen, Laoni, and a half dozen additional women in the camp to compassionately and thoroughly monitor and provide care during pregnancy. Veena felt like a lab rat, but she begrudgingly acknowledged the necessity of the training. Nate was sympathetic, and every night he listened attentively. Previously, he had made the mistake of giving unsolicited guidance to Veena, which resulted in a quarrel. Only after Doctor Joy set him straight regarding listening and offering a sincere apology without any advice was Nate able to soothe the tension.

Nate was also subject to examinations, and he soon found out that Veena was not sympathetic to his misery. He eventually learned to accept her attitude with grace and silence.

Thrown together by the necessity of the intensive training for the upcoming birth, romance began to blossom between Doctor Joy and Doc Ames. Soon, they spent their evenings together and planned a wedding.

Every evening, Kath, Roy, Abe, Veena, Nate, Miriam, Eric, and Hope would hold a session to plan the Camarillo assembly's merging with the Tierrans and their journey to Bridgeport. Frequently, Abe managed to sit near Miriam, which Miriam encouraged. The addition of Eric and Hope was a special blessing to Abe as they assisted with the daily Bible study. Their insights on the joining of their two groups also greatly enhanced the planning.

Thomas McCoy requested combat training from Carla. Seeing the wisdom in having more skilled warriors—even male ones—Carla assigned Laoni to train Thomas personally. Laoni complained about the additional responsibility. "Why do I have to do it? I'd rather be on patrol."

"Because, when you have to teach someone," said Carla, "you have to know it better than you do now, and you'll find this task will make you improve your skill and discipline. Besides, it is time you took on more responsibility."

CHAPTER 54

In late January, the Tierran leaders conferred via radio with Caleb and the Camarillo band leaders regarding the migration to the Bridgeport site, with a target start date of late April or early May. At the first planning meeting, the leaders decided to rendezvous the two groups in a shallow valley along the old United States Route 395, on the south face of the hills that overlook Kramer Junction from the south. That location was remote, and the nearby ridges would hide the encampment from anyone at ground level looking that way. The meeting place was not on the shortest route for the Camarillo group. Nevertheless, the merging had the advantage of added protection and mutual assistance as they traveled northward to Bridgeport, which outweighed the inconvenience.

"How will we get there?" asked Veena.

Roy said, "Chief Virtolli, what has your reconnaissance determined?"

"Sir, Caleb Gates and I have planned routes that circumvent the Los Angeles basin. We each have identified several diesel vehicles, primarily from the Point Loma and Point Mugu bases. We'll start moving those at night to our staging areas. We will travel slowly to keep the noise to a minimum, and we're hoping for a late winter storm in the next two weeks to help cover the sound. We've identified the routes to staging areas and have cleared any obstacles from the bases to those locations.

"That's the easy part. Each of us has a treacherous mountain road on the route away from our current encampments. We've picked these routes to make it much more difficult for any hostiles to view our movements. I know that Caleb has gotten teams to clear the mountain roads north of the Camarillo camp, which has had rock falls and flash-flood damage over the past twelve-plus years, and we have also started doing the same for the roadways selected for our passage. Fortunately, in prodigious favor to both of our groups, the pavement remains intact and only needs clearing.

"The paths we have planned are similar in distance, and we'll need to start moving the large livestock—the cattle and horses—in about two months, early April at the latest. The diesel trucks will move the equipment, facilities, food, water, and small livestock. Everyone else will have to travel on foot or by horseback. We really can't move faster than we can drive the cattle anyway, so we're hoping to achieve an average of about sixteen klicks, which is about ten miles a day.

"For us at the high camp, the first part of our route will be eastward with an ascent to Julian and then a descent on the CA-78 highway to the Salton Sea."

Interjecting, Veena said, "What about the Montezuma Valley Road that is near Lake Henshaw?"

"That pavement suffered severe flash-flood damage and is now impassable," said Chief Virtolli. "The 78 is our best option to get to the Anza-Borrego Desert and avoid the L.A. basin. We plan to stay on the roads. As I said, they are mostly intact, which should improve our progress, with less risk of injury to our livestock and ourselves. From the Salton Sea, we journey north until we reach Interstate 10. We're more exposed here, but we should move faster on the concrete highway. Even if

L.A. gang lookouts spot us, we'll be far enough beyond the L.A. basin, particularly the region controlled by the K, that it will require any attackers several days to approach us. Therefore, we should be able to move north at North Palm Springs and intercept the road to Twenty-nine Palms before any aggressors could reach us. Once we are past the mouth of the canyons ascending to Morongo Valley, we'll have natural protection from any L.A.-based gangs. We'll be able to build defensible blinds by taking the high positions along the canyon walls. That geography will funnel any pursuing bands into a kill zone. If they get that far and attempt to follow us, we're confident the losses they'll suffer will cause them to turn back.

"From that point, we'll have the natural barrier of the San Bernardino Mountains. Any bands that want to attack us will have to continue a suicidal pursuit after us or double back and climb the Cajon Pass. If they choose the latter, they'll lose days as they have to travel around.

"As for the rest of our route, we'll continue until we reach Yucca Valley, and then we'll head toward Victorville. At Victorville, we'll intercept US-395 and head north to our rendezvous point in the hills just south of Kramer Junction. The total distance from Julian to the rendezvous point is about two hundred and forty-five miles. We expect this part of the journey should take us about a month."

"Other than the gangs, what's our biggest challenge?" asked Veena.

Roy answered. "We're getting too close to the summer months, and almost all of the route is in the desert. In the first phase of our journey, we'll need to travel at night, not only for stealth but also to avoid the heat. We'll need to preposition water and food as there isn't any way to carry everything we need. If the plan is approved, we need to start that provisioning at strategic points immediately. Finally, the trek will also be strenuous as a result of all the elevation changes. For example, here at the high camp, we'll ascend to Julian and then descend to sea level as we approach Indio.

"At Indio is where it starts to get challenging. There, we'll begin a gradual rise to North Palm Springs, which we're hoping we can do in three nights. From North Palm Springs, the road into Yucca Valley will be an arduous climb. This section will be the most severe part of our journey's southern portion and where we'll be dangerously vulnerable to the L.A. gangs. Additionally, we should transition to starting travel just before dawn as we'll need the light to move along the mountain roads safely. We'll want to break around noon to avoid the hottest parts of the day, but we should be able to get at least a couple of hours of travel in the early evening.

"The good news is that once we reach Yucca Valley, the remaining route is relatively minor ups and downs until we reach the rendezvous point, which is an elevation of nearly three thousand feet. We know from our earlier reconnaissance that there isn't any gang activity in the high desert area. I suspect that is a result of too few resources to plunder. Finally, we are damn lucky that we have a few diesel trucks. I have a new appreciation for the early settlers who crossed the land with horses, cattle, and wagons."

No one spoke until the voice of Caleb crackled over the radio. "High camp, are you receiving?"

"Yes, sorry, it is a lot to take in," said Veena. "Wow, now I wish we didn't have to make the journey."

"But we do," said Abe softly, and every leader nodded.

Veena drew a deep breath. "OK, what's next?"

Roy picked up the radio. "Caleb, please tell everyone about the route from Camarillo."

A chuckle came over the radio. "Well, sir, we couldn't let the high camp have all the fun. As we are already always watched by the K and other gangs, we'll first move north to Santa Paula and burn the fields behind us to cover our movements. Then we'll start our northbound ascent to Ojai. We'll have a couple of small passes to cross, but nothing too severe. We're hoping that when we arrive at Ojai, the distance required to reach us will discourage any pursuing bands. Then, we continue on a laborious route north, ascending winding mountain roads until we enter Maricopa. It will be slow and difficult, as we must cross a high pass to get to Maricopa. There are lane blockages, mainly from landslides, along the way, and nearly half of the barriers are barely wide enough for the trucks to pass. There are also a lot of switchbacks, and we'll be exposed. Because of the road conditions, we will travel from Ojai during the daylight hours.

"The good news is that there are three tunnels, and all of them are intact and usable and not too far from Ojai. The tunnels are short and cut through solid rock ridges with steep slopes that drop to the road. We had to clear several minor rock falls. Once we get through these tunnels, we'll use explosives to create new rockfalls and block the ends. That should secure our rear from any pursuers. Then, it is just a slog up to the pass."

With road atlases they had found years ago, the high camp leaders followed Caleb's narration.

"That is an extraordinarily long route," said Veena. "What are your concerns about a more direct route?"

"The same concerns that Chief Virtolli and his scouts faced," replied Caleb. "We want to hide our movements and minimize our vulnerability to the gangs in the L.A. basin. If we head directly east to the Antelope Valley freeway, we would be marching directly into the teeth of those bands, and probably the K. If we can confuse them instead, we should be able to avoid any direct conflict. Just as your convoy will probably be relatively safe once you reach the Yucca Valley, previous observations of gang pursuits show they break off the chase once they have to start ascending into the mountains. Due to the narrow, winding road through the mountains above Ojai, we'll have to leave nearly all of our livestock in the valley. Otherwise, our progress will be too slow, and we'll be vulnerable to pursuers. Questions?"

There were none. Roy spoke to Caleb. "Continue."

The radio crackled again. "After the pass, we descend, overall, to Maricopa, and our progress should be much better. At Maricopa, we'll be in the south end of the central valley, and we'll transition to night travel as we head east, descending to Meridian.

"At Meridian, we'll work our way northeast to Arvin and then start ascending the Tehachapi Pass. Finally, from the Tehachapi Pass, we'll descend into the Mojave Desert. At that point, we'll also need to prepare hidden stores of water and supplies as we journey the final stretch to Kramer Junction. Our route's total distance is about two hundred and twenty-two miles, about twenty-three miles shorter than the high camp route. Nevertheless, the expected slowness of the ascent from Santa Paula to the pass near Pine Mountain will stretch out the entire journey to about a month."

All the leaders were quiet as they contemplated the rigors of the journey. The travel to the rendezvous point would comprise only the southern third of the trip to Bridgeport.

Finally, Roy spoke up. "It is exhausting just to consider the travel to our rendezvous point. Our routes are convoluted to add safety to our convoys. Once we join near Kramer Junction, our journey to Bridgeport will be overwhelmingly north and through areas free of gangs. We may not encounter people at all as our group's size will probably deter most, and the distance from L.A. will be an obstacle to any pursuers.

"The remaining distance to Bridgeport is about two hundred and seventy-five miles; a span longer than either of the groups traveled for the first leg of our journeys. Grievously, the first eighty miles will be across the high desert, with little vegetation for our livestock, and no water, until we reach Little Lake in the Owens Valley. Therefore, we'll also need to preposition provisions along that route. The good news is that the passage is composed of primarily small elevation changes, except for a valley south of Ridgecrest. If we average sixteen miles a day, we should get to Little Lake in five days, God willing. That's a rapid pace but will minimize our time in the desert.

"At Little Lake, we continue northward to Bishop through the Owens Valley and with the benefit of the Owens River for freshwater. We'll also have decent grazing areas there. Unhappily, it will still be a high-desert climate. We'll probably need to travel in the early morning, then break and resume in the late afternoon, especially as we expect to start the crossing in the last two weeks of June, and it could be uncomfortably hot.

"At Bishop, we'll start the long climb on the slopes of the eastern Sierra. The first thirty miles will require a steep ascent as we approach Lake Crowley. There are streams in the area, but they are not conveniently accessible, as we'll want to trek along the existing road, which will require less effort. Happily, after two-to-three days of travel, we'll start to get into pines, cooler temperatures, and more accessible mountain streams, and daytime travel will be possible.

"The last sixty-two miles, from Lake Crowley to Bridgeport, will require us to cross two passes. The first of those is just south of June Lake. We may want to make a slight deviation from Highway 395 and rest near June Lake, which will be the last freshwater for a stretch across more high-desert scrub brush until we reach Lee Vining Creek. At least that section is mainly descending.

"At Lee Vining, we'll be at Mono Lake, which is too

alkaline to drink. It is fortuitous that 395 remains passable on the west end of the lake, though there are sections that are only one lane wide due to the rock falls. Once we've passed Mono Lake, we can refresh at Mill Creek before starting the last pass before Bridgeport. Then, from the summit, it's downhill to Bridgeport.

We estimate it will take us at least two months to reach Bridgeport once we leave our camps. If we can depart during the first week of May, we should be in Bridgeport by the end of June or early July. The timing of our planned exodus will also have us abandon the camps when the moon phase transitions from waning crescent to new moon, giving us the advantage of darker nights to help cover our movements during the first two weeks.

"We recommend we send an agricultural team to Bridgeport before the departure of the main body. Since they won't be traveling with the livestock, that team should get there much quicker to plant our first crops by the end of May. That advance team will require two trucks to carry the seed and supplies and tow trailers for a tractor and a backhoe.

"Are there any questions?"

Veena looked at the leaders' faces as they came to terms with the rigors and the migration duration. It was clear that there were questions, but no one was voicing any. A firm expression of determination was also visible on each of their faces. Veena imagined that a similar scene was playing out at the Camarillo site.

Veena said, "I consider these actions to be the best that we can plan, and we should enact all of it, including the advance team, to do the first planting. Do you all agree?"

"Yes," said the leaders.

"Camarillo, what are your thoughts?" asked Veena.

"We also agree," said the voice of Michael Liu over the radio. Michael was second to Eric Zhang and led the

Camarillo band while Eric was with the Tierrans.

Then, Veena said, "Roy, please implement the plans of your team, and let's target the last week of April as the time we abandon these camps and start the migration to Bridgeport. What are the next steps?"

"As I mentioned earlier, we need to start prepositioning provisions and water along the routes to Kramer Junction," said Roy. "It appears that a storm front is moving in, and that will be to our advantage as we should move the trucks while the storms help hide our actions. We'll also start putting in defensive measures such as explosives to create rockslides after passing the strategic points we mentioned in the briefing. The agricultural teams should leave the camps by April 1. Historically, the passes we have to cross should be completely open by that date, and, hopefully, the majority of the spring storms will be over. Finally, we will move the livestock also in early April. For the Camarillo camp's herds, that should give us time to get them across the Pine Mountain pass before the people depart. A similar plan will get the high camp's stock up to Julian and then down to the desert."

"Very good. Does anyone have anything to add?" asked Veena.

After a few seconds of silence, she said, "Let's end this meeting so we can get to work. Abe, would you lead us in prayer, please?"

"I'll start it," said Abe. "Hope, will you close the prayer, please?"

Hope nodded.

"Almighty God, most Holy God, You alone are God, and You alone pour out Your mercy and grace upon our lives. LORD, we make plans, but they are all for naught if not in Your will. So, our loving Father, we pray that we stay attuned to Your direction, seeking You first in all things. Send Your Holy Spirit to breathe Your insights and truth into our lives, that everything we plan and do will honor and glorify You.

"LORD, I have a feeling that there is something else You have for us before we embark upon the journey. So, we open our hearts and souls to receive what You are bringing. In the blessed name of Your son, Y'shua HaMashiach, we pray."

After a deep breath, Hope said, "LORD, I say Amen to all that Abraham has prayed. I, too, sense that you have another blessing for us before leaving the camps where You have protected and nurtured us all these years. So, we say, 'Come, Holy Spirit.' Bless each of these leaders, and make them a blessing to Your people. May we be effective witnesses and honor You in all that we think, say, and do. Protect us from the evil one, and prepare the way before us. For as You spoke, and we affirm, it is 'not by bow, sword or battle, or by horses and horsemen,' but Your grace and mighty hand that saves us. In the precious name of Jesus, we pray. Amen."

"Amen!" the leaders said exuberantly, including those leaders in the Camarillo camp over the radio.

CHAPTER 55

About one week after the planning meeting, a delegation of non-Christians from the tribe –led by Hasan Malik and Aarav and Myra Patel– approached Abe and Veena at breakfast and asked for an audience with The Redeemed leaders.

"May I ask the nature of the audience so I can determine how soon we need to meet, please?" inquired Abe.

"Although we are not members of your faith," said Hasan, "we have lived peacefully with you for nearly twelve years, and we have shared in your hardships and contributed to the welfare of the people. Now, you are blessed with a child, and we know you are moving the camp. However, we feel excluded, and we would like to know your plans, please."

"I am dreadfully sorry," said Abe with a look of anguish. "We are so immersed in planning that we have been negligent about including those of you who are not of our faith. Please accept my humble apologies. Veena, we should call a meeting at once."

"I agree," said Veena. "You find Eric and Hope. I'll get Laoni to relieve Nate and get Kath and Roy. Let's meet in the communication room in half an hour to contact the Camarillo leadership on the radio."

Thirty minutes later, all were gathered and dialed in.

"May I speak first?" asked Abe. "First, I apologize for our failure to keep those of our people who are not of our faith abreast of the plans. Though you live apart, you have been faithful and true to our people, and we welcome you in our midst. In Holy Scripture, Exodus 22:21 states, 'Do not mistreat or oppress a foreigner,' and in Leviticus 19:34, 'The foreigner residing among you must be treated as your native-born. Love them as yourself.' We have fallen short of those commands, and we need to rectify that."

Hasan rose. "Until these recent months, you have always treated us as one of your own, and we are grateful. We have learned, secondhand, of the migration plans. We wish to go with you. Will you include us, please?"

As Hasan was returning to his seat, Veena rose. "I also echo Abraham's apologies. You, and the people you represent, have always been a part of our people, and I am ashamed that we have overlooked you in our planning. I propose that Abe bring you up to date on our plans and that you select a representative to attend all our leadership and planning meetings. Does everyone here agree to that?"

Everyone did.

"Hasan, Aarav, and Myra, will you accept our apology, and do you approve of our offer?"

Hasan looked to Aarav and Myra. "Yes, we gratefully accept your apology, and we understand that it was just an oversight brought on by the hectic activities of the planned move. So, yes, we approve of your offer. We were hoping that you'd make such accommodation, and, in anticipation, we have already selected Myra to be our representative."

"Good," said Veena. "Now, as Hasan has stated, we have much to do. Abe will stay and brief you while the rest of us leave to attend to the demands of moving our people. We are stronger for your participation, and I thank you for the kindness of your understanding."

CHAPTER 56

The weather over the next several months was favorable, and the migration preparation proceeded as planned. Light storms came for a couple of days in mid-February, allowing the prepositioning teams to move the diesel trucks quietly at night. The winds and light rains covered the engine sounds just as the groups had hoped, so no interference from outsiders occurred. The prepositioning teams started building the caches of food and water for the trip to Kramer Junction. At the camps, the daytime routines continued to provide the daily necessities while duping any spies that might be watching. At night, surreptitiously, the people performed preparations for the quick disassembly and transport of the camps. Weekly meetings of the leads monitored the progress and addressed any new challenges in the migration preparations.

Veena became more incommodious, not wanting to leave their shelter as everyone watched for her child's birth. Even the weekly leads' meetings included discussions on Veena's pregnancy status until Abe stopped that. Passionately, every member of The Redeemed prayed for successful childbirth and confirmation of the promise.

CHAPTER 57

Joy and Doug's wedding ceremony, held in late March, was shortened when Veena's water broke. So, as a newly wedded couple, the first activity shared by Doctor Joy and Doc Ames was assisting Veena in her delivery of David Kyle Sinclair a day after the wedding.

David was robust and quite a howler. Nate was bursting with joy, and he didn't want to release David from his loving arms. Veena, exhausted and in pain, smiled and cried with wonder as she held David close. Abe, Miriam, Joy, Kath, MaryAn, Laoni, and even Carla wept with gratification.

Eight days later, Veena and Nate presented David to Abe for dedication to God. Whoever could manage the time away from their duties attended the dedication. Abe called the assembly to order with prayer.

"Dear ones, let us present ourselves to God: Father, Son, and Holy Spirit, in worship and praise at this most blessed event.

"Almighty God, our Deliverer, our Creator, Lover of our souls, we gather today to give You all the praise, and glory, and everlasting thanks. By Your gracious hand, You have brought us through the valley of the shadow of death and given us hope. We stand before You, people made in Your image, with songs and shouts of gladness as we witness Your eternal love evidenced by the dedication of this dear child,

David Kyle Sinclair, strong evidence that 'Proven character produces hope.'"

At that, he held David high for all the assembly to see, and shouts of joy thundered the walls and roof of the shelter. Holding David close to his chest, Abe looked at Veena and Nate. "Do you, Veena and Nate, present David to be dedicated to God? Do you promise to be loving parents to him, just as our heavenly Father pours out His love on us? Will you raise him as a child of God, teaching him right from wrong, filling him with scripture and knowledge, demonstrating compassion and wisdom, and disciplining him with kindness so he will grow fully into what God has planned for him? If so, please say, 'We do and we shall.'"

With tears running down their cheeks, yet grateful smiles on their faces, Veena and Nate answered in unison, "We do, and we shall."

Giving David back to Veena, Abe turned the new family to face the assembly. With a loud, clear voice, he said, "Do you, sisters and brothers in Y'shua HaMashiach, promise to care, protect, and assist our new family in their journey with God? Will you nurture, teach, lovingly correct, and, above all, hold up in prayer, David, Veena, and Nate? Will you hold steadfast to God's promises and the hope that David represents and live in God-honoring ways? In all things, will you model and demonstrate the love of Y'shua? If so, please say, 'We do and we shall.'"

The volume of the responsive "We do, and we shall" shook the shelter walls. The shouts of "Glory!" and "Hallelujah!" and "Amen!" continued for several minutes. Clutched to her chest, David eyed Veena. Veena and Nate felt the love of God and the congregation wash over them.

The celebration that night was one for the ages. The people's hope was renewed and restored.

CHAPTER 58

A week later, during the weekly status update meeting, Abe asked to speak. He had requested that Carla and MaryAn attend to David so Veena and Nate could partake in the discussion.

"Now that God has blessed us with a child, there are several points to consider," said Abe. "First, we need to follow God's leading regarding whether it is His will that we use artificial insemination to help co-create children. No passages in Holy Scripture explicitly address the possibility; therefore, it is a gray area of our Christian ethics and moral walk, and we should discuss it."

There was a heaviness in the room, and after a moment, Hope Zhang rose to speak.

"Eric and I have searched scriptures, and we can also affirm that there isn't any specific prohibition. By the grace of Almighty God, we now know a medical procedure that God has revealed in His timing and the God-given skills bestowed upon Doctor Joy to serve our people in performing the procedure, one that will not stain the marriage bed. Eric and I have prayed about the challenge, and we sense that the Holy Spirit is telling us it is permissible for established couples. As confirmation of the revelation, we offer that after we have all persevered in faith for over eleven years, God blessed us with Nathanael and the miraculous gift of God that he embodies. We humbly ask for confirmation." Hope sat.

No one said anything, but Abe could see that everyone was considering what Hope had said. Then, the voice of Kath, who was with Roy at the forward camp, came over the radio and broke the silence.

"Roy and I have selfish desires for a child, so you'll have to weigh my remarks knowing that. Nevertheless, Roy and I have also searched the Bible, and we agree with the assessment of Eric and Hope. Therefore, we confirm the revelation of the Holy Spirit."

When Kath paused, Abe spoke into the mike. "Roy, most of the men of our San Diego-based people arrived with you from the *Des Moines*. I know you lead a men's prayer and accountability group, has the topic, and the impact on the men, been discussed?"

"Yes, Abe, we have talked and prayed about it. To a man, all the married men and their wives eagerly embrace the possibility of children we would be privileged to raise as our own. The single men speak with hope for a future family that was impossible just a year ago. We all feel that God has poured out His mercy and grace on us after years of struggling to walk in faith through a barren land. Praise God for his love."

Abe noticed the looks of yearning on the assembled leaders, and he suspected that there were similar sentiments at each of the locations connected by radio. He waited for a moment, and then Miriam rose to speak.

"Dear sisters and brothers, I know that these concerns have been in all of your hearts. Certainly, Doctor Joy, Doc Ames, and I have listened to most of these questions over the past months. I am sure that each of you has also received inquiries from our flock members that you represent. I suspect that all of us have already put in considerable time in prayer and thought. I suggest we take an additional moment to pray as a gathered body before we make a decision."

Miriam returned to her seat, but before Abe could call

everyone into prayer, Veena rose and spoke.

"Nate and I have also had prolonged discussions about the procedure and what it means to our marriage, and we have come to the same understanding that Hope expressed. I will not tell you that this conclusion is without uneasiness for both of us, but we will be faithful to God's leading. Notwithstanding, I have a request, as the wife of Nate, that if we confirm to move forward with the procedure, we make a special exception so that MaryAn can get pregnant. She has been my sister, teammate, and personal guard all these years, and it will grieve me if we exclude her."

Veena looked at each of her leaders before she sat down. Abe could tell, by the solemn silence, the request put a new wrinkle in the discussion. Abe stood up and spoke into the mike.

"Camarillo, forward camp, and sub base, wait a moment, please." Then, turning and looking into Nate's face, he said, "Nate, your thoughts?"

"My dear Veena has expressed our attitude, and I confirm that I fully support her desire for MaryAn. I know that it is an odd and unexpected request, but I desire to honor her request and submit to God's leading."

"All right, then," said Abe. "Unless there is something someone else wants to add. I suggest we now spend time in prayer, listening to God's leading, before we proceed."

Met with silence, Abe said, "OK, let us pray in silence and allow God to lead us."

After several minutes, Abe spoke "Amen" and rose again. After confirming that everyone was ready to discuss, Abe asked, "How shall we proceed?"

Michael Liu's voice came clearly over the radio, "Dear saints, here at Camarillo, we also confirm the revelation given to our sister Hope. We agree that Hope's criteria for moving forward and accepting candidates do not violate scripture.

We don't know MaryAn, but if her inclusion as a candidate is satisfactory to everyone else, we join wholeheartedly to accept that decision. May God's will be done."

Doctor Joy unexpectedly spoke up, "Unless someone has an objection, I ask that we call for confirmation."

Abe hadn't expected the discussion to proceed in this manner' although he was pleased that it did.

"Is there any objection?" he asked. Met with only silence, after a short wait he added, "Then I'd ask each group to affirm unanimous acceptance?"

Each group confirmed acceptance.

"OK, may God bless this undertaking, and we pray that we are always attentive to His leading." Silently, Abe let out a relaxing breath. "Now that we have agreed, we must consider how to implement the plan. With the successful birth of David Sinclair, and his healthy growth, I have conferred with Doctor Joy, Miriam, and Doc Ames, and they are confident that we, with the blessings of God, may start additional pregnancies. Nate, in conversations you and I have had before, you have expressed your discomfort with the demand upon you and your relationship with Veena and David. Despite that, you have accepted that you will walk in faith to meet your service, and we want you to know that we, all the members of The Redeemed, will walk with you and intercede for Veena, David, and you."

Nate nodded and looked to Veena, who also nodded.

"To that end," continued Abe, "Doctor Joy, Miriam, Doc Ames, and I propose a selection committee, composed of five of our people that you call to this duty, to guide the conception process. The committee must be composed of the wisest, emotionally strongest, and most dedicated of us, to safeguard and promote the welfare of the children and the people. Consider that the selection of mother candidates will have to weigh the potential mother's health and age as part of the determination criteria. This task will be difficult, so please carefully choose whom you will support fully on the committee. Any thoughts?"

Hope stood again. "I do not think we need five people on a selection committee. Instead, I propose that we elect Doctor Joy, Miriam, and Doc Ames as the committee and delegate the criteria and decisions to them. They are our medical staff and not directly involved in The Redeemed's leadership. They already know our people's medical conditions, and they are responsible for maintaining their patient's privacy. They understand the necessity of time spacing the pregnancies for our people. Additionally, among our priority criteria should be the age of the candidate new mothers, especially those women approaching the age of menopause."

Abe and the rest of the leaders smiled. It was the best solution to a difficult challenge. "Camarillo, any thoughts?" Abe said into the radio microphone.

The voice of Michael Liu said, "We wholeheartedly agree with our sister Hope."

Abe looked at the leaders, and his heart soared with joy as he thought about the persons that God had appointed to the task. "Doctor Joy, Doc Ames, and Miriam, will you accept the additional responsibility?"

Each responded, "Yes."

"Good. Then I ask you all now, as leaders of our people, shall we proceed with the proposal by acclamation?"

"Yes," said the leaders in a loud voice.

"Is there any dissent?" After twenty seconds of silence, Abe said, "Praise God for His wisdom. The next item may feel premature, but I believe we need to be prepared for God to bless us bountifully with children. We should plan the education of the children. If anyone in our combined groups has primary or secondary education teaching experience, we should ask them to consider joining a team to build an educational program. Also, we'll need to scour any surviving buildings to find books and instructional materials. Any thoughts?"

The radio speaker broke the silence as Michael Liu said, "Both my wife Ruth and I have experience teaching primary grades. We will be delighted to work on the team, and we can help train additional volunteers on how to be good teachers."

"Excellent," said Abe. "Let's put the word out and find volunteers. Once we meet at Kramer Junction, the education team can begin planning as we continue our travel to Bridgeport."

Caleb's voice sounded over the radio. "Regarding gathering books, I recommend we locate them, identify and catalog them as well as the condition of the book, and bury them safely here, so we don't have to bring them with us during our migration. After we are safely in Bridgeport, our scouting teams can return and retrieve the volumes that the educators deem needed."

Abe looked at the gathered leaders and saw the nods of agreement. "Great suggestion, Caleb, we will do that," said Abe. Then turning to look directly at Nate, Abe said, "Nate, I'm sorry to put you on the spot. With your science and math background, as well as your NASA experience, would you join the education team to help construct the science and math studies?"

"Um," Nate stammered. "I don't have any teaching experience."

Over the radio, Michael Liu said, "Nate, we can guide you. I'm sure you had to help train people in the Navy."

"Well, yes," said Nate. "However, I was dealing with adults, not children."

"Nate, I am confident that you can contribute greatly in the role," said Abe. Then, softly, he added, "Consider, Nate, these are your children that we are instructing."

Nate blushed, but then, courage and strength filled him. "I will do my best."

"Good," said Abe. "I surrender the floor."

Veena stood up. "Is there any pressing business?" When no one responded, she continued, "OK, get the word out on finding books. Michael, Ruth, and Caleb, please create procedures to identify, catalog, preserve, and cache the books for later retrieval. Please respond with your recommendations during the evening's status update. Michael and Ruth, you will be the focal point of the education team, especially in recruiting and evaluating volunteers with the Camarillo group. Camarillo, will you do that?"

"Yes," replied the voices of Michael, Ruth, and Caleb over the radio.

Then, the voice of Roy came over the radio. "Veena, Chief Virtolli might have relevant experience from his previous duties in training new sailors in the Navy. If Michael and Ruth can guide us in examining teaching volunteers, he might help lead that effort here in the high camp. I could ask him."

"That's a great idea," said Nate. "Maybe Abe should ask him, so he doesn't feel like it is a directive from his commander."

Guffaws roared through the room.

"OK, I'll do that," said Abe with a grin on his face after the laughter ceased.

"Nate, my love," said Veena tenderly, "You should be on that education committee for our camp, too."

Nate stood, gently grasped Veena's hand, and, with a nod, squeezed it.

Sensing it was a good time to end the discussion, Veena said, "Let us pray. Come Holy Spirit and fill us with the wisdom of God to fulfill His plans. Send us out with a clarity of vision, understanding of purpose, and strength in our conviction. Prepare those You have called to Your intent, and may we all serve gladly. In the blessed name of Y'shua HaMashiach, Amen."

CHAPTER 59

For anonymity, Doctor Joy, Doc Ames, and Miriam decided to call their committee "the Wellness Committee." Additionally, although the Wellness Committee selected the candidate mothers, the actual invitation for an impregnation procedure would come from The Redeemed leadership committee. Regardless, it was also the kind of secret that everyone knew.

The Wellness Committee established the criteria that there would be only two new pregnancies every three months. Per The Redeemed leadership's suggestion, the impregnation would be only for well-established couples. However, the Committee, honoring Veena's request, also selected MaryAn as one of the first mothers. Additionally, the Committee would consider the candidate's mother's advancing age to prioritize pregnancies. To promote harmony between The Redeemed members, they would select candidates equally from both camps. As a result, the Committee chose Hope and Eric Zhang as one of the first candidate couples.

The Wellness Committee interviewed the selected candidates and charted their ovulation cycle to schedule an artificial insemination date to coincide with their expected maximum fertility period. The planned procedure required Nate to produce semen earlier on that day to allow time for chemical washing. The candidate mothers-to-be would arrive later that same day for the application.

At Doctor Joy's suggestion, Veena also came with Nate to provide support and encouragement. Nate and Veena felt awkward about the whole process, but in trusting God, they served. It was good that Veena accompanied Nate because he could not provide his supply without her help.

In late April, Dr. Joy performed the first procedure on Hope, and a week later, on the last day of April, on MaryAn. God blessed their faithfulness with confirmed pregnancies before the end of May.

CHAPTER 60

On May 1, both camps started the consolidation of their members and the evacuation's final stages. Morning and afternoon fog helped hide their movements. As Roy had foretold, the moon was waning and hid their night operations. The agricultural teams had indeed left on April 1 and planted corn, tomatoes, spinach, broccoli, beets, green onions, bell peppers, and sweet peas in Bridgeport that same week. Additional units started herding the livestock onto the route a week before May 1, and their progress was also according to schedule.

When the camps started the migration, David was already the happy and healthy baby that people imagine and dream of, an infant that deceives the parents into thinking that all babies behave in this manner. He cried little and grew abundantly. The parenting ordeal tested Veena and Nate as they had to learn about it the hard way, through experience with dirty diapers and wiggly baths and restless nights before David grew accustomed to the day/night schedule. Regardless, they were filled with joy, as was the whole camp. David's health and growth reaffirmed the hope they all held for the future.

Nate cherished his one-on-one time with David almost as much as Veena appreciated the brief breaks from the new demands of motherhood. Abe and Miriam became surrogate grandparents, and Veena and Nate gratefully accepted their offers of babysitting. Several in the camp, including MaryAn, Laoni, and even Carla, cheerfully volunteered to care for David. Safekeeping David became an honor, though nearly everyone was unprepared for an infant's challenges, especially a newborn. It was a good learning experience for all.

CHAPTER 61

BLESSINGS AND BLENDING

A week and a half before the start of the main migration, the Navy crew at Point Loma secured the *Des Moines* in a dry dock hidden within a hardened bunker in the hillside adjacent to the submarine docks. Everything they needed- such as viable diesel fuel, machine shop equipment, extra batteries, and spare parts for their vehicles- was in transit from the base, with most of it already safely in Bridgeport. To disguise the intention of abandonment, the Tierran forward camp members wouldn't travel to the high camp until four days before the planned exodus date.

On the planned date, however, Kath and Roy were at the forward camp when they radioed the leaders with a request to convene in Ramona regarding a recent development: a contingent of newcomers had approached, and they wanted to meet. The leadership agreed, and the next day Kath and Roy led a smaller procession, with the new arrivals, from the forward camp to Ramona. Two days later, Veena, Abe, Eric, and Hope watched from a rise on the road to Julian as Kath, Roy, three SEALs, and seven strangers separated from the main party and walked up to meet them. In seclusion, on opposite flanks of the approach path, Carla and Laoni watched the two groups get within talking distance.

"Veena, Abe, Eric, and Hope," said Kath, "may I introduce Lucia Sanchez, leader of a group that resides in the region around Yuma, Arizona, and San Luis Rio Colorado, Mexico."

Abe stepped forward. "Blessings of our LORD Y'shua upon you, and may His joy pour over you."

Lucia Sanchez was about twenty-five, short with black hair —vibrant despite the journey's dust—and flashing brown eyes. Advancing to Abe, she shook his hand. "May our Savior, Jesucristo, reward your faithfulness and gracious greeting. I greet you with a holy kiss," and quickly kissed Abe on each cheek.

Lucia stepped back. "I would like to introduce the members of our pilgrimage; on my right is Esmeralda Contreras, and next to her is Roberto Vargas. We are emissaries from our people, and these four men with us are our protectors." Esmeralda was taller than Lucia, in her late teens with a thin frame, long brown hair in a ponytail, and big brown eyes. Roberto looked to be in his early twenties, slightly taller than Esmeralda. His appearance seemed almost gaunt, and his brown eyes watched everything intently.

Abe, followed by Veena, Hope, and Eric, greeted each one and shook their hands.

Turning back to Lucia, Abe said, "You said 'pilgrimage.' Would you tell us more, please?"

"Gladly," said Lucia. "News of pregnancy and live birth have reached us in San Luis. We also heard that the blessing came to a body of believers in Jesucristo. So, we have come as representatives of our flock to see if it is true. If it is, we wish to offer our prayers and blessings. Truthfully, we desire to share in the blessing."

At that moment, both Carla and Laoni came out of hiding with weapons down but ready. The newcomers were alarmed, but Abe calmed things. "Everyone relax, please.

Kath and Roy, how much have you told them?"

Kath spoke first. "We haven't told them anything besides that they should meet with our leadership."

Abe glanced at Kath, Roy, Veena, Hope, and Eric, before returning his gaze to Lucia. "Ms. Sanchez, we need to discuss amongst ourselves before we continue." Then, motioning to a nearby awning, he said, "Would you and your delegation wait over in the shade of that covering at the park picnic table while we withdraw for that discussion, please?"

Abe motioned Kath and Roy to join the leadership team, and they moved up the road as Carla and Laoni accompanied Lucia and her team to the picnic table. When they were out of earshot, Veena asked Kath and Roy, "What is your assessment?"

Kath looked at Roy before turning back to the leaders. "Roy and I have observed them for about four days. One of our scouting teams found them and brought them to the forward camp. They immediately surrendered all their weapons and offered to help in any way we desired. They pray twice a day, and their faith seems sincere. Their understanding of scripture is excellent. We have always accompanied them with our team members who are fluent in Spanish, including Vince, who is already giving special consideration to Esmeralda," Kath said with a smile. "I'm pretty sure that she is enjoying that attention.

"Anyway, they have always conversed in English in our presence, even when they are praying. Lucia and Roberto are sister and brother and the leaders of their people. Like us, they formed with a need to protect the women from attacks by gangs. They merged with a local congregation of Christians early on, and their spiritual leader remains in San Luis with about two hundred believers.

"They crushed the threat of the local gangs, and the remoteness of their location in the desert has been a natural barrier for them against others. The San Luis area is adjacent to the Colorado River, and there is good farmland there. Roy has been in Yuma and can confirm that." Roy nodded.

"They say they have good seed, farming expertise, a dentist, and several auto mechanics. They heard about Veena's pregnancy and David's birth from traders. They also learned that the pregnancy is within a body of Christian believers. I don't think they realize that Nate is the reason God has blessed us with children. Anyway, I assess that they are authentic Christians, and their purpose is to confirm the rumors they have heard and to join in the body if possible."

"I agree," said Roy.

Veena looked at Abe. "What do you think?"

"We should talk with them and investigate further. If these people in San Luis are believers and are sincere, we should afford them the same opportunity that God offered to us when he sent us Eric, Hope, Joy, and the Camarillo delegation," said Abe. "Eric and Hope, what are your thoughts?"

Eric looked to Hope, who spoke, "Yes, we agree. I also suggest we send a couple of our people with them, taking one of the trucks, and see if they can meet us on the journey."

"Does everyone agree?" asked Abe.

"Yes," was the unanimous answer. Then Roy added, "If they return right now by truck, they may be able to meet us near the Salton Sea."

"OK," said Veena. "Let's go talk."

CHAPTER 62

Lucia and her team listened to the proposal that Abe gave them to join The Redeemed. After a short prayer, Lucia's delegation gladly accepted the offer. Abe then told them of the imminent migration and the urgency of their return to collect their people and equipment and meet near the Salton Sea. Lucia resolved that her team should depart at sunrise to return to San Luis to gather their people, supplies, materials, and equipment and then race to meet The Redeemed body near the southern end of the Salton Sea. Vince and Chief Virtolli volunteered to accompany them. By God's grace, the San Luis settlement also had access to diesel trucks, along with trailers, tractors, and various farming equipment.

On May 7 -the same day San Luis emissaries met with San Diego's leaders- the Camarillo branch started moving from Santa Paula to Ojai. Before they left their settlement, they burned their fields to cover their departure and provide a barrier between them and any gangs from L.A. One week later, the high camp embarked on the road up to Julian.

CHAPTER 63

From his penthouse observatory in Santa Monica, Rex pondered the smoke he saw rising in the west and drifting straight toward L.A. *Now, what are those damn, self-righteous, Bible-thumping fools doing?* His gang's food supply depended heavily on the crops pilfered from Camarillo's fields, and now it appeared those fields were ablaze. "Just one problem after the other," he sighed.

Not that Rex had ever met any of the Camarillo camp members, except for a woman he killed nearly nine years ago when he led a group stealing the Camarillo crops. Killing women was distasteful, but she surprised him when she came running and screaming at him through the corn stalks. Even then, the whole interaction with her was predominantly her death screams when he murdered her with a machete. Still, it's easier to justify the slaughter when you demonize whoever would oppose you. Rationalizing senseless killing should have been abhorrent to him since Rex's mother tried to take her kids to church every Sunday and bring them up as God-fearing and compassionate members of Christ. However, Rex's righteous course fell apart after the neighborhood bullies caused Tyler's death. After that, he had a hard time "holding on to Jesus," and it was a lot easier to go along with the world, especially in his neighborhood. His mother would be horrified, but he bet she saw it coming.

He ran his gang, the Killers, and was ruthless against competing groups, especially if caught in K territory. Early on, after Rex formed the K, Fred, a recent recruit, foolishly remarked out loud that the K should kill all those from whom they plundered. Rex's policy was to leave survivors and enough crops for the survivors to continue their subsistence existence. Rex had a long-term view and wanted easy resources to pick from instead of having the K produce foodstuffs for themselves. In the morning, Fred was found dead with an arrow embedded deep in his left ear. Rex pronounced that the arrow's shaft bore the markings of the Diablo Devils in Long Beach. Everyone knew there wasn't any group known as the Diablo Devils in Long Beach, only a tiny band of survivors who could barely eat. The K also knew that an arrow shot into an ear was a ridiculously impossible shot, so it had probably been driven there by Rex. To contradict Rex was a foolish act, so no one dared to say anything to Rex about Fred's death or the Diablo Devils.

Rex commanded the K, "Brutalize those Long Beach Diablo Devils. Strip their possessions as plunder. If you want to be a member of the K, you have to kill at least two people." Rex branded those warriors who made the required kills with "K" on their upper left arm. The K scar identified them as full-fledged members. To dissuade any dissent, Rex got his brand first. No one dared to challenge Rex, for existing members discreetly passed to recruits the warning of Fred's trespass.

The Fires provided the raw material for Rex and the K to become the central L.A. powerhouse. Over the years, disease, food shortages, and constant gang wars had reduced the K to a bunch of malcontents who preyed on survivors for scraps. The Camarillo fields were the richest ground, but the Asian Bible-thumpers proved too strong for the K to overtake. He had to resort to quick forays on the edges of fields. Even with that, the K was barely better than starving and Rex, who always took the more generous portion of any bounty, was now a skeletal two hundred pounds.

I assumed we'd get relief when we absorbed the Clairens and demanded their tribute, thought Rex. The latest news from down south is that the tribe called the Tierrans crushed the Clairens, so that option is lost. *I should have insisted that Jamir stay there and lead that group. Now we lost that food supply, and Jamir is watching my every move.* Rex slammed his fist into the wallboard, puncturing it. Numerous indentations testified this was not an uncommon outburst.

Thinking of the Tierrans, he wondered about a rumor that a child had been born? *That's big news if it is true. I probably should investigate. If confirmed, I should snatch the children to rebuild the K. Not for a few years, though; we don't want to nursemaid toddlers.*

Rex sighed again as he started down the stairs from the twenty-first floor. *Damn, I wish the elevator worked.* At least, going down the stairs was less exhausting than climbing them, and it did help keep him in shape. The lack of food made it harder all the time, and his starving body had consumed his former muscle mass. Therefore, he kept his residence on the third floor to minimize his stair-climbing.

What to do about Camarillo? Something odd is going on there; they never burned their fields before, thought Rex. A couple of years after the worldwide fires, the K tried to burn them out, but those Bible-thumpers had excellent fire control and doused the flames in no time. Soon he realized that burning them out would have been a mistake as they depended on the foodstuffs his gang pillaged from there. He could wait for his scouts to describe what was happening in Camarillo, but that would take at least three days. Rex rested on the tenth-floor landing; his breathing labored even in the descent down the stairs. *I better gather the K and head that way.*

—⁓—

It took three days for the K to reach the edge of the burned Camarillo fields. The Camarillo Redeemed had already assembled in Ojai and were starting their journey north on State Route 33. Regarding the livestock that the Camarillo Redeemed thought they would have to leave behind, they traded their animals for diesel fuel with a community near Santa Barbara. Therefore, the K found hardly anything of value at the Camarillo camp. It took four more days before discovering where the Camarillo Redeemed had gone when a scouting group returned and reported they had extracted that information from a reluctant farmer near Santa Paula. As a result, the K pursuers were hungry, thirsty, and a week behind.

CHAPTER 64

For the San Diego branch of The Redeemed, the journey from Julian to the desert floor to the east was faster and not as strenuous. There were places on the winding road where only a single lane was available. Veena, Kath, and Roy ensured the caravan stayed close to singlefile to prevent slowdowns at the pinch points. The first day, they went to the section known as The Narrows, which was a long, tiring trip in one day, even though chiefly downhill. They camped there to rest and let the rear guard create landslides to block the road behind them.

They heard from Chief Virtolli that the journey by truck to San Luis took less than a day. Though some of the San Luis people were initially reluctant to leave the safety of their homes and join the Redeemed groups, they joyfully accepted the offer when they understood that they would share in the gift of children. In celebration, even that assembly took a brief hiatus from their labors to offer prayers and praises to the new hope and deliverance. They enjoyed a hearty fiesta that evening, with singing, some dancing, and a wide variety of dishes reflecting the cultural heritages now embodied in the people. As dawn first pierced the night sky in the east, the San Luis camp started moving the livestock to meet The Redeemed near the Salton Sea. Three days later, the trucks –loaded with all the supplies and materials they could salvage and towing trailers with tractors and backhoes– followed the livestock route. Favorably, they had enough diesel trucks and fuel to transport the people. Nevertheless, their pace was defined by how fast they could drive the livestock. Regardless, as they were able to leave four days before the San Diego Redeemed abandoned high camp, all held high hopes that they would rendezvous simultaneously as each group reached the Salton Sea.

The wranglers moved San Diego herds to the fields next to the northwest corner of the Salton Sea. The irrigation canals were intact and working; therefore, water was available. The advance teams had previously flooded the fields, so now the livestock had grass and shrubs to eat. The mountains to the west also provided a welcomed relief from the late afternoon sun.

After the extra day at The Narrows, the San Diego Redeemed traveled to Ocotillo Wells, continuing their descent. They set up camp in the late morning and rested in the shade from the afternoon heat. That evening, Chief Virtolli announced that the San Luis group should arrive at the rendezvous by early evening the next day. The San Luis group had pushed through to make the meeting and join the San Diego branch of The Redeemed.

In the morning, the San Diego Redeemed left Ocotillo Wells and traveled across the desert to the intersection of California Routes 78 and 86. The road was straight and easy, and the slope continued downward, reaching below sea level at the meeting spot. They put up awnings for shade as they waited for the San Luis group. As the shadows of the mountains to the west fell on their camp, the first members of the San Luis group entered the camp. By twilight, The Redeemed had swelled as the San Diego and San Luis groups merged. Though the celebration, prayers, and thanksgiving were uncommonly loud, there wasn't a fear of attack as there weren't any outsiders within the audible range of the din. "God is good" was exclaimed, both in English and Spanish, repeatedly.

CHAPTER 65

It was already dark when the nearly forty members of the K, hot and tired, completed their long, one-day climb from Santa Paula to Ojai. After lighting the evening fires, members of the K pointed out to Rex the cold ashes of the extinguished campfires of the Camarillo Redeemed. *Damn,* he thought, *it's too dark, and we're too tired and thirsty to keep chasing these guys tonight. We might miss their trail in the dark.* So, reluctantly, he told the K to get water, food, and rest for the night. It was a strangely quiet night for the K, who habitually were wild, boisterous chaos of testosterone-fueled males. That night, they just collapsed wherever they were and fell into an exhausted sleep.

Rex awoke to sore muscles about an hour after dawn. His gang remained asleep; not even sentries were awake. He kicked the nearest thug and told him to wake the rest. His throat dry and scratchy, he guzzled the remaining water in his canteen. "Find that trail!" he barked. Thirty minutes later, one of the scouts informed him that their prey had headed north. Rex didn't know the area, and as he accompanied his gang onto Route 33, he soon grimaced as he realized they had more climbing. At least there was a stream nearby, but it was muddy due to runoff from recent rains draining down the slopes denuded by wildfires that had swept through in the past month. *Damn those Bible-thumpers.*

They had barely started the ascent when the booms from distant explosives shattered the morning air. Rex's lungs heaved for air from the exertion, and he gasped in anger, "Now what?" The nearest K members stepped out of Rex's reach; it wasn't wise to be too close to Rex when he was upset. Warily, the K moved at a slower pace up the grade, ever watchful for an ambush.

It was already evening by the time they reached the first tunnel. Huffing and puffing, Rex couldn't believe their poor luck. He thought these people would be easy pickings while they were on the move, and the K had left so quickly that they only brought whatever food and water they could carry. As the skies darkened, they were without food and had only a muddy stream nearby for their thirst. Getting down to the water was a treacherous descent from the roadbed, supported by loose, jagged rocks on a steep slope, to the small stream. Rex ordered three of his gang to fetch water to keep the bulk of his forces on alert and ready to attack. Even then, one of the hapless, drained gofers slipped and went crashing down the slope and into the stream, breaking his leg during the fall. Rex gave orders to kill the injured, screaming cretin. *Not that the cries matter. I'm sure those bastards already have eyes on us.* No, it didn't matter, except Rex was too tired to hear those howls of pain, and they weren't going to carry that fool back to L.A.

Soon, the forward scouts of the K reported that rubble and dirt blocked the far side of the tunnel. They didn't know how much debris was there or how long it would take to clear an opening. Angrily, Rex sent two of them to climb the steep hill above the tunnel and inspect the far side. When the sky was illuminated only by starlight, Rex saw torches coming back over the ridge a couple of hours later. One of the two lost his footing and fell, landing with a sickening smack as the impact broke his skull. *Two dead already, and we haven't even seen those damn Bible-thumpers.*

The second scout made it down about half an hour later. "A big wedge of rock blocks the first tunnel," he said. "We can probably dig around it and crawl through by the end of the day tomorrow."

"Wait!" exclaimed Rex. "You said the first tunnel. Are there more?"

The scout stepped back. "Yeah, there's at least a second tunnel, and it appears to be blocked at the far end, too."

Rex let out a long, outraged roar. He wanted to hit something, but there was nothing here except for rocks and the road. The K members jumped back, with several sprinting away into the cloak of the night. Finally, he picked up a big rock and heaved it over the guardrail that separated the road from the steep slope to the stream, screaming again as he flung it into the night's blackness. The crack of the thrown projectile impacting other rocks resounded through the narrow canyon, and then the cascading sounds of debris as it slid into the stream. After several heaving breaths, Rex commanded, "Head back!" With a mood as dark as night, he stomped down the road back to Ojai, enraged that their quarry had eluded their grasp.

Five days later, the single file of thirsty, famished, and stumbling members of the K stretched for miles. They reached the last rise between Topanga Canyon and the Pacific Ocean as a runner from the Santa Monica camp brought word of a large body of people and cattle near Palm Springs. Exasperated, Rex looked at his scraggly gang. *We're still a day away from Santa Monica, and these fools look like they can barely make it. In the old days, we could drive from Santa*

Monica to Palm Springs in a few hours. Now, the best we can do is ride bicycles like teenage posers. We've done it before, but that was years ago, and we were rested, well-fed, and at the top of our game. Even then, it took us a whole day.

Members of the K shambled past him making their way downhill toward Santa Monica. Rex grimaced and thought, *I won't be able to get these turkeys moving until they've eaten and rested at least a day. A day to get to Santa Monica, another day to eat and recuperate, and at least two, probably three days to ride bikes to Palm Springs. Then, we have to hope that we don't run into the Riverside Raiders. That'd mean war. Damn, if we didn't need those cattle and that booty so bad, I wouldn't even attempt an attack. If only we had overcome those Bible-thumpers. If we don't get more food, we're done.*

Rex put on a fierce face with a sadistic smile and extorted the K members as they slunk past him. "C'mon, you Killers, get to the hood and grab food and rest. We're going to score beef and punks in two days. Now, move your asses." The men looked wearily and warily at Rex and shuffled down the road a little faster.

CHAPTER 66

With the merging of the San Luis and San Diego groups, the procession slowed a bit. Although the trucks and diesel fuel from San Luis allowed the people and the equipment to move faster, herding the additional livestock set the pace. The advanced team prepositioned provisions, particularly water stores, scaled to the San Diego branch's needs. Those supplies needed to increase in proportion to include all the San Luis group people and livestock. Therefore, additional teams needed to move ahead and replenish the cache sites to ensure sufficient supplies.

When the merged group, now known as the eastern branch of The Redeemed, passed Coolidge Springs, they reached the irrigated fields that were already nourishing San Diego's livestock. Everyone rested for an extra day on the Palm Desert valley's southern pastures to feed the San Luis livestock. The next part of the journey would more likely expose the caravan to sentries and scouts of the L.A. gangs, who might be up in the San Jacinto mountains watching them; therefore, they planned a rapid advance of the convoy across the Palm Desert valley area. After Indio, the fields would give way again to the harsh desert with scant vegetation. Since it was late May, the leaders limited travel to the early morning and evening hours to avoid the midday heat. Mercifully, The Redeemed eastern branch made it to Indio in three days after leaving Coolidge Springs.

At approximately the same time, The Redeemed Camarillo contingent, also known as the western branch, had completed the summit of Route 33, moved down to Maricopa and Meridian, and was marching toward Arvin. Caleb reported that blocking the tunnels had indeed stopped pursuers. All the nightly updates were now given by Michael Liu, with occasional remarks by Caleb.

Both western and eastern groups traveled without any threats, their assemblies' sheer size discouraging any attacks. Caleb had been concerned that they might encounter gangs in the central valley before the convoy crossed the Tehachapi Mountains and reached the Mojave Desert. Instead, small bands, typically four to twenty people, would approach the procession, often carrying a white flag of truce. Traders had propagated the rumors of pregnancy and birth. For outsiders, the desire to confirm those rumors, and the observed presence of women in the migration body, were enough to overcome any fears they held about approaching the caravan.

Michael and Ruth Liu would meet with the delegates, guarded by Caleb and his newly trained SEALs from Camarillo. The majority of the outsiders were also Christians. Discovering that shared bond, both parties broke into broad smiles and, sometimes, tears. The delegates signaled the rest of their companions to join them. Together they traveled with the procession for a day to hear how God had moved in The Redeemed. The love and sense of purpose that the whole body of The Redeemed displayed was refreshing for those who approached. When they heard that the pregnancy and birth rumors were true, nearly all begged to join the convoy. The Redeemed leaders explained the acceptable behavior and responsibilities, and it was rare when anyone did not accept those terms. Anyone who didn't agree to the conditions would not be allowed to continue with the procession. The western branch became confident enough to travel across the central valley during the daylight hours.

Similarly, as the eastern branch moved from Coolidge Springs to Indio, they also had people approach, and several joined. Both processions grew, and the newly received friends provided valuable knowledge regarding safety and water sources.

CHAPTER 67

Rex was fuming. He was riding a bicycle for approximately one hundred twenty-five miles from Santa Monica to Palm Springs. When he had access to gasoline, he would ride in style and make the trip in a couple of hours instead of at least two days. Gas hadn't been available for twelve years, and vehicle hulks clogged the roads, especially in sections where traffic accidents blocked all the lanes. In those places, it was a challenge even to get the bikes through. Fortunately, after negotiating the maze in those rusting wreckage sites, the road would have a long stretch of open lanes until the next cluster.

Moreover, he could only order thirty of his gang to make the assault. The rest of the K had to stay back and protect their turf, though Rex insisted Jamir come along so he could keep an eye on him. *These guys are worthless*, he thought, *and I have to lead them myself since none of them are smart enough to see a job through.* Big thugs were all he had left in the K, and several struggled to ride a bike. They stayed on I-10 as much as possible and only made it to West Covina after the first day of riding, just beyond the K territory. All night long, Rex had to listen to several bemoaning how sore their butts were from riding on the bicycles all day. "Idiots and wimps," he muttered under his breath.

The following day, Rex discovered that four of his K were missing, including their bikes and supplies. "They're dead meat!" he screamed. Fear and distrust appeared on the faces of the remaining K members at their leader's outburst. Rex commanded his warriors to ride ahead of him that morning to make it clear that he was watching them.

CHAPTER 68

In Riverside, Paco Gonzalez was in a nasty mood. Raised in San Bernardino, Paco felt as though he had to fight for everything. At age twelve, he dropped out of school and bummed around with the local cholos (neighborhood Latino gang members). The Fires left nothing in his 'hood in San Bernardino, so Paco headed to the hills above Riverside and found a house that remained intact. Now, he was El Jefe, The Boss, of the Riverside Raiders, and his gang wore the Raiders' football team's colors.

The Raiders had just returned late last night from a foray to the south. News had come that the Tierrans had abandoned their camp. Altercations in previous years with the Tierrans had gone badly for the Raiders, and Paco didn't want to lose any more of his *eses* (brothers), so they didn't venture south much. With the news that the Tierrans were gone, he felt it was safe to swoop in, claim territory, and scavenge whatever they could.

Unexpectedly, after five days of travel and picking through the abandoned camps, they found nothing of value. The trip back left Paco and all his gangsters tired, hot, hungry, and thirsty, just the kind of situations that could make the underlings question El Jefe. Paco was agitated, and he slept fitfully, with one eye open. Now, the morning was hot already, and Paco was exhausted.

One of his men ran in the door. "Chino lookout has

signaled that the K on the move on bicycles, on the I-10, heading into our turf."

"How many?"

"Less than thirty."

That's it. Those damn K are making another run on our territory. We had barely kept our pocito turf out of the hands of those bastards. Walking to the door, he grabbed his homeboy and pulled him outside. At the top of his lungs, he screamed, "Raiders, we ride north to stomp the K's asses! Grab your weapons and bikes." Then he reached back next to his doorway to grab his crossbow, quiver of bolts, and a machete. *I'll show them who is 'El Jefe.'*

CHAPTER 69

Since leaving West Covina, the K made faster progress, even with the gradual climb, as they rode east to San Bernardino. Rex was feeling better about their progress. By good fortune, the hardest part of the ride through the pass on the San Jose Hills was completed in the early daylight hours, while the air was cool. Now, it was close to noon as they approached San Bernardino, and the temperature started climbing quickly. Sweat glistened on every K rider, and the salty moisture dripped from their foreheads, stinging their eyes and impairing their vision.

The K's lead riders didn't see the cars placed as a barricade on the I-10, hidden in the shadow of the I-215 overpass, until they were right upon them, and that's where the Raiders hid in ambush. The lead riders had to brake hard to avoid crashing into the ruins, and the entire column started to smash together. The Raiders rose and loosed a volley of arrows and crossbow bolts, dropping the first six riders.

Rex quickly noticed the I-10 was clear on the far side of the blockade and screamed at his gang, "Ride, don't fight! Ride!" He plowed through his lead riders' wreckage and weaved through the blockade. The K riders who survived the initial ambush quickly followed.

The Raiders didn't expect the K to flee, and they were notching bolts into their crossbows when Rex and the rest of the K flew past them. "Run, you cowards!" they shouted as they haplessly fired their projectiles at the fleeing K. Two more of the K dropped, but soon the rest were out of range. Paco decided they weren't worth the chase. "Take your trophies, and let's get out of the sun," he said as the Raiders finished off the survivors among the fallen K's and stripped them bare. Paco didn't realize that his lieutenants were irritated about the week's lack of booty and that tonight would be his last.

———∿∿———

When Rex realized they were clear, he started to pull over to the side of the freeway. Pain shot down his right arm when he tried to brake; he nearly flew over his handlebars as his left hand squeezed the front brake more strongly than he could with his right hand. One of the Raiders' bolts stuck through his right shoulder, and blood trickled down from each side where the arrow pierced his skin. "Get this thing out of me!" he screamed.

Jamir -brooding, sadistic, but shrewd- came over with bolt cutters. He scowled at Rex as he roughly snipped the protruding rod in two behind Rex's shoulder and placed his left hand on Rex's chest near the remaining shaft of the dart as his right hand grasped the projectile and yanked it free. Rex let out an involuntary scream and glared back at Jamir. Jamir turned and walked off as a member of the K came up to bandage Rex's wounds.

Rex looked at his troops—only eighteen of the original thirty remained—and two of those had wounds even more severe than his own. One of those, Floyd, probably couldn't ride any further and would be dead before the night was over. The assault was an absolute nightmare, and Rex could see that Jamir was already scheming to take over. If Rex couldn't lead the K into the raid and gain prime prizes, he knew Jamir would exploit this weakness, and Rex was as good as dead.

For appearances, Rex said, "Floyd, you stay here and guard our tail. We'll pick you up on the way back tonight. Give most of your water and supplies to Ernie." Floyd was barely conscious and too weak to object as Ernie took all of Floyd's provisions. They started riding east again, and the pain in Rex's shoulder and arm was excruciating. He made sure they rode ahead of him so they wouldn't see him steering with just his left arm as his right hung ineffectively at his side.

By Beaumont, Rex was at least a mile behind the K. Deshawn, the other wounded K rider, collapsed right there, in the middle of the freeway. Rex felt both rage and sadness as he pedaled slowly past the crumpled body of Deshawn. He had known Deshawn since kindergarten; he was one of the last of the old 'hood. It was now about four in the afternoon, and the sun's intensity was relentless. Nonetheless, Rex rode on, as he knew that stopping to rest would be seen as weakness by the remaining K riders.

Mercifully, the road started descending after Beaumont. Though they picked up speed, the air was too hot to refresh them. An hour later, as the K riders passed Cabazon, they were spotted by the westernmost rearguard of The Redeemed eastern branch. The Redeemed caravan's main body was already above the lower mouth of the canyon as California Route 62 ascended from the Palm Springs valley to the Big Morongo Canyon area. Only the last livestock and the rearguard were still moving north from North Palm Springs to the canyon's mouth.

The scouts radioed for reinforcements and set up defensive positions on the knoll just west of the exit from I-10 to Route 62. Vince was nearby with a squad that included Nate. Nate, itching for activity, left David in the care of Miriam. Veena, who had happily rejoined patrol leadership, at least part-time, after David's birth, provided scouting support near the caravan point and was unaware that Nate had left the safety of the middle of the procession and joined the rearguard. Vince's team hustled to the bridge that allowed I-10 eastbound traffic to transition to Route 62 north, and they crouched behind the low bridge railings.

CHAPTER 70

Juanita Suarez was a recent squad member, joining The Redeemed as part of the San Luis merger. Juanita was African American, born in Puerto Rico, and was just shy of fifteen when The Fires began. Her father was in the Marines and a top-notch aircraft electronics technician. They had been in Yuma only six months when the infernos started. That was long enough for Juanita to truly miss the Caribbean breezes and tropical storms, as well as despise the haboobs that swept through the southwest deserts during July and August, blasting dust into every exposed space before departing with lightning blasts and a brief rain.

The flames that had ravaged everywhere else had initially skipped Yuma. Sadly, a Marine pilot, infected with the pandemic disease, became disoriented soon after takeoff, crashing his fighter into a nearby residence. As a result of that crash, Yuma also was razed by fires just two weeks later than the rest of the world.

Juanita's parents were among victims of the disease, and their deaths left her on her own. One of the Marines who recovered from the illness helped lead the survivors to the neighboring San Luis camp. Juanita, perfectly bilingual, integrated well into the new group. Nearly all the original members of the San Luis band spoke English and Spanish. Juanita's Latin name and her native tongue made the assimilation easy, especially when it became clear that she shared the same faith in Jesucristo with those in San Luis. She trained in hand-to-hand combat techniques whenever she had free time. By seventeen, she was leading a squad in defense of the San Luis encampment, protecting her new family from any raiders that were hardy enough to cross the desert.

When Juanita arrived as part of the merger, Vince quickly recognized she was a seasoned warrior and an asset to any squad. He had asked her to join his team for the rearguard defense, and she readily accepted. Now, as she watched the I-10 for the bike riders the western scouts had reported, she furtively glanced at Nate. *So, this is the guy chosen by God. I wouldn't let him venture beyond the center of the camp.* Still, she understood Nate's desire to get out and had already witnessed how capable he was as a squad member. *Well, I've protected high-value assets before, though not such a valuable one.* She returned her gaze to the west.

CHAPTER 71

The K's lead riders headed east on I-10 and slowed as they approached the overpass bridge that led to Route 62 north. The mesa ridgeline and the knoll just northwest of the junction had blocked their view of the North Palm Springs area, but now they could see a large dust cloud rising due to the movement of the tail end herd of The Redeemed's livestock. From their vantage point on the highway, they were lower than the land to the north. They couldn't see the livestock, but the dust cloud indicated a massive movement. The K riders came to a halt to wait for Rex to catch up. When Rex rolled up a couple of minutes later, overheated and woozy from the blood loss and pain of his right shoulder injury, he braked too hard again with his left hand. His bicycle careened into the center divider on his left, with its softer, sand shoulder and metal guardrail. When his bike struck the barrier, he flew over the handlebars and smacked into the roadway on the far side with a sickening crunch as his left arm snapped and his head impacted on the pavement.

Jamir looked with disgust at Rex's unmoving body. Jamir not only wanted to take Rex's place, but he also wanted to take Rex's possessions, such as his better bicycle. Now, the barrier collision had deformed the bike's front wheel and damaged the front forks. The bike was too much trouble to repair or take back. *Just like Rex,* he thought. Turning to two of the K riders, Jamir barked, "Go climb that bridge and tell me what you see."

The two riders looked from Jamir to Rex's broken body and quickly got off their bikes to cross the guardrail and climb up the bridge embankment on the north side. When they were nearing the far side of the roadway, a thin Latino man stood up on the bridge, appearing from behind the bridge's guardrail. "What are your intentions?" he shouted.

The K didn't survive so long without being able to rise to a threat. Rather than defer to Jamir, or negotiate themselves, they lifted their crossbows and fired at the challenger while yelling, "Killers!" However, they fired too soon, and both their bolts struck the bridge span, well below the man on the bridge. Suddenly, several bolts flew from defenders on the bridge and also north of the roadway. With short screams as they died, the two K dropped, each with at least two projectiles embedded in their chests.

Jamir was enraged, but he wasn't a fool. The original thirty K riders were now down to thirteen. They were exhausted, hungry, thirsty, and probably easy pickings for the unknown number of warriors that confronted them. He could also tell by the shots that killed his men that these new threats were adept warriors. It was not a fight that would be worth their losses, especially as now he had control of the K. "Killers," he said with an edge in his voice, "We're going back." The remaining K were sick of the ride and were ready to return to their turf. Jamir kept an eye on the bridge, watching for those hidden troops, as the K turned their bikes around and rode past him, heading back to Santa Monica.

Filled with fury and denied any prize, Jamir crossed over the guardrail to Rex's motionless body. "Fool," he spat out with disgust as he gave a tremendous kick to Rex's jaw and then two swift kicks to Rex's chest, audibly cracking the ribs. Keeping an eye on the bridge, he stooped to strip Rex of his jewelry and weapons. Then, he crossed back across the highway, got on his bike, and rode after the rest of the K.

CHAPTER 72

Vince watched the riders depart. He had seen brutality before with the gangs around San Diego and was sad that such behavior no longer shocked him. "Squad," he said, "Nate and Javier stay here and keep watch. The rest check those three wounded down there."

Juanita felt nauseous. Defending against the attackers was necessary and prudent, but the ruthless beating by that big man on his injured compadre was new and horrible to her. While her teammates checked on the other two motionless K members, she moved up the road to Rex's body. She saw that he had a bleeding shoulder wound. Looking closely, she saw that his chest moved faintly.

Vince stopped by the closest two and confirmed that they were dead. He spied the K brand on their upper left arms. "Retrieve your bolts, but leave the bodies," he said. Vince walked up the road to where Juanita crouched over the third body. "Is he alive?"

"Barely," she said as she glanced up at Vince. "He has a broken left arm, and it appears that his jaw, and maybe one or two ribs, might be fractured, too. He also has a recent wound on his right shoulder. Really, I'm amazed he is alive. What are we to do?"

Vince grimaced. Every previous encounter with gang attacks customarily had members dragging off their wounded cohorts. These miscreants were part of the K, a gang he knew only by their infamous accounts of savagery. The Redeemers didn't seek to kill, but they did defend. Now, for the first time since he started leading a squad, they had an attacker left behind who wasn't dead but, instead, needed medical attention. *A K member at that*, he thought.

Turning to face the bridge, Vince called out, "Nate, get Doc Ames to check up on this guy."

Then, looking back at Juanita, he said, "Don't move him until Doc Ames examines him, as we might make his injuries worse."

"Do you know these guys?"

"I know of them. See that K brand on his upper left arm? That's the mark of the Killers, a truly vicious and barbaric gang that rules most of Los Angeles. I've heard that the Camarillo camp had several horrible and deadly clashes with them. However, I've never seen gang members treat one of their own like that before. Abandon them, yes, but not ruthlessly attack injured cohorts."

"Oh yeah," said Juanita. "We've heard stories about these guys. They never crossed the desert and came our way."

Within minutes, Doc Ames was examining the limp body of Rex and said the man should survive with treatment. He sterilized and patched the wounds and put a splint on the broken left arm. Doc Ames wasn't sure, but he didn't think Rex had a fractured jaw. Nevertheless, Doc Ames noted the dislocation of the mandible, and he used cloths to wrap it until Doctor Joy and Emilio—the dentist from San Luis— could examine the injury. Additionally, it was pretty clear that Rex had at least two broken ribs, so Doc Ames tightly wrapped up the victim's torso. He didn't assess any critical injuries, so he gave Rex a shot of morphine to sedate him for transport. When the horse-drawn ambulance wagon arrived, they lifted Rex's unconscious body onto the cart and started north to rejoin the convoy.

CHAPTER 73

Rex's journey from North Palm Springs to the Victorville area was noted only in brief conscious periods, filled with intense pain now that the morphine's effects had worn off. Unbeknownst to him, the recent inclusion of Doctor Joy and Doctor Emilio Flores to The Redeemed came with the benefit of additional meds, so he was in the best place to be treated. He was unable to talk, moaning feebly, especially as the doctors had tightly wrapped his jaw. Doctor Joy and Doctor Flores responded to the radio's injury call and waited with the hospital truck for the ambulance cart to arrive. Both confirmed that Rex's jaw was dislocated and not broken. They set up a treatment tent and sedated Rex. Doctor Joy and Doc Ames reset the broken arm and cleaned and bandaged the wounds in his right shoulder, pumping Rex with a heavy dose of antibiotics. They also confirmed three broken ribs. After they ensured there weren't any additional dislocations, they rewrapped his chest and prescribed a naproxen sodium treatment. When they finished, Doctor Flores reset the jaw and wrapped Rex's mouth nearly closed with bandages. Rex would be eating through a straw, or spoon-fed at best, for several weeks.

Since she spent her years of The Thinning in the Camarillo camp and had experience with the K, Doctor Joy confirmed Vince's suspicions that the man was a K member and not just a person impersonating the K as an intimidation tactic. Since Doctor Joy came from the Camarillo band, which had a history of defending against the K, she looked closely at Rex's bruised face. She had a gut feeling, as well as anger, that the man might be Rex. She asked her fellow Camarillo members Eric and Hope Zhang to look at him, but neither could positively identify the badly injured man. They knew members of their Camarillo group could positively identify Rex, but that wouldn't happen before they merged the two groups near Kramer Junction. Despite his incapacitating injuries, as a precaution, Veena ordered guarding of the man.

For the rest of the eastern branch of The Redeemed, the remaining trip to Victorville was thankfully uneventful. It was hot; thirst and sunburn were their worst foes. Six days later, as they approached Lucerne, the nightly radio status updates from the Camarillo Redeemed announced that contingent had made it safely to the shallow valley between the hills just south of Kramer Junction and set an encampment. The next day, a couple of squads would head south on US-395 to meet the eastern group.

Two days later, near Victorville, the eastern branch's lead elements met the Camarillo squads from Kramer Junction. The meeting lifted everyone's spirits as it foreshadowed the imminent consolidation of all The Redeemed.

Rex had more moments of lucidity and tried to speak. It hurt horribly; even breathing was painful. He really couldn't use either arm, his right one wrapped in a sling and his left forearm in a cast from his elbow and over his wrist. Rex saw the swelling in both was reduced, and the fingers on his left hand no longer looked like inflated balloons. Doctor Joy watched him closely as she told him that she needed to replace his cast now that his healing was progressing well.

For the first time in years, he felt frightened and vulnerable. Though he could barely remember the bike ride toward Palm Springs, getting shot in the shoulder was sharply clear in his mind. Rex had no idea how he got his injuries or why these people were helping him.

Juanita and Nate became his primary caretakers, with Juanita feeding him and Nate assisting with Rex's toilet needs. Now and then, he would glimpse them praying before they came to tend to him. *Who are these people?* Then, in a moment of clarity, he saw Doctor Joy, and he became anxious that he was in the hands of the Camarillo camp. *That would not be good.* He also noticed that the blond, white man called him "Kevin." Rex thought it was wise to keep quiet as long as possible, and he might get a chance to escape.

———

Before they reached Victorville and the Camarillo squads sent to their caravan, Veena, Nate, Abe, Vince, Juanita, Eric, and Hope came to see Rex. Doctor Joy examined his left hand. "We should be able to replace the cast tomorrow with one that will allow him to feed himself."

Dr. Flores then gently examined Rex's jaw and replaced the wrapping with an elastic bandage that allowed adjustment. "Still only soft foods and liquids, and you'll probably feel discomfort when you eat. That should be better in another week." Doctor Joy and Emilio moved into the background as the others approached, and Nate drew up a chair to sit near Rex.

"Hi, Kevin," Nate said with a slight grin. "My name is Nate. I'm sorry, we don't know your name, and the K brand on your arm made me think of Kevin. So, who are you really?"

Rex looked at all those watching him, particularly the tall black woman who had been feeding him, before returning his gaze to Nate. "Kevin," he said thoughtfully in a hoarse whisper. "I like Kevin better than my name. Please call me Kevin, Kevin Johnson."

"OK. Kevin, are you a member of the Killers? You ought to

know that you have not received any of your injuries from us. One of your own attacked you."

After a long pause, Rex nodded and, after swallowing hard, "Did you kill all of them?"

"No, not all. When two attacked us, we did kill those two. You crashed your bike, and a tall, black man gave you at least three kicks after he ordered the rest of his companions to return to the west. I guess he didn't like you."

Rex didn't say anything at first as he thought about it. "What are you going to do with me?" Rex noticed that Nate looked at the others before he replied.

"Well, Kevin, we don't kill people unless they attack us first. Right now, it appears you won't be able to use either arm for at least another two weeks, and it may take longer before you can eat normally. We are on the move, and we will take you with us. When you can walk, we'll assign you duties. If you can abide by our rules and behave decently, you can stay as long as you contribute. If you want to leave, we'll let you go and give you three days' provisions and water. If you make trouble, we give you a day's provision and a canteen of water, and then you're on your own. Do you understand?"

"Yes," said Rex, and then to his surprise, he added, "Thank you." He closed his eyes; he felt so tired.

"We'll talk more in the days to come," Nate said. With that, they all left, except for Juanita.

The confirmation that Kevin was part of the K saddened Doctor Joy, yet she also felt compassion, and she was astonished to hear a "thank you" from any member of the K.

CHAPTER 74

Several yards away from the infirmary tent, Veena asked Hope and Eric, "Do you recognize him?"

Eric looked questioningly at Hope, and she answered, "We're not sure. The injuries to his face continue to distort his appearance. We have a suspicion, though."

"When we meet Ruth Liu, Michael's wife, we should have her look at him. Ruth's older sister, Anna, was killed by the K, by their leader, Rex," Eric explained. "Ruth saw the attack, and so did Thomas McCoy. Thomas is at the vanguard with Laoni. We should also have him there when Ruth looks at this guy."

Veena nodded, and she and Nate headed back to the wagon where Miriam was watching David. Abe walked with Veena and Nate, putting his hand on Nate's shoulder. "You handled that well. You should build a rapport with Kevin, but don't let your guard down."

Anger flashed across Veena's face. "Do you think that is wise? You just heard Eric and Hope suggest that he might be Rex."

Abe looked lovingly at both Nate and Veena. "Unless he gives us reason to respond differently, let's continue to call him Kevin and treat him with compassion. I have a feeling that it may be as important to you, Nate, as it is to Kevin. Nevertheless, you are right; Kevin's injuries incapacitate him now, but I do think a guard should always accompany you."

Nate and Veena nodded. They trusted Abe's wisdom.

CHAPTER 75

Before the caravan broke camp the next day to resume their march to the rendezvous, Doctor Joy and Doc Ames removed Rex's cast, inspected the healing of the breaks, and put on a new, lighter cast that allowed Rex to use his left hand. Rex fed himself for the first time since the injuries. Considering he was right-handed, the first feedings were challenging and messy. Juanita wouldn't allow Rex to quit, and he came to appreciate her attention.

Over the next three days, on their journey to Kramer Junction, Rex learned Juanita's name and little more. The conversations were small talk, and it was painful for Rex to utter more than a few words.

CHAPTER 76

BRIDGEPORT

Three hot, dusty days later, the nearly four hundred members of the eastern branch of The Redeemed met the two hundred strong Camarillo branch at the temporary camp in the shallow valley on the south side of Kramer Junction. Both groups had grown by including small bands into their ranks during the approximately five-week journey to this rendezvous. Isolated as they were by the expanses of the desert all around, the celebration and greetings were loud and vivacious. No longer would there be a Camarillo group, a San Luis band, or a San Diego tribe; they were simply The Redeemed. Now they were whole, strengthened, and full of hope and joy.

Since the Camarillo contingent had been in this camp for a few days already, they prepared a wonderful feast to bless the consolidation and blending. Before the festivity began, Abe called all the people to gather. With Miriam at his side, he asked that Eric, Hope, Lucia Sanchez, and Chief Virtolli join them on a rise that allowed them to overlook all the gathered.

When they were all together, Abe raised his arms for quiet and spoke with a robust and jubilant voice, "Almighty, gracious God, whose mercies are new every morning, has brought us safely here and given us new sisters and brothers. We are now one people, loved by You, God—Father, Son, and Holy Spirit—and we shall submit ourselves to Your good will, for Holy Scripture says in John 13:34-35, 'Love one another. As I have loved you, so you must love one another. By this, everyone will know that you are my disciples if you love one another.' So, let us take the scripture to heart, embrace it fully. In Ephesians 3:19, our God has revealed, 'Know this love that surpasses knowledge—that you may be filled to the measure of all the fullness of God.' God has a glorious plan for us, hidden from our sight until recently. Now, look around you at your new sisters and brothers, and rejoice.

"I have asked Hope and Lucia to offer a prayer of thanksgiving. Then, for all of you who declare Y'shua HaMashiach as LORD and Savior, one in the Holy Trinity with the Father and the Holy Spirit, a mystery beyond our comprehension, we will celebrate communion in remembrance of the deliverance so graciously given to us. Eric, Hope, Lucia, Chief Virtolli, Miriam, and I will offer you the bread and the wine. If you are with Y'shua, I ask that each of you receive communion from someone who was not in your previous body of Christ, so we may get to know one another better."

Abe stepped back, and Hope and Lucia stepped forward. Hope, predominantly a reserved person, took courage and emboldened her voice. "Let us pray. Almighty God, most Holy God, Creator and Lover of our souls, we gather as one Body in Jesus Christ to give You honor, glory, praise, admiration, love, loyalty, submission, service, and above all, thanks. LORD, You have been so good to us, keeping us in Your strong hand through all the evil times and bringing us safely here with new hope, expectation, and family. What a wonderful and loving

God You are. Come, Holy Spirit, in a magnificent way to unite Your people, that our adoption into Your family would be an effective witness of You and Your faithfulness. May we humbly give You our lives and wholeheartedly demonstrate our love for one another. Prepare us to respectfully receive Your holy communion, that the life only You can give fills us. Bless our time together, dear LORD, and make us a blessing in Your name. In the name of Your son, Y'shua HaMashiach, Jesus Christ, the only name that can save, we pray. Amen."

All the people responded, "Amen."

Hope took a step back, and Lucia raised her head. "LORD, we do indeed say amen to everything that Hope has prayed. We also want to thank You for the promise and gift of children. When we thought that all hope was gone and trials severely tested our faith, You remained true and faithful. Your plans for us are recorded in Romans 8:28, 'In all things God works for the good of those who love him, who have been called according to his purpose.' LORD, forgive us when we fall short and stumble. Put Your Spirit upon our souls and grant us insight, conviction, and courage. Lead us in compassion, justice, and love to also care for those You have brought into our midst who are outside our faith, that Your righteousness and mercy would be evident in Your saints. Now, prepare our hearts as we receive Your holy communion. In the name of Jesucristo, amen."

Again, all the people answered, "Amen."

Abe gathered Miriam, Eric, Hope, Lucia, and Chief Virtolli. First, they gave Abe communion and a blessing, and then Abe did the same for them. They broke into three pairs, putting space between each couple and presenting themselves with the communion elements before the people. Abe then called out, "Come, as the Spirit leads you."

When all who desired to participate had taken communion, Miriam, blessed with a resounding, vibrant, and beautiful voice, started singing the old Tom Inglis tune, "We Are One Body."

When they had sung it twice, they all let out an enormous cheer, praising God, and hugging.

Rex, standing on the outskirts of the congregation of people, was moved and frightened. *How will it all play out if these people find out who I am? And, God, if He is actually here, will He be forgiving? What will be my future?* With a shudder, Rex considered all these questions in his heart.

CHAPTER 77

Later, in their shelter in the center of the encampment, Veena sat next to Nate as she held David. "Sitting here with you, our son in my arms, I sometimes have difficulty in believing it is all true. Two years ago, before you appeared, we kept praying for a miracle that felt as though it would never come. I was struggling to hold onto hope, and only Abe's strength in faith nudged me on. Even though I know the world is not what it was, and I'll probably never see a time when our lives are as comfortable as they were before The Fires, I feel secure. Do you understand what I'm saying?"

"I think so," replied Nate. "Though I missed all the horrors that you experienced, this isn't the world to which I expected to awaken. The shock was so crushing at first. I'm overwhelmingly glad that you, Abe, MaryAn, Laoni, and even Carla, found me. It frightens me to think how different, and probably fatal, it would have been if the Clairens had found me first."

Veena smiled during the pause before she continued, "I have twenty-twenty hindsight of how God is moving. I find so much joy in you and our son. With the merging of our camps and all these new sisters and brothers in faith, I have such surety in how God has provided me with our family and the family of faith."

Nate thought this over, realizing his faith journey since he met Veena and Abe. "I wasn't particularly devout before; in fact, I had probably been downright indifferent. Now, I agree that I can see how God worked for my good in the past. I have the blessings of you and our son, and I have the bounty of our extended family. I am puzzled about why God chose me to help bring children into our congregation, and, frankly, it also makes me a bit distressed. Your strength, and grace, have helped me find the courage and a sense of purpose to submit to God's plan. Abe taught me Micah 6:8, you know, the verse that states, 'He has shown you, O mortal, what is good. And what does the LORD require of you? To act justly and to love mercy and to walk humbly with your God.' I'm trying to make that the way I act each day."

"You're a good man, Nate." Veena hugged him. David, in his sleep, smiled.

"I love you, Veena," said Nate. "You are a miracle from God, one that I am privileged to share."

CHAPTER 78

The following morning, as dawn dimly lit the medical tent, the camp disassembly sounds woke Rex. He sat up from his bedding and sensed Juanita's nearby presence, his guardian. *How strange that is.* Doctor Joy, as he had become accustomed to calling her, breezed in. She inspected his bandages and murmured her observation that the shoulder wounds were healing. He started to take a deep breath, but the pain from the broken ribs cut that short. "Those ribs will take time, maybe months," she said.

She then made sure the circulation looked good in both his hands, and she unwrapped the elastic bandage that bound his jaw. Satisfied, she motioned for one of the aides to clean Rex with a washcloth. The aide, a short Latina, came into Rex's bedding area and pulled a privacy curtain. Juanita stayed within the curtain as the aide worked. His face's bruising and swelling had subsided, but he remained sensitive to touch in certain spots, so the aide was gentle. Finally, the aide helped Rex put on clean clothes. Before she left, the aide said, "Please sit here," and she pointed to a folding chair.

Rex sat as the aide pulled aside the privacy curtain and left. He noticed that Nate and several others were standing just beyond the curtain. Nate approached, carrying another folding chair, and sat near but not blocking the line of sight of those who stood just outside the bedding area. Rex looked closely at those standing there and was startled to see a familiar face staring back at him. He couldn't place that face at first, but the young Asian woman gave out a little gasp and pulled back. Filled with dread, Rex realized that the woman looked like that woman he had slaughtered near Camarillo years ago. Of all the deaths that Rex was responsible for, that young woman's face was etched in his memory and ate at his soul.

To the group of observers, Nate said, "Well?"

The woman nodded, turned quickly, and left. A man went with her. A young, white man in the group spoke, "Yup, that's him."

Nate looked intently at Rex. "Well, Kevin, you have been identified as Rex."

Rex's shoulders sagged, and he looked down. "I'm not that person anymore; I don't want to be that person anymore." He noticed that several armed people were standing just outside. "What are you going to do with me?"

Nate got up and led the observers outside. Only Juanita and the additional guards remained. Not that Rex was much of a threat as he had one arm in a sling, the other in a cast, a jaw that ached every time he spoke, and sharp pains in his ribs whenever he drew a deep breath. The guards told Rex to get up, and the medical team stored the equipment for travel and took down the infirmary tent.

Rex, accompanied by the guards, walked behind the hospital wagon near the caravan's back as The Redeemed moved north up the hill that separated the camp from Kramer Junction. When he reached the top of the pass, Rex could see more desert ahead of them and the remains of a solar electrical generation station. The caravan's lead elements were already nearing that station, about six miles ahead in the valley below. As he started down toward Kramer Junction, Nate, Abe, Eric, Michael, and Lucia were waiting along the side of the road.

Nate walked in step with Rex as the rest followed, and Nate said, "First, what shall we call you?"

Rex, gritting his teeth as each step made his ribs, right arm, shoulder, and jaw ache, looked down, not wanting to face those he had previously hurt. "I like the name 'Kevin,' please keep using that. It's better than any name that I've had before. Even 'Rex' was a name I gave myself because I didn't like my given name."

"Well, Kevin, now that we know who you used to be, the decision on how to handle you has become challenging. Ruth Liu is the younger sister of Anna, a woman killed by you about eight years ago. Tom McCoy also witnessed that attack, and he confirmed Ruth's identification of you. After much prayer and listening to God's direction, both Ruth and Tom submit themselves to His will, taking big steps in faith. We are going to honor what I told you before. Now that you can walk, you will have duties. If you behave and contribute, you can travel with us. Otherwise, we'll give you one day's water and rations, and you will leave us. When your arms heal and are reasonably functional again, we'll reevaluate your status. Until then, we'll continue to keep a watch on you. So, what will you do?"

A tear ran down his cheek. Kevin was not used to compassion; he certainly never extended such mercy when he called himself Rex. "If you will let me, I'd like to travel with you and contribute. I promise that I won't cause trouble."

Nate looked at the leaders. Each one gave a slight nod, Abe first and Michael last.

"OK, Kevin, we'll give that a try. As for assigning your duties, your injuries limit how you can contribute. As your ribs and arms heal, we will expect more of you. You will walk near the convoy's end and keep an eye for any livestock that has separated from the herd." Pulling a yellow bandana from his back pocket, Nate gave it to Kevin. "If you see a problem, you hold up this bandana with your right arm, and a rider will come to you. Can you do that?"

"Yes," said Kevin softly, barely looking at the leaders.

"Juanita, show Kevin his station, por favor," said Lucia.

CHAPTER 79

It took four days to travel across the high desert to Johannesburg in the scorching mid-June sun. They rested when the heat was fiercest. The livestock handlers tried to keep them moving as the animals set the pace of the procession. The following day, the travel was into a deep valley and immediately up the opposite side. The planned trip was only about ten miles, but they would have to brake the wagons on the quick descent, followed by an equally tough climb on the far side. Everyone bedded down early that night.

During the trip, Kevin stayed near the outskirts of the camp. At nightfall, Juanita and Nate took shifts watching him, supplementing the guards assigned to monitor Kevin. Both would engage him in small conversation before he drifted to sleep. Twice, Abe came to talk with him and pray over him. Kevin felt torn; he was both uneasy with the kindness and deeply grateful. When Abe prayed, the act reminded Kevin of when he was a boy named Linus, and his mother would come to his bedroom and pray over him after she finished her late shift at the hospital. *How can these people behave this way toward me? They know who I was.*

CHAPTER 80

Before sunset, Veena and the leaders got news from Caleb, who radioed them from his outer scouting position above the entrance to Red Rock Canyon, about eighteen miles to the west of their campsite. "We've got an armed group, all men, moving up the 14 into Red Rock Canyon. It is reasonable to assume they are trying to cut us off and attack. They will be unpleasantly surprised that Red Rock Canyon is impassable due to previous flash flooding. It destroyed much of the road. They will have to navigate through that debris, making it a slow, tough hike."

"OK," said Veena. "Keep an eye on them. We will check with you at noon tomorrow."

The lead elements of the expedition broke camp before dawn and started the descent. By mid-morning, all the procession had reached the canyon's bottom and started up the far side. At noon, Caleb reported that most of the armed party had turned back at the broken road in Red Rock Canyon and were now moving toward the road that went from Route 14, through Garlock, to intersect with US-395. Caleb estimated that it would take that group at least two days to reach the 395.

However, ten of the party were continuing on foot through Red Rock Canyon. Caleb recommended taking his squad to watch that group and having the Redeemed rearguard defend against the raiders' remaining larger group. Veena, Kath, and Roy agreed.

Adopting Caleb's recommendation, the caravan's rearguard looked for the raiders but never saw them.

Two days later, as they approached Inyokern, Caleb and his squad rejoined the caravan. "They were woefully unprepared," said Caleb. "It appears that they ran out of water a day later. The ten hiking through Red Rock Canyon turned back, and even then, three of their group collapsed, probably from dehydration and heat exhaustion. Regardless, their compadres left them, taking what they could from the victims. We kept to the high ground and saw a similar scenario to the bandits' main body. When we crested a ridge overlooking the valley the main group took, we saw buzzards circling over bodies. We spied the rest shuffling south. I don't think they'll last another day."

CHAPTER 81

Beyond Inyokern, the road clung close enough to the Sierra mountains' eastern face that the late afternoon shade from the peaks relieved the convoy of the sun's intensity. Two days later, the whole procession bunched up after the short rise to Little Lake. The livestock wranglers had to watch that the animals didn't venture too far into the lake as the beasts gulped down the cold water. People shouted with joy and splashed in the waters fed by mountain runoff, a refreshing respite from the heat and thirst delivered by the desert.

Veena and Nate sat waist-deep in the cold water on rocks near the shore. David, whom Veena held on her lap with his feet in the water, squealed with delight. "Praise God, we made it across all that desert," said Veena. "I hope we never have to do that again."

Nate splashed a little water at Veena and David, who squealed again. "Amen, and praise God. I forgot how vast that desert is."

⸺∿⸺

Not far away and overhearing their conversation, Kevin smiled as he watched Veena, Nate, and David. He looked at Juanita, who was also sitting nearby. "I never knew that there was an immense desert. I spent all my life in L.A. and never got north of Dodger Stadium. I thought that L.A. was hot, but it's a paradise compared to the desert."

Juanita smiled back. "I spent the last thirteen years near Yuma, so I'm used to the desert. At least there, we had the Colorado River. After leaving Puerto Rico and all the rain that it would get, I assumed that Yuma and San Luis were as close to hell as you could get on Earth. But even there, we could always jump in the Colorado River, or one of the canals, to cool off. This last month has been brutal, and I kiss it goodbye." She blew a kiss toward the south.

Kevin laughed, and his ribs hurt. *Pain lets you know you're alive*, he told himself. He wondered who had said that to him in the past; perhaps it was his mother.

CHAPTER 82

That evening, when Doctor Joy examined Kevin's healing, she decided to remove the sling from his right arm. "It's healing well, but don't pick up anything with that arm until I tell you it's OK. It will probably be at least four more weeks before your ribs heal enough that lifting will be possible," she said.

"Thank you, doctor." Kevin tenderly stretched his arm. "How about the cast on my left arm?"

"Let's leave that on for two more weeks, and then we'll change it to a removable support brace."

Before the caravan started north in the morning, Nate and the leaders met with Kevin again to discuss his future.

"You have behaved yourself," said Nate. "You have contributed. We see that your right arm is now free, so we have come to reevaluate your status with us. What is it that you want to do?"

"You've been kind to me, and I feel so ashamed," said Kevin. "If you'll let me stay with you, I'll try to help and make amends."

The leaders withdrew a short distance and held a quiet discussion. Soon, they returned, and Nate said, "We will let you stay with us as long as you continue to behave and contribute. You will continue to work with the animals. You'll have to walk, but we expect that you will shoulder more of the burden of keeping the herd moving forward."

"Thank you," whispered Kevin. "I won't let you down."

Most of The Redeemed didn't expect that the next part of the journey was still high desert, though now they were closer to several small lakes south of Cartago. From Cartago, they stayed on the west side of Owens Lake. Before The Fires, Owens Lake was predominantly a dry lakebed, but now it had salty and undrinkable shallow water. The wranglers struggled to keep the animals away from that water.

Advantageously, north of Owens Lake was the freshwater Owens River, which roughly paralleled the road. While the people and vehicles stayed on the pavement, the herds moved closer to the river. It was late June when they reached the Owens River near Lone Pine, and the daytime temperatures were hot, though not nearly as bad as their crossing from Victorville to Little Lake. Opportunely, for the animals, it was cooler by the river, and the procession was able to reach Bishop, fifty-eight miles north of Lone Pine, in six days.

CHAPTER 83

At first, Kevin spent his time out with the herds. After the first dinner service, he was relieved and came into the camp's central body for the second service. Often, he ate with Juanita, and she talked about her life in Puerto Rico. How different it was from his childhood in the much drier, automobile-choked neighborhoods of L.A. He noticed how she gave thanks before her dinner, and it reminded him of how his mother did the same whenever she didn't have to work the night shift at the hospital. After dinner, Juanita would leave to go to Bible study. Kevin watched her leave and went back to the herds. He couldn't stop thinking about her. On the third night of their shared dinner, he asked if he could come along, and she smiled broadly. "Of course."

Kevin stayed at the back of the study group. He was surprised that Nate led the class. After the discussion ended that night, he approached Nate: "You do this, too?"

Nate laughed. "I know it's kind of odd. Abe always led these studies, but he impressed upon us that if we truly want to learn, we need to take the initiative and lead a small study. I tell you: it's a big stretch for me, but I am learning so much."

Kevin thought about that as he bedded down by the herds that night. He decided he would go again.

CHAPTER 84

At Bishop, the people rested for a day and scavenged what they could from the intact buildings. By good fortune, as they traveled to Bishop, they were able to find books in usable condition in the libraries at the Independence County building, the Big Pine school, the Bishop High School, and the Bishop library. "How to," math, science, and engineering books were prized finds, but fiction and poetry were also collected. The remoteness and desolation of these areas, which contributed to not drawing people to these locales, helped eliminate the pilfering of the publications. Additionally, the buildings were fire-resistant, so they remained silent sanctuaries. Whatever the teams didn't take immediately, they inventoried and buried the publications in water-tight containers for future retrieval.

In one corner of the Bishop High School gym, Doctor Joy removed Kevin's cast and gave him a removable, plastic brace for his left arm. "Again, I warn you, don't lift anything, especially with your left arm," she said. "How do you feel?"

"Sore, but no real pain," replied Kevin. "My arm feels incredibly light now that the cast is off. I'm also getting more movement in my right arm and, most of the time, my ribs don't hurt. Though I've made the mistake of twisting, which resulted in sharp, stabbing pain," he said with a smile. "Oh, it also doesn't hurt as much when I eat now."

"OK. You probably should have Dr. Flores check your jaw.

Otherwise, be sure to wear the brace during the day, but you can probably take it off to sleep. Go ahead and put on your shirt. Nate and the leaders want to talk with you again."

Doctor Joy signaled to Nate and his companions, standing across the gym. They came over as Kevin finished buttoning up his shirt.

"Kevin how are you feeling?" asked Nate.

"Not bad. The doctors are kind, and I'm healing well."

"Good," said Nate. "Now that you have use of your arms, it is time for another discussion about your status with us. From what we have observed, not only have you contributed and not caused any problems, you have also demonstrated good and humble behavior. Nevertheless, I'm sure that there will be residual uneasiness about your presence in our midst. Despite that, we are willing to accept you as part of our group if you continue the positive conduct you have shown over these past two weeks. If you'd rather leave, we will give you three days' supplies and water, and a knife. What are your thoughts?"

"I am grateful for all that you have done, and I'd like to remain with you. I know that there are people struggling with my presence, but I'd still like to stay. I feel at ease with the animals, and if it is all right with all of you, I'd like to continue to work with the herds."

Turning to Doctor Joy, Nate said, "Is he healed enough to ride a horse?"

"We should wait at least two more weeks to allow his ribs to mend completely."

Nate looked at Eric and Hope. "What do you think?"

"God redeemed Saul and renamed him 'Paul.' Hope and I have talked with Ruth and Michael, and we are willing to trust that God can reclaim Kevin," said Eric.

"OK," said Nate. "Kevin, you are welcome to continue with us. As you heard from Doctor Joy, you won't have a horse for now. We are about to start a pretty steep climb, and I don't think we'll be going too far each day as the herds move slowly. Are these conditions acceptable to you?"

"Yes, I'm very grateful," said Kevin. "I'll try very hard not to grieve you, and I hope, someday, to prove my character has improved."

CHAPTER 85

When the caravan started again, they moved to the pastures of Round Valley. From there, they would head uphill fifteen miles along US-395 to Toms Place. It was a long, continuous ascent, and they chose to travel along US-395 instead of any alternate routes because that climb was uniform and therefore more manageable. Months earlier, the advance teams had positioned water and feed at a few spots along the road. It took three days to reach Toms Place, where Rock Creek flowed and watered nearby pastures. The people would have liked to rest there, but it was already past the first week of July. Roy informed them that there remained about ten days of travel, including crossing two passes. Veena agreed that they needed to keep moving, and the leadership supported her decision.

The first pass was Deadman's Summit, three days from Toms Place. Two days later, they made the journey to the base of the rise to the gap. The last two miles, up the steep, winding road to the summit, took up the day. From there, they moved the herds to a spot south of June Lake Junction. It was reasonably level there, and they had the shelter of lodgepole pines that surrounded a meadow. Except for the wranglers, the people continued to the eastern shore of June Lake to camp by the clear mountain waters.

That night, Kevin partially acquitted himself with The Redeemed when he single-handedly drove back a pack of coyotes, with just a flaming torch and his pent-up rage, saving the livestock.

While the people stayed next to June Lake for an extra day, the wranglers drove the herds through the long stretch of sparse desert to Lee Vining Creek. It was a hot, arid road, but it was primarily downhill. At Lee Vining, the wranglers had to guide the livestock on the partially blocked road that continued along the west side of Mono Lake. As the scouts had described before they began the journey, the short stretch of the road cut into the Lee Vining mountainside that dropped steeply to the western shoreline of Mono Lake had rockslides that covered the lane closest to the slope. Here, the unhindered travel path was only about fifteen feet wide, so the wranglers had to keep the herds moving in a narrow column through these sections. Fortunately, it was a relatively short day of travel as they reached the cold freshwater of Mill Creek flowing out of Lundy Canyon. As the last herds departed the Lee Vining Creek area, the people's first wagons arrived from their day's rest at June Lake. When evening fell, the livestock was herded a short distance to a pasture just at the base of the Conway Summit ascent.

At first light, the people left the Lee Vining River, moved past Mono Lake and the grazing livestock, and ascended the steep but wide roadbed to the Conway Summit, the final pass before Bridgeport. Reaching the gap, they were greeted and cheered by nearly twenty advance team members, which was about half of those who had arrived in Bridgeport three months earlier to plant the fields. Many people openly wept, knowing that Bridgeport was an easy, one-day descent from this point.

The following morning, as the people started their final trek to Bridgeport, Kevin and the wranglers herded the livestock up the road to the gap. The steep climb took the whole day. Long before the first animals made it to the top of the pass, the people's lead elements were already past the narrows south of Willow Springs. Just beyond Willow Springs, they saw the open spaces and fields, green with the plantings, around Bridgeport. The sight of the young crops spurred the people into singing "America the Beautiful," a song that grew louder as more of the procession came upon the view of their new home. The sound was so loud that even the wranglers at the top of the summit could hear it above the herds' bellowing.

The next day the herds finally entered the southern pastures. The Redeemed celebrated the gift of their new home with praise, adoration, and a banquet. For an hour, the wranglers left the herds to roam the fields while they attended the festivity, and Kevin went with them. He saw Juanita standing with Veena, Nate, and David, and he quietly joined their group. Juanita and Nate glanced at Kevin and smiled.

Abe stood on a wagon. "Precious people of God, let us join hands as dear sisters and brothers in His family, and we shall give thanks." All the people, including those outside the faith, closed in, held hands, and bowed their heads. Then, Abe said, "Almighty God, omnipotent and gracious, by Your everlasting mercy You brought us all safely here. You kept every one of us safe from harm, and all, including our livestock, arrived by Your good plan. You added to our number with new sisters and brothers as we traveled. What a wondrous, loving God You are.

"We offer our praise, adoration, love, loyalty, service, and surrender. May we live in unison and peace in honor of You, and as Your good and faithful servants. Pour out Your provision and wisdom on all of us. May our community, both believers and those outside the faith, be a living testimony to Your glorious Name. Send Your Holy Spirit to write Your laws upon our hearts. Finally, may the light of the Body of Christ shine to all, bringing Your hope to replace their despair and draw them to You.

"To the Glory of God the Father, God the Son, and God the Holy Spirit, we pray. Amen."

The answering "Amen" thundered across the valley.

Kevin looked at the hands he was holding, Juanita on one side and an Asian-American on the other, and he felt a warmth he hadn't felt since before The Fires. *Perhaps here is home*, he mused. Then he thought of something he often heard Abe say, *Proven character produces hope.*

CHAPTER 86

NINE MONTHS AFTER ARRIVING IN BRIDGEPORT

The sun dropped below the mountains' ridges, and the Sinclairs finished their evening meal. Veena watched Nate playing with David, now a toddler who trundled around at full speed on his chubby legs. Less than three months ago, MaryAn delivered Joel Rodriquez, who would be raised jointly with Carla. The thought of Carla rising to the challenge of rearing a boy amused Veena. Nonetheless, she had observed maturing in Carla, along with a more moderate attitude than Veena would have surmised just two years ago. Veena marveled at the tremendous changes she had witnessed in that time.

Then, a day after Joel was born, Hope and Eric welcomed Luke Zhang into the world. Veena smiled as she marveled at the blessings of children and was glad that David would have playmates within a couple of years. Likely within the month, The Redeemed looked forward to the birth of children to Kath and Roy Haines and Doctor Joy and Doc Ames. God had graced the people with additional pregnancies, and everyone offered praises to new babies expected every three months. God is good.

As that last thought crossed her mind, the child in her

bulging womb kicked, and Veena involuntarily said, "Oof." Nate glanced her way, but Veena waved off any concern with a bit of grin. "David's sister is active tonight. I suspect we can expect an arrival soon."

Chuckling, Nate got up, came over to Veena, put his arms around her, and gave her a warm, loving hug. Veena gently guided his hands to her protuberant belly, and Nate felt their baby kick.

"Wow," he said. "You're right; that is a powerful kick. Does that hurt?"

"Not really."

"What makes you think our baby is a girl?"

"I'm just anticipating that God wants to bring balance," said Veena with a smirk. "I mean, our people have already received the gift of three boys; it's about time He gave us a girl so we can have parity and leadership."

"Ha! Or should I say 'Ouch.'" Then, after a short silence, he added, "I'm still getting used to being a dad. Did you ever dream of being a mom?"

Veena looked wistful. "No. Before you arrived, we had pushed that hope far beneath our thoughts. It hurt too much to dwell on it. Besides, every day was already a constant struggle. The peace we've enjoyed in Bridgeport is quite a refreshing change from the constant state of readiness that formed our day-to-day life in San Diego. I'm slowly accepting that being a mom is part of my life now. I have to admit, being a mom genuinely brings its own set of challenges. If we ever get pregnant again, it's your turn to carry the baby for nine months." Veena laughed hard enough that tears formed in her eyes.

Nate rewrapped his arms around Veena. "I cannot comprehend the evils and struggles you, Abe, and all the others survived. Even after spending two years with you, everything remains so new to me. And how different is a life of farming, hunting, building, defending, and teaching compared to the plans that I made when I was in the Navy. Before, I didn't face dangers such as those all of you overcame. Then, even after I awoke to a new reality, my life was, and is, on the whole, safe."

"There were times when I was frightened for you," Veena said softly. "Such as when you went on the patrols. Additionally, when you first met with Kevin, I was extremely uneasy about your safety, and I was glad that Juanita was there. Abe prayed with me about that, and God put assurance in my heart. Now, look how well Kevin is becoming part of our extended family. What mysterious ways and events have unfolded."

"I love you, Veena," Nate said as he nuzzled his wife's cheek.

"And I love you, Nate," Veena responded. "Numerous times, I have thought about how I would feel about the additional children that you have helped bring into our world. I was a bit possessive and selfish, and the thought of you fathering those children bothered me. Now, I'm glad that our children will have playmates and friends. Every child has a bit of you in them, so I love them too."

"You're a good woman," said Nate tenderly, and they embraced in the evening stillness that was occasionally broken by David's squeals as he played nearby.

CHAPTER 87

FOUR YEARS AFTER ARRIVING IN BRIDGEPORT

Now just over four years old, David gazed at his younger sister, Hannah Dawn Sinclair, as Veena stroked the hair on his forehead and Nate read them a bedtime story. David and Hannah loved their family time and adventures. Their chores, as well as lots of playtime with the other children –their half-brothers and sisters– filled the day. Wherever David and Hannah went, an inseparable band that included Joel Rodriquez, Luke Zhang, Blossom Ames, and Ezra Haines was with them. The parents took shifts in watching and feeding the group. Additional children would temporarily join them throughout the day, but the six were an enduring pack. Only at bedtime were the parents able to separate them back to their respective homes.

When Nate finished reading, he kissed them both on their foreheads. Many nights, the kids would clamor for more stories, but tonight they both were already drifting to sleep from the exertions of the day's activities. As Nate stood in the doorway of the kids' room, Veena tucked each of them in, caressed the hair on their heads, and gave each a soft kiss.

It was late July, and the evenings were long. Veena and Nate sat outside their simple house on a small porch protected by mosquito netting and looked over Bridgeport's fields. Dusk was coming, and the breezes picked up to cool the day's heat. The cares of the world faded away.

"Will you be ready for school in a month?" Veena asked. Nate, Miriam Cohen-Jones, Michael Liu, and Ruth Liu were starting the first of the children's formal classes at the beginning of September. "Herding cats" was the common expression used around the community. Happily, Chief Virtolli and Laoni Wright-McCoy were assisting with fitness activities and had plenty of that planned.

"Oh, how did I ever let all of you rope me into this?" Nate said, faking exasperation. "Yes, I think we're ready. We all realize that we will have to adapt and rework our plans to meet the kids' needs. They're good kids; the schooling should all work out and be fun."

"You will do well. You always do. Besides, Miriam, Michael, and Ruth will keep you on the right path. Hopefully, Chief Virtolli and Laoni will help those little bodies burn up that excess energy. Oh my gosh, I'm talking like an old lady already. I suspect Chief Virtolli will be spent by the end of the day trying to keep those wild ones focused. I'm glad Laoni is also working with them."

Nate chuckled. "Yes, I hope to take a nap while Chief Virtolli and Laoni have them running all over the schoolyard." With an expanding grin, he added, "Maybe I should suggest lots of field trips."

Veena guffawed.

"I saw you talking with Eric earlier. Anything you want to share?" asked Nate.

Veena sighed. "Eric thinks he should set precedence and retire next year from the civil leadership of The Redeemed. He wants me to intern with him and be prepared take over when he steps down. Eric feels confident I will be elected as the next president. I don't know how I feel about that, and I wanted to talk with you first. I'm not sure I'm up to it, and I wish that Abe would accept that role."

Nate reflected on what Veena told him and pondered the changes. "Veena, you have always been able to lead and meet any challenge confronting you and our people. Abe has made it abundantly clear that he wants to remain removed from the civil leadership and focus on the spiritual needs of The Redeemed. I believe that if you ask him, he will wholeheartedly bless you in taking on a new challenge. I also think that Eric is impressed with your leadership skills and feels it fits you and our people. I agree with that assessment, and I will support whatever you decide."

Veena thought about Nate's words before she said in a soft tone, "OK, I'll consider it. First, I want also to get Abe's thoughts and blessing. If he agrees, too, then I'll do it. You realize, don't you, that will mean you will have to watch Hannah and David more?" she added emphatically with a grin.

"I'll be delighted to do that," Nate replied. Then, with a smile that spread from ear to ear, he said, "So, if 'the First Lady' is the wife of a male president, then, future Madam President, am I the 'First Gentleman?'"

"Oh, in *so* many ways!" Veena's loud laugh nearly woke the kids.

CHAPTER 88

Not far from Veena and Nate's cabin was the home of Abe and Miriam, who also sat on their screened porch as the twilight faded. Their sitting porch made a fine addition to their otherwise crude shelter. Miriam sat close to Abe, snuggling in his warmth as the evening temperatures started to drop quickly. They sat in silence for nearly an hour as they enjoyed watching the community finish supper and begin the bedtime routines. Only a few hours earlier, the howls of children at play had filled the air, and the glee of the laughter and shrieks smothered the memories of the recent past.

Abe looked at Miriam by his side. "I'd say a penny for your thoughts, but I don't have any coin money. How about an apple for your thoughts?"

With a broad smile, Miriam looked at Abe and hugged him. "The sounds of the children just make my heart soar. None of what has happened is how I thought God might move."

"Me neither," said Abe. "Nevertheless, it is so much more than I could have imagined. God is good."

"Yes, He is," Miriam said warmly. Then, with a sober tone, she added, "Abe, even with the blessing of these children, I am struggling with the consequences of low genetic diversity since Nate fathers all of them. What are we going to do when the children mature and want mates of their own? They shouldn't be intermarrying."

Abe paused for a moment to reflect on the quandary before expressing his thoughts. "I know that people see me as a man of strong faith, though you probably have a better insight than most regarding my struggles. However, sitting in peace here, having witnessed the children at play, knowing the safety and prosperity we are enjoying, I have learned to wait on God's timing. Our God will watch out for His people, and especially these children. I don't have the faintest idea of how He will do it, but I have confidence that He will provide future mates for these children. I believe our job is to train the children rightly, instill the skills they need to survive, explore, and thrive, trusting God to give us all direction and meet our needs. When the time comes, He will provide. Does that seem naïve and foolish?"

"Not at all," said Miriam. "After all we've witnessed and survived, I understand your trust in God. I'm sorry for fearing the future. Just hearing your words has renewed my trust in Him, and I'm so glad He brought you to me."

"And you to me," replied Abe with a loving smile. "God is good."

"All the time," said Miriam, and she pulled Abe closer.

CHAPTER 89

THREE WEEKS LATER

Kevin and Nate were hiking the old road from Saddlebag Lake to Ellery Lake near the Tioga Pass. A week ago, Caleb, Vince, Nate, and he had left Bridgeport to spend two weeks enjoying the Lundy Canyon area, as well as hunt game. Part of their adventure had been the strenuous climb up the canyon, scrambling up the goat trail to the tallest waterfall at the canyon's ridge. They had left at dawn and made it to the top of the waterfall and the plateau with many lakes that fed the waterfall and Mill Creek in Lundy Canyon. The view from the top of the waterfall was breathtaking, and the plethora of little lakes on the plateau was a special treat. While Caleb and Vince were fishing on Saddlebag, Kevin and Nate decided to head to Ellery Lake, Tioga Lake, and the eastern entry into Yosemite.

"Nate, I never could have imagined that one day I'd be strolling casually in the mountains with clear water lakes and pine trees, hearing the swish of the breeze through the branches and tickling the lake surfaces. Growing up in L.A., such scenery was just a fantasy, captured in pictures I saw in schoolbooks."

"Incredible, isn't it? I had been to Yosemite before, but I

was a young boy traveling with my family, and I don't think we ever left the Yosemite Valley. I had no idea we missed so much. I'm glad Vince and Caleb convinced us to take the trip, and I greatly appreciate that our wives let us go. How did Juanita feel about your taking two weeks off?"

"She is a godly wife, and I'm convinced that she felt I'd be a better man by spending the time with Caleb, Vince, and you. Besides, she probably appreciates the time spent alone with Natalie, Veena, and Hannah. I tell you: I had no idea that taking care of toddlers was so exhausting. The climb up that goat trail was easier than running after Natalie all day. I don't know how Juanita does it."

Nate chuckled. "Yeah, the same with Hannah. We're fortunate we married good women. Whew, the altitude is getting to me. Let's sit for a moment."

Resting on a low boulder, they enjoyed the fresh breezes and overall quiet that was only interrupted by a bird song or a stronger gust of wind.

"Nate," Kevin said softly. "I don't know if I ever properly thanked you for saving my life."

"I didn't save your life, Kevin. I was only there when God brought you low, and He used me to help reclaim you. Your wife, Juanita, and Vince walked in faith and made sure you got medical attention."

"That's true, and to both of them, and especially Juanita, I am deeply grateful. What I'm talking about is after that, when you interviewed me. Whether you consciously meant to or not, you acted as my advocate when I was especially vulnerable. More than that, I've learned from your life, how you act, and the Bible studies you've led, how to be a man. I'm a changed person."

"Me, too, Kevin. I was stumbling until Abe and Veena took risks and intervened in my life. It warms my heart to hear that I've improved enough that God can use me to help people in their walk with Him. Thank you, Kevin, for telling me that; it's a real encouragement."

Moments after Nate spoke, they both heard voices that were not too far away. Advancing slowly and low to the ground, they reached a hill to observe the Tioga Pass road covertly. Lying prone and hidden by shrubs, they peered over the edge of the rise at a scraggly band of men walking down the highway from Yosemite through the Tioga Pass, headed down to Lee Vining. They were heavily armed but moving listlessly. It was evident they were exhausted from the ascent to the Pass and the nearly ten-thousand-foot elevation. With alarm, Kevin recognized Jamir and realized the disheveled band must be the K.

Kevin counted about thirty. They looked scrawny and malnourished, struggling with the altitude, but they remained a horrible threat. Kevin never thought he'd see the K again, and the sight of them both angered and saddened him. Things must be untenable in L.A. for the K to come all the way here. Kevin realized that the band must be planning to raid The Redeemed, as there weren't any other tribes, especially any as wealthy as The Redeemed, anywhere along the eastern Sierra.

From what he had heard in scouting reports, Kevin knew that if the K just stayed on the road, they would reach an impassable section where storms and avalanches had wiped out a narrow bridge spanning a break in the shear wall. At that same point, the K should see that rockslides obliterated the roadway further down Lee Vining Canyon. Kevin whispered to Nate, "It's the K, and I bet they're coming for us. Perhaps they'll give up when they see the bridge is out."

"I wondered if they might be the K. See that big guy at the end? He's the one that kicked you when you were down."

Nate just confirmed what Kevin had long suspected.

"Yeah, Jamir. He's going to be trouble. You better get

Caleb and Vince, and I'll make sure they don't double back."

"OK, but don't you confront them. Caleb will have a better idea of how to deal with them."

Kevin nodded, and Nate scooted back and then ran up the road to Saddlebag Lake.

Kevin couldn't believe it; he never thought he'd hear or see the K again. Yet, here they were, obviously headed to raid and plunder. *It feels like so long ago; it was another lifetime. I had almost begun to forget my life as Rex and the leader of the K. I still feel guilt and shame for that past, even though both Abe and Nate remind me that God has forgiven me and made me a new man. Now, here they are, with Jamir leading them.*

Waiting for Nate to return with Caleb and Vince, Kevin considered his change over the last four years. He continued to work with the animals. Doctor John Williams, the veterinarian who came with the Yuma and San Luis band, took Kevin under his wing and trained him extensively in animal care, well enough that he now handled all the animal care for the southern regions. That wasn't even the most significant change. He continued attending Bible study with Juanita and Nate, eventually reading the Bible without prompting and genuinely digging into the Word. Within six months of arrival at Bridgeport, Kevin's heart had changed so much that he asked Nate to mentor him and hold him accountable. Now, Nate was his closest friend, well, in addition to Juanita. The June after they arrived in Bridgeport, Kevin asked Y'shua into his life and was baptized by Abe in the cold water of the Twin Lakes. Witnessing Kevin's changed life was enough evidence to Hasan Malik, Aarav Patel, and Myra Patel that they also embraced Christ. Together they formed a fellowship group led by Nate, and their jubilant growth in the community served as a witness to newcomers and established members alike.

Then, six weeks later, on the first anniversary of their

arrival in Bridgeport, Juanita Suarez and Kevin married. Even Ruth Liu and Thomas McCoy attended the wedding, as Kevin's transformation was so remarkable that "the old man" who Kevin used to be was no longer recognizable. Two years ago, Juanita and Kevin welcomed Natalie Johnson into their family, named in honor of Nathanael. *I'm now a new man of God, a husband, a father, and part of a growing, joyful community. Only God could redeem the old me and make me new.*

Kevin thought about his daughter, now a toddler who raced about, giggling frequently and bringing such joy into his life. He treasured his new life, one that was unimaginable just over four years ago. Watching Jamir round a corner and move out of sight, Kevin felt heartsick that anything could happen to Natalie, Juanita, or any of his newfound family in The Redeemed. Despite his indications to Nate, he decided he better discreetly follow the K to see what they did when confronted by the destroyed bridge.

CHAPTER 90

Storm clouds started rolling over the Sierra as Kevin stealthily made his way down to the Tioga road. Though he couldn't see them, Kevin could hear the K as they noisily moved down the sinuous road ahead of him. The discipline that Kevin instilled in the K when he was its leader as Rex was lacking.

It was one of those typical August storms in the Sierra, with numerous bolts of lightning and micro-bursts of heavy rainfall. By the time he passed Ellery Lake, one of the downpours had soaked him. Hugging the steep wall of the canyon slope as he edged along the mountain road, Kevin traveled only about three-quarters of a mile along the road before he spied the K around a bend. He crept forward and watched the K use ropes to cross the gap left by the destroyed bridge. The rain had let up, but flashes and booms of the lightning and thunder foretold that another microburst was closing in. Kevin looked around the bend and saw Jamir, screaming at his reluctant gang to keep moving, even though one of them had already fallen to his death. *Can't they see that the road is gone ahead? They must really be desperate.* Finally, only Jamir remained on the same side of the gap as Kevin.

Caleb, Nate, and Vince had not arrived yet. Kevin realized that once Jamir crossed the gap, he wouldn't have the opportunity to reason with him one-on-one. Kevin couldn't wait any longer to confront Jamir and try to stop the K. He thought again of Natalie and Juanita, said a short prayer for wisdom and strength, and rose to meet Jamir just as a heavier rain started to fall.

"Jamir, we should talk."

Jamir had one hand on the ropes when Rex's familiar voice reached him. Shocked, he whipped around to face the figure in the rain behind him. Even after four years, Jamir could recognize Rex.

"I thought you were long dead. I heard rumors you were now with the Bible-thumpers, but I didn't believe them. How the mighty have fallen. Are you here to challenge me for the K?"

"No. I can offer you a better life, a life of peace, and a future."

Several of the K on the far side of the gap crowded the edge. Eyeing Jamir and the nearly forgotten figure across the chasm, they raised their crossbows until Jamir waved them off.

"Are you going to sell me on Jesus?" Jamir sneered. "I've already got the K, peace as I demand it, and a stranglehold on the future."

"Jamir, I can't sell you on Jesus, but I can tell you about how my life has changed, changed for the better if you are willing to listen."

"I have a better idea myself. Why don't I finish what I started years ago and deliver you to your precious Jesus right now," he said as he started advancing toward Kevin.

Kevin also took a step forward. "Jamir, if you don't want to hear about Jesus, let me at least offer you peace between us. We can give you livestock and seed and teach you how to survive without hate and cruelty."

"Farmers, ha, that's not a future! I think we'll just take what we want." Jamir rushed Kevin as lightning flashed, and a storm cell unleashed a deluge.

CHAPTER 91

When Nate, Caleb, and Vince didn't find Kevin where Nate last saw him, they also headed down the road to look for him and the band of the K. They rounded the bend near the missing bridge just after the heavy rain started falling. Lightning flashed all around them and, through the downpour, they saw Kevin wrestling with another man.

"That's the brute that kicked Kevin all those years ago," shouted Vince above the din of the rainfall. "He must have taken over the K."

Kevin and the man were struggling uncomfortably close to the edge of the gap. Before Nate, Caleb, and Vince could rush to intercede, a lightning bolt hit the wet roadway between them and the fighting pair. The electric shock knocked Nate, Caleb, and Vince to the ground and temporarily clouded their vision. When Nate could see again, the combatants were gone. Caleb was first to get up and rush to the edge. The K on the far side of the chasm were also stunned. When they saw the three men across the gap running to the edge, they scrambled down the road to get out of range.

"Where are they?" Nate shouted urgently.

Caleb grasped the ropes bridging the gap and peered over the edge.

"They've fallen, Nate. It doesn't look good."

Nate edged closer to where Caleb was standing as Caleb retreated to let him grasp the ropes. Kevin and his assailant lay about fifty feet below, splayed across the broken rocks and twisted bridge sections. Nate could see streams of red flowing from the bodies and across the rocks. Nate wept.

CHAPTER 92

The remainder of the K continued running down the Tioga Road and started scrambling across a section of scree that had obliterated the roadway. As the storm cell moved over to that area, the same deluge caused another rockslide. The cascading debris swept more than half of the remaining K down the steep canyon wall, killing them. What happened to the survivors, no one knew.

Using the ropes left behind on the gap by the K, Caleb descended to Kevin and Jamir. He confirmed that Jamir was dead. Thankfully, Kevin was still alive but unconscious and severely injured. Caleb determined that Kevin could be moved, but the injury to his right knee appeared to be debilitating. Carefully, Caleb splinted Kevin's leg. They bound him in ponchos to reduce movement and hoisted him back up to the road. It took them two days to carry Kevin, who moaned every time they jostled him, back past the upper falls of Mill Creek and to their base in Lundy Canyon. Before they descended the falls, Caleb was able to radio the campsite where a couple of his SEALs were safeguarding their supplies and horses, and he told them to get the doctors to the camp to meet them. Two days after that, the weary party arrived in Bridgeport with Kevin, who was rarely awake and in extreme pain whenever he was.

The doctors confirmed that the fall had shattered Kevin's knee. He had several other broken bones and some internal injuries that made his recovery touch and go for a week. However, the knee injury meant that Kevin would need a cane to help him walk for the rest of his life.

One night after he knew that Kevin would survive, Nate thought back over the last four years and softly spoke to Veena as they lay on their bed in the warm summer night.

"Reflecting on how Kevin's life has changed since we've known him, I feel that I've never fully given myself to God and sacrificed my way to submit to Him. Because Kevin came into our lives and embraced our faith, I have a new understanding of commitment and sacrifice."

"What are you talking about? You lead Bible studies, shepherd men's accountability groups, and have submitted to His people to help produce all these children with whom we are so blessed. Your commitment and sacrifice are carved in stone for all to see."

"One of the countless things I love about you, Veena, is your support and faith in me. Yes, I do all those things, but I also realize that I have been holding back. I no longer want to be on the fence; I want to be as dedicated as Kevin."

"God redeemed Kevin, redeemed us all, and gave us strength. I know He will continue to work in your life, our life together, and our people. Every day we just need to renew that commitment to walk in faith."

"You're profoundly wise, Veena. Thank you for that encouragement. I'm so fortunate to be united with you."

"Jointly, we are blessed, Nate. We should never forget God's grace poured onto our family and our life together."

"Amen."

CHAPTER 93

GROWTH, SWEET SADNESS,
AND A NEW BEGINNING

Eighteen years after arriving in Bridgeport

Over the past eighteen years, the growth and blessings poured upon The Redeemed are all worthy to be recognized as miracles. Due to the scarcity of paper and pen, I, Ezra, summarize them to document those most valuable to this record.

The arrival of the main body of The Redeemed was early in the second half of July. The weather stayed dry and warm enough until mid-December, allowing the construction of a large meeting hall, a grain storage building, and several barns. The first buildings were all log structures. The following spring, we built a lumber mill, and all future buildings were wood frame and plank construction. The grain storage building is the only construction that now remains in its original form, a memorial to the blessing of that first winter, which was unusually mild and allowed the people to stay in tents except for one week in January.

Pastor Abraham regularly quotes scripture, "Proven character produces hope." The end of that first January in Bridgeport was also the occasion of the births of Joel Rodriquez to MaryAn Hedgemore and Carla Rodriquez, and Luke Zhang to Hope and Eric Zhang. Veena and Nathanael Sinclair's second and last child, Hannah Dawn Sinclair, was born in late April. Less than two weeks later, Blossom Ames came into this world to Doctor Joy and Doc Ames, and I, Ezra Haines, to Kathy and Roy Haines.

Initially, our artificial insemination guidelines restricted performing the procedure to a maximum of two women every three months. Joyfully, the addition of the San Luis community and those who joined The Redeemed during the migration made it feasible to increase the pregnancy rate safely. Father Sinclair served God to co-create one hundred and fifty children over sixteen years. A handful of couples, such as Hope and Eric Zhang, were blessed with a second child. The Zhang's second child is Elizabeth, who was born sixteen months after her brother, Luke.

As an aside, I should explain that 'Father Sinclair' is an endearing nickname the people gave to Nate. Just as Pastor Abraham would begrudgingly acknowledge the epithet 'Old Abe,' the combined forces of Nate, Veena, and Abraham could not dissuade people from using 'Father Sinclair.' The ubiquitous label stuck to Nate, and he surrendered to it. The name was a shocking surprise to us children when we learned the implicit meaning of the moniker. We continue to call him Father Sinclair because that is who he is to us, both by custom as well as by service.

After arriving in Bridgeport, romances bloomed, and marriages abounded. The first wedding was that of Miriam Cohen to Pastor Abraham Jones. Miriam was beyond child-bearing age, but she and Abraham have been grandparents to all of us. Quickly following were the marriages of Lucia Sanchez to Chief Virtolli, Esmeralda Contreras to Vincent Ramon, and Laoni Wright to Thomas McCoy. These unions were enriched with children, producing Bethany Virtolli, Emmanuel Ramon, Rebecca McCoy, and Belinda Ramon. Caleb Gates married Shiloh Williams, an African-American newcomer who, with twenty survivors, joined the migration near Arvin, and they have a son, Zev Gates.

The whole community prospered, too. The advance teams were able to salvage enough equipment from the hydroelectric plant near June Lake and the geothermal power generation facility at Mammoth Lakes to create small hydroelectric generating stations at the Bridgeport Reservoir and the Twin Lakes. We scavenged photoelectric cells wherever we could, with our biggest trophy recovered from a solar generation field near Olancha. All the "firsters," as we—their offspring—are prone to call them, remarked just how good it is to have ample power, warm houses, abundant crops, and a reliable source of good freshwater. For us, as the second generation, it is all we have known.

As predicted, the notorious gangs have virtually vanished, killed off by inter-gang warfare and natural attrition. The Clairens were the first to fade from memory, followed soon after by the Riverside Raiders. After exhausting their sources of plunder in the Los Angeles basin, the remnants of the K trudged north through the central valley of California to scavenge whatever they could. Eventually, the remaining group, who numbered fewer than forty, crossed the Sierra through Yosemite, seeking to pillage the bounty God had bestowed on us. As recorded earlier, by the courage of Kevin Johnson and the hand of God on the Tioga road, that foray ended in disaster for them. Their memories are now recalled only as history lessons and warnings on the importance of being prepared and careful.

The firsters also reported that a large gang from Stockton tried to raid our community in November of the second year. As told, the band fell victim to early, heavy snowfall in the Sierra, and the storm wiped them out. There were those among us in the second generation who believed the narrative was one that parents tell their children to keep them from straying. Or so we thought until about four years ago, when David, Joel, Hannah, and I saw bones and weapons scattered along the 108 on the western slopes of the Sierra. Now, we're inclined to believe the account.

New groups of survivors came periodically into our community. In the spring of the third year, the animals –except for the horses, dogs, and cats– were relocated to expansion areas. This change of pasture allowed the cultivation of the nearby fields solely for crops while reserving higher pasture areas in the summer for the horses. Under the guidance of President Veena Sinclair, the northern boundary of our community reaches Topaz Lake, north of Coleville and the Walker River. There, we have cattle, sheep, and fields of grains. On the southern side, the extent is Round Valley and Bishop, where we have cotton fields and several revived fruit tree orchards. The Sierra Mountains limits growth to the west, and the desert is our eastern boundary.

Father Sinclair, Michael, and Ruth Liu developed a school program and trained us from the time we could walk. It was through the school that each of us built a personal, close relationship with Father Sinclair. He was our teacher, guide, and advocate. He had a knack for making mathematics and science fun. He was not unique in that aspect as all our teachers were loving, kind, and gifted in educating us.

Additionally, Father Sinclair routinely spiced his instruction with stories of the old world and the journey to Bridgeport. Somehow, he would demonstrate how his lessons applied to those tales. Imagine our surprise when we learned about his special kinship to each of us.

Joel Rodriquez, David's closest friend, has been favored with dream visions from God. In response to one of his earliest revelations, we sent an expedition to Pecos, Texas, where a small community with a working oil refinery welcomed us. God blessed us in leading us to a people who shared our faith in God—Father, Son, and Holy Spirit—and we have formed a loving partnership with them. We have been able to share our surplus of crops and livestock with them, and, in return, they provided us with containers of lubricating oils and a tanker truck filled with diesel fuel. The Virtolli family, and Luke Zhang, have moved there, with Chief Virtolli and Luke working in the oil fields and refinery. Luke, at his young age, is quickly becoming the best engineer in The Redeemed.

In another of Joel's visions, eight years ago, we sent an exploratory squad to the region around Rosario, Mexico, where we encountered hamlets of sheepherders. As directed by God in the vision, Michael and Ruth Liu traveled with Kevin, Juanita, and Natalie Johnson to that community. Despite Kevin's injury and difficulty walking, he became as proficient as Doctor Williams in treating animals. Due to Kevin's injury, Juanita worked with him as a veterinary apprentice, and the locals at Rosario were thrilled to receive their skills. Since the initial visit, the Liu and the Johnson families return twice a year, in late spring and October, to help with veterinary needs and build trade. At Bridgeport, we benefit in early November when they return with wool garments in time for winter.

Not all our time has been without sorrow. Several of the firsters have passed. Though we should be rejoicing that they are now with our LORD, the grieving is, as Pastor Abraham has reminded us, part of being created in the image of God and a sign that we are to treat human life as precious.

The saddest of these losses happened just two years ago. The second wave of MR swept through our fellowship, perhaps introduced unintentionally by one of the travelers who have peacefully passed through our area, eager to confirm the miracle of children. Several of The Redeemed, but none of the children, got sick. The sole fatality, though, was our dear Father Sinclair, whom we buried on a bluff overlooking Bridgeport. The anguish to our whole congregation was devastating. Even when Abraham, in a loving eulogy, spoke of God's unwavering favor and grace and how He had sent Father Sinclair as a promise of hope and steadfast love, scores of us felt inconsolable. Only after President Veena Sinclair, with an unwavering voice and full of purpose, spoke that we cannot fall short, that we must endure and thrive. Demonstrating our trust in God's plan and His gift of Nate, we channeled our grief into shouts of acclamation and resolve. Veena testified of her love of Nate, of his maturing walk with our LORD, how she will always cherish the time they shared, and how she looks forward to their reunion in our LORD. When she finished, David and Hannah stood with her, and strengthened by her charge to us, we all surrounded them, with hands outstretched and making contact, raising our voices in prayer and blessing. Then, starting softly and growing continually, Miriam lifted a song, Agnus Dei, that was one of Nate's favorites. Before the second stanza, the whole congregation overcame grief with voices of praise and renewed hope.

As I write, we, the children, range from David Sinclair at eighteen to the youngest, Belinda Ramon, at fifteen months. By submitting to God and His divine plan, Father Sinclair has served God's people and renewed our faith and hope. May each of us be counted as worthy of His gift.

As we in the second generation reach young adulthood, we must travel in faith to find our future spouses, a necessity as all in our community are already sisters and brothers by faith and blood. In a recent vision to Joel, God gave a glimpse of another body of believers graced with children, in Minnesota. A week later, pilgrims visited Bridgeport and told us about an encounter with young adults near Spirit Lake, Iowa, led by a tall young woman named Abigail Stumpp.

Next week, Laoni and Thomas McCoy will escort an exploration to Minnesota to validate God's revelation to Joel. Our party will include David and Hannah Sinclair, Joel Rodriquez, Blossom Ames, Elizabeth Zhang, Rebecca McCoy, and myself. In a symbolic gesture of our trust in God, we will leave on May 7, the exact date the Camarillo camp started their journey to merge with the rest of The Redeemed and claim Bridgeport. May Almighty God, who promises in Romans 8:28, "In all things God works for the good of those who love Him, who have been called according to His purpose," guide us, preserve us, and deliver us to His good plans.

I have interviewed our history witnesses, and I testify that this is a trustworthy recounting of all.

Faithfully submitted in the service of Y'shua,
Ezra Haines

ACKNOWLEDGMENTS

M y sincere appreciation to the following who have helped and encouraged me in completing this work:

Authors: Eva Shaw, Ph.D.; Caitlin Jans; and Emmanuel Jeremiah Etunim from Nigeria.

Editors: Jim Thomsen, Daphne Santos-Vieira, and Meghan Bowker.

Readers: Marie C. Keiser, Christopher L. Kincaid, Joanne McCoy, Sherry Clarke-Perry, Belinda Silvey, and Margaret Walter.

ABOUT THE AUTHOR

RV Minkler is a Christian, husband, father, grandfather, software engineer, private pilot, guitar hobbyist, worship and praise team member, deacon, and joyful traveler.

Born in Iowa, he completed elementary school in Des Moines before his family moved to Phoenix, AZ, where he lived until he completed his degree in Engineering from Arizona State University. After college, he moved to San Diego, CA, where he worked as a software engineer and raised a family. Now retired, he volunteers with the local police department to visit shut-ins, leads a bible study fellowship, and writes fiction.

He has written articles for the local flying club, and this story is his debut novel.

Connect with the author:
facebook.com/rv.minkler
goodreads.com/ rv.minkler

APPENDIX: NAMES

THE ELDERS

Nathanael Sinclair (A.K.A. Father Sinclair)
The father of the new-generation children, Nathanael (Nate) was a member of NASA who participated in a suspended animation program to prove the concept for deep-space travel. The test was planned to last six months, but world events caused the experiment to continue unattended for eleven years until the monitoring computers detected anomalies and woke Nathanael. Nathanael awoke to a world utterly foreign to the one he knew when he entered the experiment, and when he awoke, he was alone.

Veena Osborne (A.K.A. Captain Veena)
Veena, pronounced "VEE-nah," is the leader of the Tierrans, a tribe in the new world composed primarily of women; the only daughter of African-American decathlete Kyle Osborne and his Caucasian wife, Dawn. Both parents died when Veena was eleven, during the world cataclysms that occurred soon after Nathanael entered the suspended animation experiment. Veena has been raised and guided by Old Abe.

Abraham Jones (A.K.A. Old Abe)
Abraham Jones is an African American and Doctor of Physical Therapy. Known affectionately as "Old Abe," he is the

intellectual and spiritual leader of the Tierrans. Old Abe was a close friend of Veena's father and mother, and when they died in the cataclysm, he became Veena's guardian. Though Veena now leads the tribe, she looks to Abe for wisdom, discernment, and advice.

Originally from Virginia, Abe has a crisp, clear, and educated manner of speaking and vocabulary. He sounds more like a college professor than a former Marine.

Kath(y) (Arlain) Haines

Veena's "right hand," Kath, is two years older than Veena and quick-witted. Though she isn't as skilled in combat as Veena or Carla, her cunning has often saved the Tierrans without any losses. Her husband is Lieutenant Commander Royce (Roy) Haines, and she is the mother of Old Abe's apprentice, Ezra Haines.

Kathy's family came from Georgia, and she has a Southern accent in her speech.

Carla Rodriquez

One of the oldest women in the Tierrans, Carla and her team buddy, MaryAn, were early victims of the Clairens' cruelty. Second in skill only to Veena, she is part of the Tierran defense force Archangels under the direction of Veena. She is emotionally tied to MaryAn and acutely distrustful of men; the latter trait has saved her team countless times in the treacherous new world.

MaryAn Hedgemore

MaryAn is Carla's companion, close to Carla's age, and has also suffered the Clairens' cruelty. Although she is a good warrior, especially fierce and daring when she feels Carla is endangered, she is so dependent upon Carla that she cannot lead a team. MaryAn is the mother of Joel Rodriquez.

Laoni Wright

One of the youngest members of the Tierran tribe, Laoni was only three years old when the world changed. Veena's squad, the Archangels, found her half-dead, next to the body of her mother. The members of that team have raised her jointly.

Lieutenant Commander Royce Haines, U.S.N. (A.K.A. LCDR Haines)

Originally the Executive Officer of the U.S. Navy Nuclear Attack Submarine *Des Moines*, LCDR Royce (Roy) Haines is the leader of the survivors from the original crew. After arriving in San Diego two years after The Thinning, they encountered a battle between the Tierrans and Clairens and came to the aid of the Tierrans. Roy married Kath (neé Arlain). Roy and the surviving crew stayed with the Tierrans. Roy retains his rank in the U.S.N., but he follows orders from Veena.

THE CHILDREN

Ezra Haines (Izzy)

Ezra (Izzy) is the son of Nathanael and 1st Lt Kath. Kath and her husband, LCDR Roy Haines, raised him. Ezra is an apprentice to Old Abe.

Joel Rodriquez (The Prophet)

Second-born child of the new world, Joel is the son of Nathanael and MaryAn. Raised by MaryAn and Carla, he is David's closest friend. Joel is known as "The Prophet."

David Kyle Sinclair

David, the first-born child of the new world, is Nathanael and Veena's son and the future leader of The Redeemed.

Hannah Dawn Sinclair

Hannah is the second and last child of Nathanael and Veena. Hannah has her mother's strength of character, athleticism, and beauty, and her father's intelligence and wit.

OTHERS

Hospital Corpsman First Class Douglas Ames (*A.K.A. "Doc Ames"*)

Doc Ames is a Tierran tribe member and husband of Dr. Joy Shimizu.

Miriam Cohen

Tierran tribe member, chief botanist, and, at forty-six, Miriam is the oldest woman in the tribe. The future wife of Abraham Jones.

Esmeralda Contreras

Esmeralda is a Latina tribe member and the future wife of Vincent Ramon.

Walter Duncan (A.K.A. "Dunkin' Donuts")

Walter is the leader of the Clairens. Before The Fires, Walter was an overweight shoe store night manager. A teenage employee mockingly called Walter "Dunkin' Donuts" due to his affection for pastry sweets. He is a bitter and conniving person who knows how to manipulate people. He survived in the gangs because he had a desired skill: he can brew beer. He rose to the top when the other gang leaders killed each other off.

Emilio Flores (A.K.A. "Doc Flores")

Latino tribe member, and a dentist.

1st Lt Caleb Gates

U.S. Marines 1st Lt Gates is the senior officer of the U.S. Navy SEAL team attached to the U.S.S. *Des Moines*, and one of the African-American members of the Tierrans. He follows orders from LCDR Haines but operates independently with his SEAL team on any assignments.

Jody Higgins

Tierran member who tries to usurp the tribe leadership.

Linus Johnson (A.K.A. "Rex," A.K.A. Kevin)

A sadistic leader of the Killers, the largest and fiercest gang remaining in the Los Angeles basin, Linus is an African American who grew up in the South Los Angeles neighborhood. He also adopted the name "Rex" and named his gang the "Killers," A.K.A. 'the K.'

Michael Liu

Second, in leadership, to Eric Zhang of the Asian-American tribe and married to Ruth Liu.

Hasan Malik

One of the leaders of the non-Christian members of the Tierrans.

Thomas McCoy

Adopted son of Eric and Hope Zhang, and future husband to Laoni Wright.

Aarav and Myra Patel

Other leaders, along with Hasan Malik, of the non-Christian members of the Tierrans.

Vincent Ramon (A.K.A. Vince)

Tierran tribe member, future husband of Esmeralda Contreras. Close friend to Nate, he was Nate's best man at the wedding of Veena and Nate.

Lucia Sanchez
Latina tribe member, future wife of Chief Paul Virtolli.

Dr. Joy Shimizu (A.K.A. Doctor Joy)
Pediatrician and one of the first members of the Asian-American tribe to join the Tierrans. She weds Douglas Ames and is the mother of Blossom Ames.

Juanita Suarez
Latina tribe member and future wife of Kevin Johnson.

Chief Petty Officer Paul Virtolli (A.K.A. Chief Virtolli)
Tierran tribe member, future husband of Lucia Sanchez.

John Williams, Doctor of Veterinary Medicine
Veterinary who lived in Yuma, AZ, before The Fires, and later became a member of the San Luis Latino tribe.

Eric Zhang
Leader of the Asian-American tribe from Camarillo.

Hope Zhang
Wife of Eric Zhang and gifted with spiritual insight.

Y'SHUA HAMASHIACH

The Hebrew name, pronounced "ye-shoo-AH haw-mash-she-ACK," of the more widely used, Anglicized form of the Greek name, Jesus Christ. In Christianity, He is one with the triune God (Yahweh) in revealing God as Father, Son (Y'shua), and Holy Spirit.

It was clear that God has cleansed with fire when we read scriptures such as Genesis 19:24-25, Numbers 11:1-3, Numbers 16, Deuteronomy 32:19-22, 2 Kings 1:10-12, Job 1:16, Psalm 21:8-10, Psalm 78:63, Psalm 97:3, Isaiah 9:19, Isaiah 29:5-6, Jeremiah 21:12-14, Ezekiel 15:7-8, Joel 2:2-3, and Amos 7:4.